POLLS APART

CLARE JOHNSTON

www.bloodhoundbooks.com

Print ISBN 978-1-914614-64-4

ALSO BY CLARE JOHNSTON

From The Outside

1

LLOYD'S MURDERESS ROLE "COULD THROW ELECTION CAMPAIGN"

FRIDAY, MARCH 13TH 2009, UK NEWSWIRE

Anna Lloyd, wife of SDP leader Richard Williams, today faced further criticism over her decision to appear nude in a controversial TV drama to be screened just weeks before a widely-expected General Election.

In the ITV thriller, *Dancing With Danger*, Lloyd plays a serial killer who cuts the throats of her clients while performing for them in private at a lap-dancing club.

The 37-year-old actress's decision to appear in the show has angered many in the Social Democratic Party who fear the controversy could throw their campaign off course before it has even begun.

Mr Williams has yet to comment on his wife's role, but sources close to the opposition leader say he is concerned about the public's possible reaction to her performance which comes as Prime Minister Kelvin Davis looks set to call a May 7th General Election.

Joy Gooding, spokesperson for Lloyd, dismissed the controversy as "nothing but a storm in a teacup", and said the actress was "hugely proud of the production and of her performance".

A nna held her hand up protectively in front of her as she battled her way through the throng of reporters, photographers and TV crews all jostling to get close. Her PR agent, Joy Gooding, walked directly ahead and tried valiantly to get the crowd to clear a path. One particularly persistent TV reporter kept thrusting her microphone under Anna's chin whilst repeating the same question over and over: "Are you hampering your husband's bid to become prime minister, Ms Lloyd?"

Anna hated people getting too close and she felt panic surge as she struggled to dodge the reporter's microphone only to stumble into the path of a photographer. She tried to correct her footing, but her left ankle twisted under her and within seconds she was heading for the ground. She gasped and thrust her hands out to break her fall, but the inevitable thump against the pavement was halted by a sudden firm grip around her left arm. She looked up into the face of the man pulling her to her feet. He was staring intently and mouthing words she couldn't make out above the sound of the crowd and the blood rushing around her head. His eyes were a piercing, icy blue that cut straight into her, drawing out a sickening mix of emotions she hadn't experienced in twenty years. It couldn't be, she thought. He was dead. But the man clasping her arm and staring at her in confusion was a terrible reminder of him.

She flailed momentarily then pulled herself sharply from the man's grasp, unable even to offer a simple thank you.

"Don't mention it," she heard him call after her but she didn't look back – she wanted to get as far away from him, and the memory he evoked, as possible. No doubt he would think her rude. After all, it wasn't his fault he happened to bear a striking resemblance to the man who still haunted her in her dreams, but it was too late to make amends now.

She saw Joy holding the car door open and quickly climbed inside.

With the door now shut behind them, Anna closed her eyes and began the breathing exercises taught to her by her therapist.

Joy sat quietly next to her, aware she shouldn't interrupt the ritual.

Anna tried to focus only on the sound of her breath and to put the afternoon behind her. She had been helping launch a new homeless charity initiative which Joy had promised would take under an hour but had, in fact, ended up running to more than three times that. By the time she'd toured the women's hostel, met some of the volunteers and residents, posed for pictures inside and out, and generally been shoved around, all she wanted to do was go home, relax and leave the exhausting public persona outside. Her jaws ached from smiling and her head throbbed from the sheer effort of constantly having to talk and listen.

The breathing was beginning to work its magic and she felt a sense of inner calm return. She drifted into a semi-sleep only to be brought back to reality seconds later by a tugging on her sleeve.

Anna opened her eyes and turned to look sharply at her friend and PR representative.

"It's Richard," Joy said, waving her mobile phone in front of her. "Did you not hear your phone ringing?"

"I was trying to relax." She flashed Joy an annoyed glance as she reached out to take her phone, hoping she would get the hint that she hadn't appreciated the extended outing.

Anna hastily answered, confident Richard would be calling to praise her on the hostel trip.

"Hi Richard," she said breezily.

"Happy now?" he barked.

"I beg your pardon?"

"You heard."

"Richard," Anna answered calmly, no stranger to his stress-induced rants. "I'm in the car with Joy at the moment. Can I call you back later?"

"No you bloody can't call me back, Anna. I have two minutes before I have to go into yet another planning meeting that will more than likely last hours. Top of the agenda is sure to be my actress wife grabbing the headlines again and threatening to overshadow every ounce of effort I've spent the last two years putting in to winning this damn election."

Anna turned to look at Joy and rolled her eyes. She knew her assistant had become used to overhearing her spats with Richard. Privately she was embarrassed that their rows were so frequently overheard, whilst publicly she would make light of them.

"Don't be ridiculous, Richard. It's only a TV role – how could that possibly throw your campaign off track?" Anna winked at Joy again, indicating she felt she had the upper hand in the argument.

"Because, who I'm married to and what they do matters, Anna. Everything you do, I have to defend. Today, instead of answering questions on our new Young and Working initiative, I had to explain why my wife would be appearing nude as a psychotic lap dancer before millions of TV viewers."

Deep down, Anna could see that her latest role didn't exactly fit with the straight-and-narrow persona the Social Democrats expected from a leader's wife, but she'd done it now and she wasn't going to let Joy hear her backing down to Richard again. She cleared her throat and prepared to strike back. "Well, you should be grateful you finally had something interesting to talk about, Richard. Look, I'll never be Barbara Bush, okay? Twinset and pearls are not my style. I'm an actress, not a nun. And anyway, I've just spent the whole afternoon in a refuge for the homeless; my every blink picked up by the cameras. That's bound to make up for any negative coverage today." Anna smiled again, satisfied she'd done enough to win Richard over; but her husband was not for turning.

"Nice idea, but you have to do a lot more than hang out in a homeless hostel for a couple of hours to win over a sceptical electorate. I have to go. See you tonight."

"Okay," said Anna, with more than a hint of meekness. "Richard..."

"Yes."

"I love you."

"I love you too, darling. I'm just bloody stressed to the eyeballs."

Anna tossed her mobile phone into her handbag before leaning back against the headrest and letting out a long, frustrated sigh.

"Take it Richard's having another bad day?" Joy asked with a raised eyebrow.

"Richard is always having a bad day at the moment, and I usually seem to be at the centre of it. I blame Henry Morton, personally."

"Yes, he is a total shit, isn't he," agreed Joy, her New York accent still dominating what had become an anglicised drawl after fifteen years of living in the UK.

"Why are you married to him then?"

"Gotta have someone to split the mortgage with, haven't you?"

Joy laughed. "Course, you won't have that problem when you're living at Number 10."

"No, but even more than now I'll be expected to keep my mouth shut and swap Dolce and Gabbana for an M&S twinset."

"His expectations of what you'll wear aren't really that severe are they?"

"Well." Anna shrugged. "Henry has already warned me about my 'alternative look'. In his view, I'm expected to look 'uncomplicated', keep my mouth shut and do whatever I'm told."

"Just stick to who you are, Anna, and you'll be fine. You've got a terrific career in your own right, and Richard should count himself damned lucky to have you by his side. The best celebrity endorsement poor old Kelvin can come up with is a half-extinct *Dad's Army* star. I wouldn't swap you for that."

"Thanks, Joy." Anna smiled. "That's good to know."

Anna poured herself a glass of red and happily sank into her favourite leather armchair while she waited for Richard to get home and berate her further. On the rare evenings he was in they would often sit with a glass of wine and pick over that day's controversy, sometimes involving them but more often – and more fun – involving Kelvin and the Alliance Party.

That was what she relished about her relationship with Richard most – the fact that, despite all the pressure, they could still laugh together. She glanced at the antique clock proudly taking centre stage on their mantelpiece. It was nearly nine o'clock, so she guessed Richard would have already eaten on his way home from his constituency or wherever he was tonight; she rarely asked any more. At least it's a Friday, she thought.

She sat back and tapped her fingers on the arm of the chair as she waited, before suddenly springing upright again after spotting an enormous cobweb covering the corner of her ceiling. Anna made a mental note to ask Joanna the cleaner to get rid of it when she arrived on Monday. As her eyes trailed around the rest of the room, she felt a pang of sadness at the thought they would more than likely have to leave their house in what felt like the sheltered suburb of Highgate soon to live in Downing Street. They had bought their home together when they married six years ago. Anna had decorated each room herself, choosing traditional styles, splashing out on thick, heavy curtains, luxurious merino throws, Persian rugs and fine furnishings. Not very SDP, she realised, but then she had paid for most of it herself. Tonight, she took an extra moment to appreciate her handiwork.

She heard Richard's key in the lock and waited as he hung up his coat in the hallway. When he finally appeared in the doorway to the lounge he looked as soaked from the rain as he did frazzled.

"I'm guessing you could use one of these," Anna said, dangling her glass in front of her.

"I need more than one."

"Help yourself," she said, pointing to the glass and bottle she'd left for him on the coffee table.

"Thanks." He quickly poured his drink and sat back against the luxurious mass of cushions that lined their sofa. Anna could tell by the way he was staring blankly at the ceiling that he was stewing on something.

"Is it all my fault today then?" she enquired.

"Mostly you, if I'm honest."

"What. All over a bloody acting job?"

"Not just that, no." He turned to look at her. "You're increasingly being seen as a liability. It's very difficult to paint a picture of a man firmly in control of his party – and soon country, hopefully – when I don't appear to be able to get a grip on my own wife."

"Get a grip on me. What does THAT mean?"

"It means you never stop to think how your behaviour might reflect on me. You run around taking any acting job you like and are too busy attending showbusiness gatherings with Joy to come to official functions with me."

"Oh, this is just Henry talking now," Anna said, flapping her hand as though batting his criticism away.

"No, Anna. This is not Henry talking. This is me talking."

Richard leaned forward and stared into his wine glass which he now clasped firmly between his hands, the vein at the top of his temple pulsing as it always did when he became highly agitated. "What are you going to do when we get to Downing Street, Anna? Have you thought about that?"

Anna watched Richard take several large gulps from his glass before running his right hand through his increasingly-thinning hair. Although he was only forty-four, she noticed the last two years of party leadership had not been kind to his once youthful looks. He'd given up the gym several months previously when his timetable could no longer afford it, with the direct consequence that his once lean and solid frame had now settled for just lean. The greys sprouting through his jet-black hair were strengthening in number and intensifying their march across his scalp.

Anna, on the other hand, was faring considerably better at thirty-seven, and was still being cast as women ten years younger. Regular visits to her hairdresser, Torquin Sellars, ensured no one need ever know she, too, was harbouring greys among her once-natural blonde locks. And she was still clinging on to her place in the top ten of the annual "most beautiful women" polls – though she knew those days were numbered. While critics had regularly questioned her acting ability, none had ever questioned her looks and she frequently wondered – feared – her face and figure were the sole reasons she'd ever got anywhere in life. To many she appeared as the vacuous, trophy wife with the easy life. But she knew the truth: life was anything but easy when you had a destructive secret boring its way a little further into your soul with every passing day. The burden of tortured days left behind, but never forgotten.

She turned to look at Richard who was by now staring intently at her awaiting an answer to his last question which she desperately tried to remember. But it didn't take her long to work it out considering it was a question he'd repeated almost daily in the last few weeks: "How will you behave if we reach Number 10?"

"I don't know what I'll do, Richard." She sighed. "I guess it'll just have to be whatever I'm told. You obviously won't settle for anything less."

Richard woke early with a knot of worry firmly embedded in the pit of his stomach. It was all going too damn well. It was just a bit too easy. He spoke, people applauded, he made a suggestion, everyone agreed. Even the old dinosaurs who lined the back benches were singing his praises. It can't last, Richard fretted. Somehow he had to keep the good headlines going until the election. Kelvin looked almost certain to call a May vote because he'd been warned the polls were only going one way, and if he left it to September he'd be lucky to beat the also-rans.

Richard knew if he could just keep things at a level, maintaining both the country's favour and the sense of confidence amongst the party, then an election win was firmly within his grasp. Still, the pressure was often gut-wrenchingly intense. It just took one very public slip-up and the pendulum could swing again. Kelvin had a reputation as a political bruiser who would stop at nothing to take out an opponent – a fact that left Richard feeling very unsettled as he wondered when the first major blow would land.

He stretched his arms above his head and turned to look at Anna peacefully sleeping next to him. She never looked more beautiful or more innocent than when she was out for the count, silent and unable to create trouble. He admired once again the smooth skin, carefully groomed eyebrows and pursed, angelic lips that had given rise to so many column inches on the beauty pages. The fragile features and tiny frame that belied a more defiant nature, carved out by the years of suffering about which they rarely now spoke. He just needed her to toe the line for a few weeks until they made it past the election. She was volatile, he knew, but surely she could do this for him. The knot in his stomach further tightened when he thought of how hard he'd worked first to become an MP when he won Bristol South eight years ago, and then to beat the odds – and the party hardliners – to become SDP leader. It was hard to accept that beyond Kelvin Davis and the Alliance Party, his own wife could be the greatest threat as he prepared for his biggest political battle.

The tension between them now was in sharp contrast to their early romance when they had talked endlessly of their shared dreams. Curled up in bed, staring into each other's eyes, Anna would smile excitedly as he told her of all the wrongs he wanted to put right in society. How he would face down the toughest of challenges in a job he believed he was born to do. She had believed it too. And, before the headiness of fame and adulation had set in, she, too, had spoken passionately of trying to help those who had shared her past pain of poverty and neglect. He reached out and lightly touched her arm as he remembered their closeness, their complete devotion.

Somehow he had to try and convince her to get behind him again. This could only work if they shared the vision once so vivid in their minds. But how to win her over, Richard just didn't know.

He sighed, tossed the covers back and headed for the shower.

Anna bristled as, for yet another Sunday, she had to endure Henry's signature doorbell ring – finger solidly on the buzzer until the occupant answered. Today's was even more aggravating than usual as she realised he would almost certainly have a go at her over the recent coverage in the tabloids. *Actress in gritty TV role shock* – hardly the news story of the century, but her every move was under scrutiny at the moment and the natural rebel in Anna just wanted to kick out.

Richard made it to the front door first, dressed for the weekend in his open-neck shirt and crisply ironed jeans. Casual, Anna thought, but never relaxed.

As Anna followed Richard down the stairs she spotted Joy standing sheepishly behind Henry, all too aware his buzzer antics would have riled her hosts.

"Good morning," Richard greeted them with typical enthusiasm.

"Morning Dicky," Henry boomed in reply before quickly making his way past Richard, almost managing to flatten him against the wall with the enormous pile of newspapers he was carrying under his left arm. He was typically dressed in a crumpled shirt and jeans – a look that was only marginally upgraded in the week when he would wear chinos instead and add an ill-matched tie. It was a style that only he could carry off in the SDP circle where he was regarded as something of an indulged schoolboy, his foppish hair and gentrified good looks masking his otherwise low-maintenance appearance.

Richard shook his head as he watched his guests make their way towards the living area. No matter how many times he told Henry not to call him Dicky, he still insisted on doing it – unless in public. At least Richard had that to be thankful for.

Anna reached the bottom of the stairs in time to kiss Joy on the cheek before escorting her to the sofas.

"Coffee all round then," Anna called as she made her way towards the kitchen.

"Actually, I'll have a tea," said Joy, "it's just dawned on me that my years of insomnia might actually be down to the fact I've been drinking up to ten cups of coffee a day."

"Yes. Might just be something in that." Richard laughed.

"You can't sleep because of your relentless desire for me," quipped Henry.

"That must be it, dear. Why hadn't I thought of that earlier," she replied, adding a sarcastic smirk.

Anna smiled to herself as she watched the scene unfolding in the living room. The serving hatch that had annoyed her so much when they first moved in had actually proved to be a very useful spyhole when they had visitors, and Anna had overheard many an interesting conversation from the very position she was now standing in setting out coffee cups.

She studied Joy for a moment; a vision in a cerise-pink wool dress, matching pink lipstick and black stiletto boots. Anna often wondered what brought her and Henry together as, style-wise, they were such polar opposites, but she figured that was part of the attraction. Like Henry, Joy took a no-nonsense approach to life and called things as she saw them, which often made for lively conversation between the four of them.

"What are the papers saying today then, Henry?" asked Richard.

"Better than yesterday, but not much." Henry sniffed as he spread the array of mastheads out on the coffee table between them. Joy was perched attentively in an armchair next to her husband while Richard leaned forward on the sofa opposite.

"Anna comes in for further criticism over her career choices, and even her fashion sense is questioned in this feature." He triumphantly waved the highlighted article in front of Richard. "An expert describes your style as 'rebellious', Anna. They say it's a 'public statement of your refusal to conform to the more traditional style demanded of a leader's spouse'."

"Is that right?" Anna said scathingly as she carefully made her way towards the coffee table before abruptly setting the tray down. "To think someone actually gets paid to come up with that crap."

"You dress the way you've always dressed," Joy chipped in, "and you've not always been a politician's wife."

"As hard as that is to believe now." Anna sighed.

"Maybe they've got a point, Anna." Henry fixed his target with a meaningful glare. "I know an excellent stylist who could work with your tastes but bring them in line to be something that sits better with the press and public."

"You mean the press and politicians, Henry. Let's face it." Anna returned his glare, thrusting his cup of coffee towards him and sending the liquid sloshing into the saucer.

"Now, now, children." Richard smiled. "Let's not fall out over a choice of blouse. It wouldn't do any harm for you to meet with a stylist, Anna. We're only talking about a few weeks until the election."

"There's nothing wrong with the way Anna looks," Joy said firmly. "The public love her for who she is and the press are just looking for something to write, so let's drop this."

"All right," said Henry, a steely glint suddenly coming into his eyes. "In that case why don't we talk about the phone call I took last night from Damian Blunt of the *Sunday Echo* asking me exactly how and when you two met."

"What about how we met?" asked Richard, furiously stirring his coffee.

"That's what I can't work out. Why would the editor of a Sunday paper suddenly start asking me about that?" Henry's eyes darted between Richard and Anna as he searched for clues.

"Well, did you ask him?" Anna said impatiently.

"Yes, Anna. And he said he was considering doing a warm, cuddly feature on how this public partnership first came into being."

"What's wrong with that?" asked Joy.

"What's wrong is that the *Sunday Echo* don't do warm and cuddly. There's something up but I haven't figured it out yet."

"Don't be so bloody dramatic, Henry," said Joy. "They met at an awards ceremony seven years ago, it's hardly earth-shattering is it?"

"No." Henry pulled at his closely-shaven chin. "But when Damian Blunt starts asking unusual questions it's time to worry."

"Well, you certainly know how to cheer up a rainy Sunday morning, don't you." Anna frowned at Henry as she reached for a biscuit to dip in her coffee.

"Just trying to stay ahead and prevent us getting eaten alive by the wolves."

"You're paranoid, Henry." Joy laughed, instantly riling her husband.

"Oh, I know in the la-la land of showbusiness that all publicity is good publicity, Joy," he hissed, "but in the world of politics – where the stakes are genuinely high – we tend to take muck-raking a little more seriously."

Anna cringed as she watched her PR's mouth fall open in shock at the vitriol behind her husband's harsh remark. Joy looked over helplessly, her eyes signalling for back-up. But to confront Henry now would only make things worse between her and Richard so Anna opted for the coward's way out; she averted her gaze and stood up to get a refill of coffee.

Richard coughed and shuffled uncomfortably in his chair. "Pass the sports section will you, Henry?" he asked, nodding towards the object of his desire on the coffee table. "I want to find out what's going on in the real world."

"All yours, Dicky," Henry said, thrusting the supplement in his hand.

As Anna stopped to pour herself another cup she chanced a glance in Joy's direction, then wished she hadn't. For in the few seconds that she studied her friend's face she had caught a mixture of hurt, humiliation and isolation. Anna knew all three emotions like old companions. She guessed she'd let her friend down by not stepping in to defend her. But Joy would get over it, she thought. She wasn't the type to hold a grudge.

2

DOWNING STREET WON'T CHANGE ME, INSISTS LLOYD

FRIDAY, MARCH 20TH, 2009, UK NEWSWIRE

Anna Lloyd, the actress wife of Social Democrat leader Richard Williams, today appeared to take for granted that her husband's ambition to reach Number 10 would become a reality, as she spoke of her future life in Downing Street.

Talking at a press conference ahead of tomorrow night's ITV screening of the controversial thriller *Dancing with Danger* in which she stars, Lloyd told reporters that a spell at Number 10 wouldn't change her.

"I am who I am", she said. "Some people don't see me as the traditional Prime Minister's wife, but that doesn't bother me. I won't change just because of a new address".

Asked whether her husband shared her open-mindedness when it came to public image, Lloyd replied: "Richard and I are two separate people, united in one goal; to see each other live our dreams and fulfil our potential as human beings".

And the 37-year-old actress refused to be drawn on

suggestions that she had been rowing with her husband over her decision to play a serial-killing lap dancer in her latest TV project, saying only: "My husband is as supportive of my career as I am his".

But Lloyd did little to appease her critics today who accused her of arrogance in her apparent assumption that she would be living at Number 10 after the next election.

Alliance Party backbencher Lizzie Ancroft said the actress was "living with her head in the clouds".

"Both Anna Lloyd and her husband have a long way to go to convince the public they belong in Downing Street", the MP added. "She is clearly already planning where to put the furniture, but the British voters are now seeing what some of us at Westminster have known for a long time – that, as on screen, this actress can only ever pretend to be something she's not".

Henry drummed his fingers over the desk, furiously studying the press clippings laid out over the meeting desk in Richard's office, positioned on the top floor of the SDP's Victoria HQ. Richard was meanwhile left to exchange expectant glances with Sandra Mackenzie, senior policy advisor, and his campaign organiser and deputy party leader Ray Molsley. After a few moments' deliberation, Henry looked up towards the ceiling as he first inhaled and then exhaled a long, troubled breath. They had called the meeting to run through some changes to their manifesto but, instead of talking politics, he had again been forced to put Richard's wife at the top of their agenda.

Turning to his colleagues, his long frown let it be known that he was not happy.

"We have a handful of days to go before we're into this campaign and, once again, I'm spending my every waking moment defending this party against the flippant remarks and behaviour of one person."

"And there's no prizes for guessing who he's talking about." Sandra chuckled, her Glaswegian accent never stronger than when she was at her sarcastic best.

"Well, quite." Henry turned in his chair to look directly at the man seated next to him – his boss. "I'm at a loss, Richard. We keep ending up in the same place and nothing or no one seems to be able to rein her in."

"Well, we could start with your wife, Henry, if we're going to get personal." Richard clasped his hands together and leaned forward to show poise – something that was essential in trying to gain the political upper hand. His old friend and head of communications was beginning to rise above his station and Richard knew the rest of the shadow cabinet were baying for him to be brought under control.

"Joy is supposed to be Anna's PR advisor, yet she continues to preside over one public relations disaster after another. So perhaps you should be directing the criticism closer to home, Henry."

"Might I make a point?" Ray Moseley's thick Cockney accent always commanded silence from an audience, an attribute which, along with his portly frame and no-nonsense manner, ensured even the least tameable MPs found it hard to refuse his orders when they were cornered. "Anna has her own successful career and isn't the least bit bothered about being the wife of a Prime Minister."

"And?" asked Richard.

"And I just wonder if we gave her an incentive to become more involved with the campaign, whether that might just make the difference?" Ray rested smugly back into his seat and watched as the pennies dropped around him. At fifty-eight, he'd been in the game of politics long enough to tell a winning idea from a lame one – and he had a reputation for backing political winners.

"What kind of incentive did you have in mind, Ray?" Henry enquired nonchalantly, briefly glancing at the clock to indicate time was at a premium.

"She happened to mention to me one evening that she had always wanted to work with the director Don Monteith but, although her agent had put her forward many times for roles in his films, he had never once even as much as asked her to audition. It 'eats away at her', she said." Ray dramatically raised his right eyebrow to emphasise his point.

"What *are* you getting at, Ray?" Sandra piped up with typical forthrightness. She had been a loyal friend and follower of Richard's for several years and always jumped to his defence. As an attractive woman in her early-forties, Sandra had managed to intimidate most of the predominantly male shadow cabinet, but Ray's thick skin and enormous ego meant he was scared of no one and so he continued unabated.

"Don Monteith has just today become a major supporter of the Social Democratic Party who he has vowed, in any way he can, to help win the next General Election."

"Why the hell didn't you mention this earlier?" barked Henry.

"I've only just got the chance. But it's turning out to be a real coup. He's prepared to do a press conference, and he's up for appearing alongside Richard at a couple of campaign events."

"That's fantastic news." Richard beamed. "At last something to celebrate."

"Indeed," said Ray, pausing further to bask in the glory of his idea. "I like to think I was pretty instrumental in getting him on board..." Sandra interrupted his blatant gloating with a loud groan, prompting Ray to cut to the chase. "And I think Anna will be quite excited about the idea of getting behind this campaign now, don't you think? She can have special responsibility for hosting Don on the campaign trail."

"You're smarter than you look, Ray." Richard chuckled.

"Bloody smug with it though," joked Henry, winning collective laughter from around the table.

"Come in here a minute will you, Marie?" Damian barked into the telephone receiver before slamming it back into the cradle. He looked once again over the small piece of notepaper gripped in his hands, bearing only a name and telephone number. He carefully placed it down on the desk in front of him and continued to pore over it as he weighed up the pros and cons of running a story such as this. It would, of course, strike a major blow to the Social Democrats – which would please the paper's staunch Alliance-supporting owner, Viktor Nemov, no end – but would also mean if, as likely, Williams won the election, the *Sunday Echo* would be all but blacklisted when it came to briefings. Damian, however, knew he had to do what would please his owner and shift copies off the news stands – and this story would certainly do both. In these tough times for the newspaper industry, that alone would be worth ticking off Henry and his mob. They weren't going to blacklist a national Sunday newspaper for long no matter how pissed off they were. In fact, the more Damian thought about it he couldn't see a downside. As long as the story was true. And that was where Marie would come in. She would have to get her facts straight and, even then, they'd need to get it direct from the horse's mouth. That would involve a carefully-crafted phone call to Anna Lloyd that could not go wrong. Marie was fairly new to his team, having moved from another Sunday tabloid just three months ago, but Damian had no doubt she was the right woman for the job. He had hired her based on the reputation she'd earned for getting a story between her teeth and refusing to let it go if there was an ounce of mileage in it. That was what he needed here. Someone with enough pluck and tenacity to pull this thing off.

"You wanted to see me, Damian?"

Marie stood smiling in the doorway wearing a bright-red halterneck top, black cardigan and what looked to Damian to be some kind of rah-rah skirt – the kind he hadn't seen since the eighties. As he took in the petite vision standing before him, notepad clutched in her left hand, ready for business, Damian momentarily lost track of what he was about to say.

"Yes..." He beamed broadly, showing his nicotine-stained teeth in their full glory. "Come in, Marie. I've got a job and a half for you, so why don't you take a seat and make a few notes because this one could be a career changer."

Anna carefully applied a second layer of lipstick and smoothed her hair over for the final time. Her hairdresser, Torquin, had left only minutes earlier having spent more than an hour and a half styling her shoulder-length locks. Tonight was the *Sunday Echo's* much-heralded *Great Britains* awards ceremony and Anna was fully aware how much scrutiny both she and Richard would be under. They were jointly presenting an award tonight – something Henry had hailed as a terrific idea – until the last couple of weeks when tensions over her 'behaviour' had reached new heights. Richard paced the floor behind her, fervently reciting the few introductory lines he had planned for his time in the spotlight.

"Tonight is so much more than just an awards ceremony," he murmured. "It's a celebration of all that is good in British society..."

Anna deliberately zoned out, choosing instead to focus on squeezing her feet into the three-inch stilettos that Henry's newly-appointed stylist had chosen for her. Much to Henry's dismay – as Anna felt sure he hoped the two women would be at each other's throats – the stylist, Camilla, had actually proved a popular addition to Richard and Anna's rapidly growing advisory team, having picked out some particularly stunning outfits, including tonight's silk Amanda Wakeley dress.

Things were looking up, thought Anna.

"Are you ready yet?" Richard barked nervously.

"Yes. I've been ready for the past five minutes."

"You've only just put your shoes on."

"Well, I wasn't rushing because it looked like you were about to practise your introduction for the fiftieth time." Anna flashed a sarcastic grin.

Richard sighed. "Let's go then. The car's waiting outside."

Anna sensed Richard's tension growing steadily throughout the twenty-minute journey to the studios in Southbank where the ceremony was being held.

He had spent the first ten minutes staring at his notes until Anna could stand the silence no longer.

"What's the matter, Richard? You seem incredibly nervous."

"I just need tonight to go well, that's all. We're pretty damn sure Davis is going to the Palace tomorrow to call the election so all eyes are on us. This thing gets a big TV audience and it's a tough one to judge. I don't want to come across like a stuffed shirt, but then I'm not Russell Brand either."

"Well, that's true." Anna laughed, before adopting a more sympathetic approach. "Look, you're incredibly good with people, Richard. That's why you're leading the Democrats, so just be yourself and act like you do when we're hosting guests in our own home. Be open, friendly but respectful."

Richard finally looked up from the crumpled notepaper in his hands to give Anna his full attention.

"Thank you." He touched her cheek softly. "I'm glad you're by my side tonight. I'm hoping you'll be able to do a lot more of this over the coming weeks, just until we're through the campaign."

"I'll do my best," Anna said, gently patting Richard's hand.

He looked back down at his notes for a moment before folding them up and putting them in his pocket. "We had some good news today."

"That's good, darling," Anna replied vaguely as she turned her focus to polishing a tiny mark on the front of her stiletto with her finger.

"Yes, Don Monteith has publicly pledged his support to the SDP."

Anna sat up straight, her eyes wide with sudden interest.

"Don Monteith the film director?"

"Yes. Henry's even lined him up to do a couple of appearances with me out on the road."

"Well that's fantastic. Perhaps I could help there?"

"What do you mean?" Richard asked, feigning confusion whilst privately celebrating the obvious success of Ray's plan.

"I mean," Anna gushed, "if I'm going to be out campaigning with you, then I should definitely help organise the appearances with Don Monteith because I understand his world and how he operates."

"Oh, so you will be campaigning with me?"

"Of course I will, Richard. When have I ever said anything to the contrary?"

~

Flashlights lit up the night sky as Richard and Anna slowly made their way along the red carpet, well-rehearsed grins fixed on their faces. The strobe effect of the camera flashes created a surreal world in which they were half-blinded and thrown into slow motion.

Anna was used to photographers, but even she hadn't encountered anything like this before. She beamed from the inside out as she realised she was finally tasting what world-class movie stars took for granted. Suddenly another flashbulb lit up; this time in her head. This is it, she thought. This is the big time.

Once inside, the room throbbed with celebrities all clamouring to be seen with the small and frightened group of award winners who were being treated to a glass of champagne to loosen them up before they were paraded in front of the cameras. As Richard made his way through the predominantly celebrity guests who were standing around the dining tables set out in front of the stage, he took care to hold Anna's hand tightly. He was afraid that, if left to her own devices, she would stop and talk to every second 'industry' person they passed. Along the way he overheard one bottle-blonde actress caked in make-up who he was sure he'd seen on a soap, eulogising about a previously unsung hero who she "just adored".

Clutching the rather startled fifteen-year-old close to her chest – in what Richard noticed was quite a proprietary way – he overheard the actress telling a TV reporter: "I'm just so thrilled to be presenting an award to Jamie. He's such an inspiration to us all in the way he fearlessly fought over a pensioner's wallet."

One of the organisers stepped in to whisper something to the actress that Richard assumed must have been a correction by the way her face further contorted with every word he uttered. He slowed to a snail's pace as he made his way past the scene so he could watch the full spectacle unfold.

The actress was waving her hands in front of her now.

"Can we start again?" she asked in her thick Yorkshire accent. "I didn't get that quite right." She tossed her long hair to the other side and cleared her throat. "I'm just so thrilled to be presenting an award to Jamie. He's such an inspiration to us all in the way he bravely fought off thugs who were trying to steal a pensioner's wallet."

Richard couldn't help but laugh out loud which earned him a very dirty look from the now mortified actress. He turned to Anna behind him who was so busy scouring the room she had missed the entertainment right in front of their noses.

"Mr Williams." A very smiley young lady was standing in front of him and, judging from her headset and clipboard, he guessed she was from the production crew.

"I'm Mary Waterman, the assistant producer. Pleased to meet you – and you, Miss Lloyd."

Anna returned her smile but, Richard noticed, she still hadn't lost that distracted look as she half-heartedly tried to listen to Mary's instructions whilst star-spotting.

"If you follow me to your table, I can introduce you to Ruth," Mary continued. "I'll then call you fifteen minutes before you're due to present the award and take you backstage where there will be make-up artists on hand should you need freshening up."

"Lovely, thank you," Richard said as he dutifully followed the assistant producer to his chair.

"This is Ruth," Mary said, pointing to a young woman who was the total opposite of what Richard had been expecting.

"My goodness," he blurted as he shook the girl's hand. "How did such a petite young lady like you chase two armed robbers from a bank?"

"I used shock tactics." Ruth giggled. "I'd read an article in a magazine a few weeks earlier saying if you were ever assaulted then the best thing to do was to act all weird and make a lot of noise as it would throw your attackers off course."

"So what did you do?" Richard asked.

"I just started screaming my head off and waving my arms around to attract the attention of passers-by. Before I knew it the robbers were running in the opposite direction."

"Weren't you afraid it wouldn't work?" Anna chipped in from behind Richard. "Some robbers would have shot you for less."

"Oh, hello," Ruth said shyly as she realised who Anna was. "I didn't really think about it, I just went on automatic. Looking back at it, I was very lucky that it worked and everyone escaped unhurt."

"I'd say." Richard laughed. "What a wonderful story though. We need more people like you who are willing to stand up to the bad guys."

Suddenly an announcement cut across their conversation: "Ladies and gentlemen. Will you please take your seats as the *Great Britains* awards ceremony is about to begin."

Richard spotted his place card beside Ruth's while Anna was seated between her husband and the sponsor's very straight-looking chairman who she realised she would be stuck talking to for the next couple of hours. She sighed quietly to herself and glanced at who was placed on the nearby tables. She was quickly cheered to see she had been seated at a preferential table to several so-called A-list singers and actresses who were positioned behind them.

Once she had taken her seat, Anna leaned close and whispered in Richard's ear: "I didn't realise there were going to be so many major celebrities here."

"Yes. It's become quite a high-profile event. That's why Henry insisted we present the award."

"He's much more in touch than I thought." Anna laughed. "In fact, I'm quite looking forward to this campaign now. I think we'll make a dynamic team." She winked at Richard and gave him a teasing nudge.

Anna woke early the following morning to the sound of their radio alarm and immediately regretted the fifth glass of champagne she had carelessly swigged shortly before they left the awards ceremony. Richard – ever sensible – had advised her against drinking it, but she'd got carried away as she enjoyed all the attention that accompanied her increasing celebrity. Finally, she was starting to get the kind of admiration she had always craved. Even directors who had once looked down on her as a two-bit soap actress were now actively courting her because of the kind of publicity she could generate. All this meant Anna was no longer nervous about her nine-thirty meeting that morning with a production company in Soho. They were interested in casting her as a single mother who turns to armed robbery to support her family. Her agent had told her it was a six-part drama which they were to begin filming in June but, while only last week she'd been desperate to get the part, last night had made her realise she could now pretty much choose whatever role she wanted. In fact, she'd decided she was going to invest her all in helping Richard on the election campaign and, once happily ensconced at Number 10, she'd start knocking on Hollywood's door; if the directors of Tinseltown weren't already lining up to talk to her by then.

Richard was stirring in the bed next to her and, feeling the warmth of abounding opportunity, Anna cuddled up behind him, her hands linking across his chest. She kissed him softly between his shoulder blades. "Morning darling," she whispered in his ear.

Richard turned towards her, staying in his wife's embrace. "Good morning, my love," he said wearily. "You seem very happy for six-thirty in the morning."

"That's because I'm very proud to be your wife." She kissed him firmly, folding herself even closer into him.

"You're not rushing are you?" he asked with a devilish smile whilst maneuvering himself to lie over her.

"Not anymore." She giggled, drawing his face towards hers until their lips met.

"Richard," she whispered. "How about we try again for a Downing Street baby?" The brief silence that followed almost deafened Anna, who held her breath as she waited for an answer. For the last couple of months she had been pleading with Richard to try and start a family, fearing the ticking clock, but he had wanted to wait until after the election.

"I thought you were getting all excited about your career again?" Richard asked, then immediately realised he was shooting himself in the foot by discouraging her from a family life when that is exactly what Henry and all his closest colleagues were encouraging him to go for.

"I can combine the two," she said in a quiet voice that spoke loudly of her true desire. "I just want us to be a family, Richard. I want to give what I never had."

He studied her for a moment, her eyes imploring him to understand, to commit. "We can try, darling." He smiled, kissing her gently on the forehead. "I mean, I've always said we could do with encouraging more young people into the party."

"Thank you," she whispered, still wrapped in his embrace. As Richard leaned in to kiss his wife again he thought he could see a single tear run down the side of her cheek and disappear into the pillow.

~

Two hours later Anna bounced into the back seat of the Mercedes and bid a cheerful good morning to John, her regular driver with the chauffeur firm she'd been using for the last five years.

"How's life treating you today, John?" she asked as she rifled through her Tardis of a handbag to try and find her mobile. It was only eight forty-five but already she noticed she had two missed calls from a number she didn't recognise. With a little buzz of excitement at the thought it might be one of the directors she met last night trying to reach her, she hastily hit the redial button.

A woman answered after a couple of rings but spoke hesitantly. "Hello."

"Hi. It's Anna Lloyd. You dialled my mobile a couple of times this morning?"

"Yes... Anna, it's Sylvia Levine here. I hope you don't mind me calling."

Anna's heart plunged as she realised who she was talking to.

"What do you want, Sylvia?" she demanded coldly.

"I didn't know what else to do." Sylvia's aged voice sounded shaky and panicked as she got to the point of her call. "A newspaper reporter's been calling me these last few days telling me she knows all about your work for the agency and asking me all these questions. I didn't know what to say to her, Anna. I thought I should tell you."

Anna clutched the edge of the car seat in a futile attempt to stop the world from spinning around her. Her breathing sped up to a pant as the implications of what Sylvia was telling her played through her mind.

"What paper is she from?" Anna asked icily.

"The *Sunday Echo*."

"Shit. Have you told them anything?"

"No, nothing, Anna. But they know you worked for me for six months and they know what kind of work you did."

"This is a bloody nightmare," Anna shrieked. "We're just about to go into a general election campaign and this blows up in my face. I knew the past would come back to haunt me, I knew it." Anna's voice sounded strangled now and she fought hard to regain some kind of composure. She could see John giving her alarmed glances in his mirror and she realised quickly that she would have to try and avoid more people finding out or the evidence against her would start piling up.

"I'm so sorry, Anna. They already know the names of some of your regulars."

"Don't say it like that, Sylvia. You make me sound like a hooker." Anna could feel the cold sweat breaking out across her brow. "Look. I need you to just stay quiet and never call me again, do you understand?"

"Perfectly," Sylvia replied calmly, and Anna instantly detected the shift in her voice. Her stomach lurched when she realised what had just happened. Sylvia had set her up – and, having inadvertently just confirmed the story during what must have surely been a taped call, she had no doubt she was well and truly stuffed.

❧

"Well, Dicky, this is really it. The moment we've been waiting for." But Henry quickly realised he was talking to himself. Richard's attention was firmly locked on the TV screen hanging precariously on the wall above the filing cabinet in his office. A blonde newsreader with a perfect bob spoke earnestly into the camera as a ticker running beneath her proclaimed: *PM set to announce General Election date.*

Henry moved silently to sit next to Richard as they watched Kelvin Davis emerge through the front doors of a primary school and make his way towards the crowd of waiting photographers and reporters.

"Look at him," scoffed Richard, shuffling uncomfortably on the edge of the meeting table where they were both now perched. "Not a hair out of place while there's a bloody gale raging around him. How does he manage it?"

"Hairspray I expect."

Richard glanced at his head of communications, but decided there was no time to analyse whether his comment had been genuine or in jest. Henry's dry wit and deadpan delivery often left Richard a little bewildered as to how he was supposed to respond.

Kelvin smiled like a well-practised Hollywood star as he approached the cameras, the teeth-whitening for which he'd recently been ridiculed by the press now in full view.

He took a moment to nod in acknowledgment to the hundreds of schoolchildren who were gathered all around him.

"Trust him to surround himself with kids as well," said Richard. "Is there no stunt too low for him to pull?"

"Doubt it," replied Henry.

Kelvin fixed the cameras with a look that said, *"I'm about to say something really important",* and began his prepared speech.

"Earlier today, I saw the Queen at Buckingham Palace to ask for a dissolution of Parliament so there could be a General

Election on May 7th. My goal is to continue to secure a better future for all, but most especially the children and young people of this country who deserve the best start a nation can offer."

Kelvin paused to smile affectionately at the children gathered directly to his side, but was forced to cut what was meant to be a poignant moment short when one of them embarked on a rigorous effort to release a bogey from his right nostril.

"Ha! Make that child an honorary member of the Social Democratic Party. He's created one of the most well-executed diversions ever to be seen in British politics," Henry roared.

"Beautiful." Richard beamed, smacking Henry triumphantly between the shoulder blades.

"This is our time, Dicky. I can feel it," said Henry.

"Yes," replied Richard in a near whisper as he pushed the mere mortal he was behind him and summoned the man who would be Prime Minister. "We're going to expose Davis for the fraud he is and send him running back to the Home Counties. He's not even fit for the fight."

"That's right my friend," Henry said, throwing an arm of comradeship around Richard's shoulder. "We'll show those amateurs how a real election campaign is run."

3

SOCIAL DEMOCRATS ROCKED BY LLOYD "ESCORT GIRL" CLAIMS

MONDAY, MARCH 30TH, 2009, UK NEWSWIRE

Opposition leader Richard Williams' hopes of leading the SDP to an election victory in May suffered a severe blow after a Sunday newspaper printed claims his wife previously worked as a professional escort.

The allegations, published in yesterday's *Sunday Echo* newspaper, came just three days after Kelvin Davis announced that a General Election would be held on Thursday, May 7th. The newspaper claimed that Lloyd worked for the Mademoiselles escort agency in 1994 for a period of six months.

The timing of the claims about the actress Anna Lloyd, who has been married to Williams for six years, could not have been worse for the opposition leader or his party who have, to this point, been riding high in the opinion polls.

The allegations were firmly denied by Lloyd and an SDP spokesman who dismissed the article as "ludicrous", but the

Sunday Echo last night released a statement saying it stood by its story which, it maintains, is supported by several sources.

The *Sunday Echo* editor, Damian Blunt, added there were "more revelations to come" on Lloyd's past which, he says, will be published in the newspaper this Sunday.

Williams is expected to make a personal statement about the claims following a visit to City of Bristol College later today where he was due to talk about the Democrats' pledges on further education.

R ichard stared mournfully at the newspaper pages in front of him, still trying to absorb the magnitude of his problem. He was sitting in his party HQ office, flanked by Henry on one side and Ray on the other. Sandra was making her way through the Monday morning rush-hour traffic, but they had decided to start without her as Henry was determined to prepare a "statement of intent" before they left – in little over an hour – to catch a train to Bristol where Richard was due to make a speech to college students and staff later that morning.

Richard had been informed in a phone call by Henry on Saturday afternoon that the *Sunday Echo* would be running the story the following day. Henry had picked up an early edition and read it word for word to Richard late on Saturday night as Anna lay on the sofa across from him, sobbing into a cushion. Richard had sat in complete silence as he heard how Sylvia Levine had damned his wife with praise as she described the time Anna had spent working for her. "She was a very beautiful young lady and the punters absolutely loved her", she'd been quoted as saying. "I could have booked her every night of the week if she'd been available". And while the paper hadn't actually stated whether any of Anna's encounters had been sexual, it had strongly hinted that way.

"Anna was a very obliging employee", Sylvia had cryptically added. "She had no problem with the work and was good at keeping the customers happy".

Once Henry had finished reading the article – which had been spread over three pages – the two men had hastily prepared a statement in Richard's name, designed to distance the Opposition leader from the allegations whilst simultaneously downplaying them.

"While I was shocked to hear the claims made against my wife, Anna, in a Sunday newspaper, I was even more concerned that – at such an important point in this country's political evolution – so much time and interest should be paid to what is effectively gossip, rather than the real and very serious issues facing this nation.

"I want to assure all those people who long to see Britain stand on its economic feet again and to see the political focus shift to some of the most pressing issues in our society – rebuilding the NHS, tackling crime and supporting families – that I will be undaunted in my determination to win the next General Election and to make this nation proud again."

Richard and Henry had been satisfied that the statement would achieve its purpose, but the UK media had other ideas. The newspaper headlines spread over the meeting table that Monday morning screamed trouble at the three men gazing forlornly down at them: "Democrats' Whitewash on Lloyd Escort Girl Claims", one tabloid shouted, while another's front page featured a large picture of Richard scowling (snapped over a year ago when he was papped leaving a restaurant) and reading: "This Looks Tricky, Dicky – SDP leader in a spin over wife's escort past".

Henry smiled unconvincingly at Richard and Ray: "Looks

like our attempts to move the news agenda on haven't quite taken hold yet."

"You're a master of stating the bloody obvious," sniped Ray. "Don't you think you'd better tell us what you're going to do to make up for the even deeper shit you've put Richard in?"

"I've not put anyone in shit, Ray," Henry hit back. "It would appear that it's Anna who's got us here." Henry then turned on Richard: "Has she told you whether it's true or not yet?" Richard continued to stare blankly at the newspapers in front of him: "She said parts of it are true."

"Parts? Which parts?" barked Henry.

"She worked for the escort agency but she didn't shag anyone, all right?" Richard's cheeks flushed with stress and embarrassment as he forced himself to look Henry in the eye.

"Do us a favour, Henry," Ray chipped in again, "and save us the self-righteous act. We're supposed to be here as a team."

"Well, that's a nice sentiment, Ray. But we need to establish all the facts and we need to think quickly. The truth is this isn't going away, Richard. The way I see it you have two choices..."

Richard continued to stare at Henry although he was unsure whether he wanted to hear the options he was about to set out.

"You can either stand by Anna and we tough this out, but risk it throwing the election campaign, *or* we ask her to step aside until the election's over."

"What do you mean step aside?" asked Richard.

"I mean you announce a separation which we'll say is giving you some space to reflect on what's happened and to focus on the campaign. The message will be loud and clear: No distractions."

"You're asking Richard to chuck his wife out until we win, in other words," said Ray, before adding: "Do he and Anna get a say in this at all?"

"Anna doesn't, no." Henry smirked. "But she's in no position

36

to argue right now. The best thing for everyone is if she takes a nice little holiday abroad until this blows over and lets us get on with the job in hand."

Ray turned to Richard, searching his face for clues as to what he could be thinking, but the opposition leader's face remained blank. "I'll back you whatever you decide to do, Richard," he said.

Then, just as Henry was about to try and force Richard's hand, the door opened and Sandra bustled into the room, laden as usual with the stack of files she carried everywhere with her.

"Sorry I'm late guys," she said breezily, before slapping the files onto the table and taking a seat next to Henry. "What have I missed?"

"You've just missed Henry suggesting I publicly dump my wife until the election's over," Richard said starkly.

"And you don't think that's a good idea?" she asked, as though they were discussing a simple policy decision.

"Well, do you?" Richard replied, surprised one of his closest confidantes had so readily sided with Henry who she would usually go to the ends of the earth to avoid agreeing with.

"I just don't think we can carry her through this, Richard," Sandra said. "Being totally blunt, Anna is a bit of a dead weight in our campaign. If she stays around, she'll drag us down."

Richard ran his hands through his hair, which he thought must be thinning by the minute, as he fought for time. He felt like an animal trapped by a pack of hyenas. And he knew there was no escape. "I don't know how I'm going to tell Anna," he said mournfully, head bowed.

"Look, you've got a very busy and important day ahead of you," said Henry. "Why don't you let me brief Anna on where we're up to, and you can talk to her properly later."

"Brief Anna on where we're up to?" Ray raised his eyes to the ceiling, despairing at the lack of feeling Henry was displaying for Richard's wife.

"He's right, Ray," said Sandra. "Now is not the time for Richard to be having a marital heart-to-heart when he's got a major campaign speech in a few hours. Henry can talk Anna through what's been discussed and we can get back to focusing on the job in hand."

Richard pushed out a quick, hard breath, before looking round his team. "Okay. Let's move on to what I'm saying this afternoon, can we? Every word counts so we need to get this absolutely right."

Anna curled up in her favourite armchair and selected the AllNews channel on the enormous flat-screen TV Richard had bought for himself as a Christmas present. Anna had thought it was the greatest monstrosity she'd ever seen when Richard had first lumbered through the front door carrying it – or attempting to – but as the months had passed she had stopped noticing its size to the point where it now looked quite neat in the corner of their living room. She turned the volume up as soon as she saw the words *Escort Claims Crisis* appear behind the presenter, Esther Yarleth. Anna bristled as she listened to Esther – a raven-haired, fiercely ambitious media darling who never missed an opportunity to flirt with Richard – clearly enjoying announcing their troubles to the world. "Social Democrat leader Richard Williams is due to make a speech during a visit to Bristol College this morning where he is expected to discuss embarrassing claims made in a Sunday newspaper about his wife's past. The newspaper alleged that actress Anna Lloyd…"

Anna turned the volume down again and peered through the cracks in the shutters at the street outside and the cluster of reporters and photographers camped out at the bottom of their driveway. They had been there since Sunday morning, seemingly only taking a few hours off to sleep, although even then there were usually a couple who lurked around overnight, just in case they missed Richard throwing Anna out the front door, followed by a sack of her belongings. So they hadn't got that shot yet, Anna mused, but she knew Richard would be under pressure to do something to distance himself from the claims. The past forty-eight hours had marked the lowest point in their marriage by far – and there had been some real lows before that as he had been forced to get to grips with the enormity of her past.

They had been getting ready for a charity dinner when Henry had called Richard on his mobile to deliver the news about the story that would shortly hit the streets. Anna had watched her husband's face turn ashen white with a mixture of panic and anger as he absorbed the full implications of what he was being told. Henry had advised them to stay in the house and not answer the door or telephone until he got there. With those words he effectively sentenced the two of them to spend the next hour caged inside while the British press set up stall outside. Richard had been too afraid to speak in anything more than a whisper in case they heard him so, instead, he paced the floor, ranting quietly to himself over and over. "That's it," he kept saying. "Everything I've worked for – mine and my family's lifelong dream – gone. Just gone and there's not a thing I can do about it."

Anna's feelings lurched from overwhelming guilt about her past to uncontrollable anger at the fact Richard was being so insensitive towards her. And as he paced in front of her for what must have been the hundredth time, she finally snapped.

"Some social conscience you've got, Richard. You preach about helping those in need, about us all being equal, but not in your own home. Poverty forced me to take that job, remember. We weren't all born middle class, Richard. Some of us have had to sell ourselves just to get out of the shit into which we were landed."

She had cried then, long and hard. She had been humiliated and degraded in front of her husband and the whole country. But worst of all, she had been reminded. Richard had looked on anxiously for a while, before eventually kneeling in front of her and taking her head into his hands. "It's not your fault, Anna. And I'm sorry if I made you feel that way. I know your life was hell. I just wish we could make people understand."

"Why can't we?" Anna had asked. "Why don't we just tell the truth about everything that happened? Then people would understand why I had to take a job like that."

Richard's face had taken a stony turn. "We can't do that," he'd replied, shaking his head. "That's just way too risky."

"So we just stay quiet and let the world think I'm a tart?" Her eyes explored his, urging him to see her position.

"Henry will think of something," was all he could muster in response.

Sitting in her armchair staring at the rabble outside, Anna knew Richard had a choice. He could stand by her and use her plight to demonstrate just why the SDP had to win, or he could cut her off and put personal gain over just cause. She thought of the man she'd fallen for at the awards ceremony seven years ago where Richard had presented Anna with her Best Actress trophy. It had not been the first time they'd met, but the difference that night was they were both single and looking for a new partner. She had been attracted by his sharp mind and sense of social justice, and he – so he had told her – had been instantly hooked on the sound of her laughter, her ease within her own skin, and the way she managed to turn the head of every other man in the room without seeming to notice. Anna had thought they made the perfect pair. They had talked of being an indestructible force in politics.

Sitting in her armchair, waiting for her husband to make his announcement on the steps of Bristol College, she felt sure he would remember all they'd set out to conquer together. They would get through this, she knew they would.

Henry glanced nervously at his watch as he waited for Richard to finish his meet and greet with the college staff and students. He needed to get clear of them within the next two minutes if they were to start the announcement by five past one which would mean they'd get a live slot right at the top of the lunchtime news programmes. As Richard caught his eye, Henry nodded twice – their code for "get a move on" – and watched the opposition leader skillfully round up his brief chat with those assembled in the main lecture hall. But just as Henry started to relax into their plan, he was soon filled with horror as he realised he'd forgotten to call Anna to tell her what was happening. If he didn't call her now, she'd have to find out from the TV news. He reached for his mobile and shook it in frustration when there was no signal in the hall. He thought about quickly running out into the street, but he knew he would panic Richard if he did and cause them to miss their all-important time slot. It was a harsh decision, even by his own standards, but he'd just have to abandon the call to Anna. After all, he reasoned, she'd brought this situation on herself – and, worse, the party.

Richard was by Henry's side now as they made their way to the front door of the college flanked by security and the ever-increasing team of press officers and aides who now accompanied the two men on each outing.

"How did Anna take the news?" Richard asked, his eyes bulging slightly with the pressure of what lay before him.

"Everything's fine, Richard. Let's focus on your speech and we'll talk afterwards."

Henry heard Richard's sharp intake of breath when they reached the doors of the college and were confronted by a sea of press all keenly waiting for an update on the state of his marriage.

"You'll be fine," Henry whispered. "Just stick to the wording we agreed and don't take questions."

Richard executed a well-practised *"I'm in control"* smile as he reached the podium at the top of the college steps. He cleared his throat before leaning into the microphone.

"Bristol College can be proud of its place as a centre for educational excellence; an achievement that was reflected in the enthusiasm of all the staff and students I met here this morning," he began.

"Every child and young person deserves the very best education but, sadly, still all too few will be privileged enough to benefit from state-of-the-art facilities such as the ones I have seen here today."

Richard remembered his speech training and deliberately slowed his next line down to accentuate every word. "It is my desire to change that. And it is my desire to make sure that every single child who has a career ambition will be given the very best chance of achieving it."

Richard paused for a moment, allowing his message to sink in with those watching and listening. He looked around the wall of cameras in front of him, hoping to make eye contact with every single viewer before he ventured further. Both he and Henry knew how important it was that they trusted him right now.

"We cannot... will not, be distracted from our goals. Britain needs the Social Democratic Party and I will not stop until we deliver the very best for the people of this country. There will be challenges along the way – and there will be those who try to throw me off course. I spoke with my wife Anna this morning. She has been deeply hurt by the recent allegations thrown at her but she knows, too, that we cannot let such gossip stand in our way. She has decided today that she would like to withdraw from the glare of the cameras for the next few weeks, during which time I will be one hundred per cent focused on the task in hand. The task of renewal, of courage and of victory. I thank you."

Anna continued to stare into the screen long after she had turned the picture off. Her mind spun like cherries on a slot machine as she tried to sort through what Richard's statement actually meant for their marriage. By the time her thoughts had settled she was clear on the answer: she had just been dumped on national TV without even a hint of prior warning. Six years of marriage cast aside in an instant – all to save Richard's face. She had thought when they'd talked things through the night before that she had convinced him they could come through this together. Before they switched the light out to go to sleep he had stroked her arm and said: "We'll come out fighting tomorrow, Anna. We're a winning team and it'll take more than a shoddy little tabloid tale to finish us."

He'd got up at five-thirty that morning and kissed her softly on the cheek as she lay dozing. She'd heard him confidently bidding the press pack outside a good morning before getting into his car and speeding off to the party HQ. Anna had told herself how lucky she was to be married to such a loyal man yet, just a few hours later, he'd betrayed her without so much as a warning.

Her mobile rang on the coffee table in front of her and she saw Joy's name flash up on the screen.

"Hello," she answered.

"Anna, I just saw Richard's speech," Joy said breathlessly like she was running to get somewhere. "I'm on my way over to pick you up."

"Where are we going?" replied Anna with the meekness and uncertainty of a small child.

"You can't stay where you are, Anna. You'll be hounded by reporters trying to work out the answer to what everyone is now asking, *'Did he just try to separate himself from you in the public eye?'* We need to get you somewhere safe and quiet where you can think things through. Do you have anywhere in mind?"

Anna went quiet for a moment as she tried to think of a place she'd feel secure – and comfortable. Then it came to her. "I want to go to Libby's," she said. "I need to be with my sister."

4

LLOYD "THROWN OUT OF MARITAL HOME", CLAIMS FRIENDS

TUESDAY, MARCH 31ST, 2009, UK NEWSWIRE

The actress wife of SDP leader Richard Williams was forced to leave their home to save her husband's political career, according to tabloid reports.

In a speech on Monday, Williams said Anna Lloyd had "decided she would like to withdraw from the glare of the cameras", but unnamed friends of the actress claim the announcement was made out of the blue and against her wishes.

Williams was forced to make an announcement on the state of his marriage after allegations were printed in a Sunday newspaper claiming Lloyd had previously worked as a professional escort.

The story came just days after Prime Minister Kelvin Davis announced a General Election would be held on Thursday,

May 7th. The newspaper claimed that Lloyd worked for the Mademoiselles escort agency in 1994 for a period of six months.

SDP spokesperson Henry Morton denied Lloyd had been forced into a separation saying her move from the marital home in the Highgate area of London had been a "joint decision".

He added: "As Richard Williams stated on Monday, Anna was very upset over recent newspaper allegations and decided she wanted a period of privacy away from the public spotlight. Richard supported her wishes and she was in no way forced to move out of their home".

When pressed on whether Lloyd's move constituted an official separation, Morton said: "This is simply a practical solution which allows Anna some time away from the cameras whilst Richard gets on with the important job of winning the next General Election – a task he is absolutely committed to carrying out for the people of this country".

Marie Simpson was quietly enjoying picking her way through her tuna and bean salad when she became aware of an unsettling presence nearing behind. Although Damian liked to creep up behind his staff and catch them unawares, he was rarely successful in his efforts because of his involuntary throat-clearing habit. Marie heard the familiar rasping sound from around ten paces away so made sure she shut down her Facebook page before Damian rounded the corner to her desk. The *Sunday Echo* office was mainly open-plan but Marie sat in a corner of the newsroom with several other reporters, all separated by annoying and ineffective partitions which didn't offer any privacy and meant you had to stand up to speak to your workmates.

She swivelled around in her chair just in time to catch Damian's furtive glare as he approached. Marie noticed he was even scruffier than usual today, with his creased shirt, ruffled greying hair and loose tie. All the female reporters in the office agreed that Damian had a strange kind of bad-boy appeal, but the lines on his face – the product of years of chain-smoking – made him look older than his actual age of forty-one.

"Marie," he said, in a falsely cheerful voice. "How's the Lloyd story coming along? You tracked down any of her ex-clients yet?"

"I've tried to contact everyone Sylvia named, but they're either ex-directory or they won't talk. Most of them are highly-paid professionals who don't need the money."

"Right, time for plan B then."

"What's that?" Marie asked, already afraid of the answer.

"We run an interview with Lloyd. The heartbreaking story of how she was betrayed in her hour of need by the man she loves."

"Have you spoken to her then? Has she agreed to do it?"

"This needs a woman's touch, Marie." Damian winked in what Marie found to be a patronising way. "You give her a call and – in the nicest possible fashion – let her know that unless she does an interview we'll let her old clients do the talking."

"But we don't have any of her clients."

"Use your loaf, Marie." Damian leaned forward, eyes wide with agitation. "She doesn't know that does she? Now I want this sorted by the end of today so I need you to get onto it as soon as you've finished your birdseed." With that, Damian took off and left Marie to watch him saunter back to his office with all the affectation of a man trying to appear comfortable in his own skin.

Marie swallowed back a wave of nausea as she considered the prospect of trying to talk to Anna Lloyd – who, she felt, must surely hate her more than anyone else in the whole world right now – into divulging her innermost secrets to the *Sunday Echo*.

She knew the outcome would rest on how well she managed to veil her threats, keeping her tone friendly whilst leaving Lloyd in no doubt she had little choice.

This was the type of task Marie hated – particularly when her heart was just not in this story. The "scurrilous end" of tabloid journalism as her father called it. She would much rather have been chasing stories on important social issues, rather than harassing politicians' wives, but Marie also knew the only way out of this kind of work was to resign and she simply couldn't afford to do that right now. While this job was hardly feeding her soul it paid the mortgage and that was what mattered most. At twenty-nine, this could also mark a much-needed turning point in her career. Until last week she'd never worked on a really massive exclusive – those jobs were always handed to the chief reporter or other favoured hack. So this was her chance to get up the ladder and start regularly working on the kind of stories that would move her from the middle to front pages. And she supposed that was where she should be. If she could get to the top of her game, perhaps then her father would drop the snobbery against what he called her "type of work" and finally be proud of her. As the only man in her life, her father's approval meant everything – perhaps even helping her conquer the desperate insecurity and lack of self-worth that had shadowed her since childhood.

She sighed then opened up her contacts file on her desktop and typed in the name of her target. Taking a deep breath, she picked up the phone and dialled.

Bob Guthrie was the first person to raise a smile out of Richard in forty-eight hours with his unintentionally humorous attempts to flag down a passing waiter or waitress. Bob was Shadow

Chancellor, with a deceptively bumbling exterior that masked the agility of his knowledge-packed mind. With Ray Molsley sitting to his left, sharing the moment, Richard let all the tension of the past few days go and laughed raucously at Bob's feeble finger ripple which couldn't attract a passing bee if his hand was covered in honey. Feeling a mixture of pity and impatience, Ray finally stepped in and waved his hand vigorously as their waiter walked away from a nearby table. "Another bottle of red," he said loudly.

Bob tried to hide his obvious shame, but couldn't prevent the lighter shade of crimson from creeping up his neck into his cheeks.

"Don't worry, Bob," said Richard, patting his friend and colleague on the back. "Fortunately you have other assets to compensate your inability to order at a restaurant."

"And fortunately you have me to flag down the waiter for you." Ray chuckled. The three men had been close friends since Richard's first months in Westminster. Bob had won his seat eight years ago at the same time as Richard. They were also similar in age, though Bob's ruddy cheeks and portly frame added at least another three or four years to his looks. Ray had acted as an unofficial mentor (and drinking companion) to the young MPs. Richard knew Ray's initial hand of friendship was not purely down to kindness, but rather his ability to spot future leaders. Although publicly seen as a jovial man of the people, he was in fact a shrewd and considered character, his one handicap in politics being his big heart. He had confided in them at a similar dinner two years ago that he knew they would both go on to great things and that's why he'd stuck with them, though Richard knew the bond went much, much deeper than that. In each other they had found kindred political spirits. They had a thirst for change that would not be quenched until they achieved it.

Bundled together in the packed Italian restaurant in Highgate, the three men found a safe haven to relax and offload. It was a place they would regularly meet to bitch about colleagues and, if they weren't too drunk, talk strategy. The restaurant was dimly lit, giving it an added feel of secrecy and conspiracy.

Richard finished the last of his soup and tried to get his mind back onto the election campaign which they had met to talk about. But it was too late. Anna's face was now firmly etched in his mind. He so desperately wanted to talk to her but she wouldn't return his calls. He realised why, of course. The moment Henry had finally chosen to confess that he'd forgotten to warn her about his speech – on the train back to London – he knew he'd lost all chance of keeping her on side. He hadn't wanted a long-term separation – he hadn't actually wanted any separation – but he had foolishly accepted Henry's advice to keep their distance for a couple of months to get them through the election and into Downing Street. He had thought he was doing the right thing. He had thought that sacrificing their happiness was a selfless act, done for the good of the country. But within hours of making the announcement he had seen his decision for what it was: an act of utter panic which could only show him to be weak and disloyal.

The control was slipping away from him and he sensed their marriage was in real trouble, particularly if she wouldn't even talk to him.

"I can see we've lost you again, Richard," Bob said, offering his colleague a comforting pat on the shoulder. "Have you managed to speak to Anna yet?"

"No." Richard hung his head. "She won't answer my calls or texts."

"She'll come all right," said Ray, with a confidence Richard knew was based on nothing more than optimism. Realising his dining companions expected him to back up his statement, he added: "She's been stung by the announcement and she needs time to heal. But she'll soon see you were only trying to do the right thing for everyone."

"Do you think it was the right thing?" Bob asked, his candor jolting Richard from the safety of his depressed mood.

"I didn't know what else to do."

"Well, I guess you could have stood your ground and said that Anna's past had nothing to do with the party's future."

"Oh that's wonderful, Bob." Richard held his hands up in frustration. "You tell me this now when there's no way back. I asked you to be at that meeting on Monday morning to decide what we should do and you didn't bloody turn up so it's a bit late now to hit me with the 'stand your ground' talk."

"I didn't turn up because Henry had ordered me to talk to every TV and radio show in the country to cover your arse. The man deliberately sets things up so I can't make key meetings. I thought you would have twigged that by now."

Bob looked at Richard for a response but he stayed silent. "Richard," he continued, "Henry knew if I'd been there I'd have told you to stick with the woman you love and not go dancing to the media's fiddle."

"Look, it's done now," Ray jumped in. "There's no point sitting arguing over what's already happened. Anna's going be just fine and we're going to concentrate on winning the bloody election so let's just stay focused shall we?"

Though he had stopped talking, Richard continued to glare at Bob – partly out of anger, but mainly because he knew he was right and it was killing him.

～

Anna watched in bemused admiration as her sister raced around the kitchen piecing ham sandwiches together, grabbing drinks and yoghurts from the fridge and, moments later, producing three packed lunch boxes.

"You've managed to turn that into an art form." Anna laughed.

"Yeah, well it's the only form of art I'll ever be able to produce," Libby replied whilst trying to tame her wildly curly hair into a knot at the back of her head.

Next, Libby's husband Dan appeared at the kitchen door and collected the three lunches. Anna could tell just by watching the two of them that they had perfected a morning routine that rarely wavered by even a minute.

"Jasmine, Ollie, Rupert, let's go," Dan shouted with the authority of an army major.

Anna smiled as she heard the thunder of feet on the stairs and through the hallway until the children's faces appeared alongside Dan's and they stood together like a ramshackle Von Trapp family. Jasmine, who at eleven was the eldest, shared her mother's corkscrew curls and fox-like pointed features. Ollie, two years younger, with his tousled blond hair inherited from his father and bright blue eyes, appeared to Anna to be an exquisite urchin – an impossibly beautiful scruff. And little Rupert was a law unto himself with wide-eyed, asymmetrical features like no one else in either family. Unlike his brother and sister, Rupert was immensely well-turned-out, taking great pride in his appearance despite being only six years old.

"We're off then, ladies," said Dan.

"Bye Mummy, bye Auntie Anna," Ollie called. Libby rushed forward to kiss her children, slightly panicked at the thought they could turn around and leave without saying goodbye properly.

"Bye kids," Anna shouted after them. "Have a good day at school."

As stressful as the last few days had been, Anna couldn't help but feel glad that they had created the opportunity for her to spend some time with her family like this. In the six years she had been married to Richard, she had never stayed with Libby and had only seen the kids on the odd afternoon. She'd never stopped to imagine her sister's existence as a wrung-out housewife, always dashing here and there trying to organise her family. From where Anna was sitting she could see that Libby's life – though pretty much devoid of luxury – was worth a hundred of her own. While her sister was surrounded by people who would be bereft without her, there was no one who couldn't live without Anna. In fact, she realised, she was little more than an ageing commodity that could be as easily disposed of as an empty can of Coke.

Her breakfast duties over, Libby sat down at the kitchen table opposite Anna and let out a long sigh. "It's only quarter past eight in the morning and I'm already bloody exhausted." She laughed.

Anna smiled. She felt relaxed for the first time in as long as she could remember. Sitting there in Libby's roomy but worn kitchen she felt hugely proud of her big sister. "You do such a great job, Libby. I was sitting here watching you and wondering how such a good mother could come from such a bad one."

"Mum was mentally ill. There was never any chance of her being a good mother."

"You always did defend her. You're much more forgiving than I am."

"That's because I've less to forgive." Libby gave her sister a long and knowing look and, as Anna returned her gaze, safe in the kindness and love of someone who knew her like no one else, she knew she had come to the right place. Libby had protected her through some of the darkest days of their childhood. Anna often wondered if she'd have ever made it this far without her sister. Surely the burden of her youth would have been too much to carry alone.

"I've been wondering these last few days why we never got counselling?" Anna asked.

"Well." Libby shifted uncomfortably in her chair. "When we left Wellinghurst we agreed we'd put it behind us – separate ourselves from our past and start again. I think that's the only way, don't you?"

"I don't know." Anna shook her head. "I thought I had put it behind me, but it's back again."

"Put it out of your mind," Libby said abruptly. "I'm going to make myself another coffee. Do you want one?"

"Okay," Anna replied, struggling to hide her disappointment that her sister had shut the conversation down.

Libby had only just got to her feet when the doorbell rang. The sisters looked at each other with wide eyes, their minds quickly sifting through the possibilities of who it could be.

"I'll take a look through the peek-hole," Libby said before tiptoeing out into the hallway, only to return a few seconds later. "There's a chubby red-headed woman with black-rimmed glasses on the doorstep who looks very familiar."

"Oh." Anna leapt up and headed for the hallway. "That's Joy, my PR agent."

Anna quickly opened the front door, checking behind Joy to see if any press had found where she was staying.

"Don't worry," said Joy, kissing Anna on the cheek. "No one knows you're here, although I'm sure they'll work it out soon enough."

Anna ushered Joy in and showed her through to the kitchen where Libby was busy making the coffee. "I'd better make it three cups then." Libby smiled then reached out to shake Joy's hand. "I'm sure we've met before though I can't remember where."

"Yes," Joy replied, eyes squinting while she tried to figure it out. "I think it might have been a couple of Christmases ago at one of Anna and Richard's drinks bashes."

"That'll be it," Libby agreed. "That was probably the last one they invited me to after I slipped in their kitchen and ended up with my skirt over my head." Libby laughed unselfconsciously at her own joke as she handed out the cups of coffee and guided the women over to the kitchen table.

Joy carefully laid her huge Mulberry shopper bag on the floor and proceeded to pull out that morning's papers. "Here is the news," she said, in classic newsreader tone, slapping the papers down on the table.

Anna immediately seized a copy of a tabloid which she held close to her face, studying its front page. "The man has no shame," she said, throwing the paper over towards her sister.

Libby looked at the main image and headline and realised immediately why Anna was so upset. There, in full colour and taking up a quarter of the front page, was a picture of Richard, head thrown back and laughing raucously with his colleagues in a restaurant.

"Look at him living it up with Bob and Ray while I'm hidden away like some kind of scarlet woman." Anna jabbed her finger at the picture while Libby nodded vigorously to show her support.

"For what it's worth, Henry says Richard's mortified by that photo. He said it was the one time he cracked a smile all evening," Joy piped in.

"Yeah, right," sneered Anna. "He looks just devastated doesn't he. Well, he doesn't hold all the cards, you know."

"What do you mean?" Joy asked.

"I mean I've got about fifty messages on my mobile phone

from newspaper editors and reporters asking me to call them. And I've just decided it's time to make that call."

"To who?" Joy asked again.

"To the *Sunday Echo*." Anna stretched her arm to reach the kitchen surface behind her and grabbed her mobile phone.

"Look, Anna, don't do anything rash," Joy said, her face flushed with something that looked to Libby like panic. "Let's just talk this one over and decide if it's the right thing to do."

"I've thought it over," Anna barked. "I'm not having them run ten more pages of shit this weekend if there's a chance I can actually get the truth out there instead. You don't actually think I'm going to sit back and let the media paint me as some cheap whore who slept her way to the top when I've had to fight for every little scrap of success that's ever come my way."

Joy opened her mouth to speak but Anna fixed her with a look that said *"don't even try to dissuade me"*, so she shrugged in defeat. "You've obviously made your mind up, Anna. Maybe Henry was right to say a showbiz PR like me doesn't get the bigger picture – certainly none of you seem willing to listen to me anymore. But I've been in this game a long time and I can tell you the one thing I know; the media is like a pack of hungry dogs, and if you feed them a juicy bone they will never leave you alone."

"I think her message is clear," Libby said, suddenly cutting in. "She's been spat out by Richard like a piece of gristle when, in actual fact, she's the one person in this entire situation that has some integrity. Soon the public is going to realise that, at which point Richard, and your husband, are going to have a bit of explaining to do." Libby arched her eyebrow defiantly before flashing Joy a forced smile.

Once again, Anna found herself caught in the middle between her old friend, Joy, and someone she loved and didn't want to betray. She knew Joy was only trying to help, but she was so entwined with Henry – and Richard – that it just didn't seem right that she should be involved at this point in time. So instead, Anna sat silently and watched Joy collect her bag and jacket, make her excuses and leave, clearly put out.

Anna wanted to stand up and tell her not to be so silly and to stay. That they were all on the same side really. But it was too late. She had to stay loyal to the one person she had ever really needed. Someone who would fight to the last to protect her; Libby.

5

LLOYD WRONGED BY "MERCILESS" SDP LEADER, SAYS PM

WEDNESDAY, APRIL 1ST, 2009, UK NEWSWIRE

The Prime Minister today branded Social Democrat leader Richard Williams "merciless" for announcing a separation from his wife over claims she had previously worked as an escort girl.

Kelvin Davis said Williams had treated Anna Lloyd "like a disposable commodity that had ceased to suit his carefully-manufactured image" and called on the opposition leader to publicly apologise to the actress for his actions.

Speaking to the BBC's *For the Record* programme, Davis said: "I feel sickened by the merciless way in which Williams has treated Anna who, let's not forget, is a much-respected actress who the people of this country have a great deal of affection for.

"It is just a pity that Williams doesn't seem to share that respect or affection. What we're looking at here is a man who is willing to cast off his own wife for political gain which, in my mind, is indefensible".

Davis was speaking after a new poll carried out on behalf of the *Today* newspaper revealed a sharp fall in support for the SDP leader in the wake of his marital separation.

Meanwhile, it was reported in two tabloid papers that Lloyd is set to tell her side of the story in an interview with the *Sunday Echo*, to be published this weekend.

Social Democrat sources admitted there was a great deal of anxiety over Lloyd's decision to speak out. The actress is said to be both furious and deeply humiliated by Williams' treatment of her, and party officials fear that an unfavourable account of their marriage could seriously damage the Democrats' chance of election victory next month.

K elvin paused momentarily to button his suit jacket before stepping out into the corridors of Number 10 where he was shortly due to carry out a meet and greet with charity bosses. In the few moments he had been left alone in his office he made sure, as usual before public appearances, that he combed a little more styling product through his hair. He was meticulous about his appearance and had once sacked an advisor who accompanied him on a press trip for not telling him his hair had ruffled at the back and was standing on end. For major appearances he employed the services of a grooming assistant who was allowed to apply increasing amounts of liquid concealer and powder to his face to avoid negative comments in the press about his "flamboyant lifestyle taking its toll" as they liked to describe it, much to his irritation. Being a single Prime Minister brought both unique perks and problems.

As he stepped out into the corridors of Number 10 he was

flanked, as usual, by both his press secretary, Reggie Caldwell, and PA, Vanessa Mellor. Reggie was in buoyant mood because it was he who had suggested Kelvin publicly side with Anna and today's poll had proved him right. "I think you should call Anna Lloyd today," Reggie gushed.

Kelvin couldn't suppress a smile as he watched his aide grow increasingly excited. Reggie had always tried to butch up for political life – a veneer that slipped within seconds of hearing the slightest bit of good news, at which point his hands would begin to flap and he would become breathless with the pace of his own speech.

Kelvin weighed up Reggie's suggestion before answering. "Don't you think that's taking things a bit far? This is the sort of situation in which one little error of judgement can set the whole scale of opinion tipping the other way."

"A personal situation needs a personal touch, Kelvin," Reggie replied using a schoolmarm's tone. "We can keep this very low key. Just a five-minute call from you to tell her you hope she's coping in such difficult times. We won't send out any statements or anything; we could just offer it to *News Daily* as a leak. We owe them one after the *Echo* exclusive last week anyway."

"All right." Kelvin sighed as they approached the reception room. His mind had already moved on to the forty or so guests he was going to have to meet and mingle with. This was most certainly the one part of the job Kelvin least liked. And opening the door to the room his heart fell further as he realised there was not a single celebrity or attractive female in sight.

Anna thought Marie looked a good deal younger than she had sounded on the telephone the day before. Based on their brief conversation to set up a time for the interview, Anna had placed Marie in her early forties but that was based mainly on the mature tone of her voice and crisp south-east accent that meant her sentences were clipped and to the point. She had been assertive but polite – the latter not being typical of all journalists in Anna's experience. Standing on her sister's doorstep, Anna could see the reporter was probably not even thirty yet, and was only a slip of a thing, her small height topped up a couple of inches by her edgily-tousled black hair. She thought she would hate the pushy hack who'd steamrollered her into an interview, but looking at the little pixie-like thing in front of her, Anna couldn't help but feel something close to affection. She just looked so sweet.

"You'd better let me in quick," Marie said, waving Anna back. "I saw a couple of photographers at the top of the road looking for the house and they're not with me."

"My PR agent said they'd be onto me soon enough," Anna replied, closing the door quickly. "Come through to the kitchen."

Marie trotted along the wooden hallway behind Anna until they reached the big open-plan kitchen.

"Did you say this is your sister's home?" Marie asked.

"Yes." Anna nodded.

"What a lovely family kitchen," the reporter said, her eyes misting with nostalgia as she looked around. Anna watched Marie as she studied the scruffy floors and furnishings and knew she had already identified Libby's home as one belonging to a loving and secure family who cared little about belongings and superficial gloss.

"I'm really enjoying spending time here," Anna said, alarming herself slightly at how quickly she was opening up. "My sister, Libby, is out shopping just now but she'll be back later."

"Great. It would be nice to meet her," Marie said as she rifled through her bag looking for her voice recorder. "I've got a photographer coming later, if that's still okay?"

"Yes, that's fine."

Marie had offered Anna the opportunity to come into the *Echo's* photographic studio for the shoot, but Anna had asked that they keep it low key and just take a couple of shots in the garden. She hated that she had to attach her photo to this interview – just which facial expression was she supposed to use in this situation? Meek smile? Bereft, heartbroken and wounded pout? But she knew the rules of the game by now and there was no way around it.

Once Anna had fetched Marie a coffee, and the reporter had set up her voice recorder, the two women were ready to begin the interview. Anna had rehearsed with Libby what she wanted to get across. Her sister had told her not to sound too bitter and not to get personal in attacking others as that might alienate people who had previously taken her side. She had agreed she would talk only fleetingly about her childhood and not mention the most difficult time – the shared secret which had followed the two of them around since their teens. They both felt the burden of it every day, but while Libby had pretty much made peace with her past, for Anna, it had become a black cloud that followed her wherever she went.

Sitting at the kitchen table that sunny spring morning, Anna saw that cloud for what it was; a hazardous mix of hurt and anger and shame that had been growing inside since her youth and which was just waiting to explode.

Marie took a deep breath before launching into her first question. Starting an interview as big as this one felt like tiptoeing towards the edge of a diving board and forcing yourself to step off. She had spent several hours preparing for this; the exclusive that could make or break her. And she knew all too well that if she started on the wrong foot, she could spend the rest of the interview paying for it. So Marie called on the outer confidence she used so convincingly to mask the inner nervous wreck that she actually felt.

"Do you feel your marriage to Richard is a happy one?" she asked, almost wanting to cross her fingers as the final word left her mouth. Earlier that day she had tried to rephrase her opening question several times, but in the end decided just to ask it outright, risking immediately putting Anna's back up. Marie hoped Anna would not get cold feet or simply skirt around her questions. They only had one hour together so every question had to count.

Marie relaxed as soon as she saw Anna begin to smile, holding her head to the side as she reflected on her situation.

"I certainly thought we were happy," she began. "The Richard I married six years ago was a very kind man, driven by his desire to improve the lives of others. Until I met him, I was a very inward-looking person. But almost as soon as we started talking I knew I had met someone who I would admire and learn from. Someone who genuinely wanted to change the lives of others for the better. That was tremendously attractive to me."

"What were the early years of your marriage like?" Marie shot the question out like a bullet, afraid that to linger over any word would give Anna time to close the shutters on her life which, for now, seemed wide open.

"There was a lot of storming and forming in the first couple of years." Anna chuckled. "Richard and I are both stubborn people with very strong opinions so that could cause a lot of tension between us. But in the main we were really happy. We were very in love and very committed as a couple and that kept us going through the bad times."

"And what were the bad times?" Marie looked up from her notepad, making sure she could catch any change in emotions from Anna.

"Just times when the past would catch up with me, in particular the death of my mother which I still struggle with sometimes." Anna sighed. "My relationship with her hadn't been easy so my grief can be all the more intense because it's fuelled by rage. I often took that anger out on Richard. But he was strong and he never cracked under the pressure. He knew I needed to work the pain out of my system and he gave me space and time. A lot of men wouldn't do that."

"Where do you think things started to go wrong?"

Anna slowly took a sip of coffee while she thought through her answer. As Marie watched, she realised this was a question the actress had not yet posed to herself.

"I think... looking back, things changed a little when he became party leader. The pressure was higher, he started to become much more aware of public perception. Suddenly, if I decided to wear a revealing outfit for a shoot, that became a party issue, rather than my own personal decision. Increasingly I was expected to seek approval before accepting work and that caused a lot of tension between us."

"Did Richard know about your past work as an escort girl?"

"Yes he did," Anna replied matter-of-factly. "But when I first met Richard he didn't see a former escort girl in me, he saw someone who had been failed by her mother and by the state under which I grew up. I was the very kind of person who Richard wanted to fight for. What happened to me in my youth made him so angry – and I loved him so much for it. Richard loathes injustice, which is why I still find it so hard to believe that when I needed him most, he turned his back on me. That's not the Richard I know. That's Richard the political machine and not Richard the man."

Marie shifted in her seat slightly, her heart rate quickening as her mind signalled a major story ahead.

"What was it that happened to you that made Richard so angry?"

"I was abused by my stepfather."

Marie fought desperately to hold Anna's sustained eye contact so as to conceal her shock at what her interviewee had just revealed. She had to maintain Anna's trust or the actress could shut down at any moment.

"Was it verbal or physical abuse?"

"It was verbal, physical and sexual. He targeted me the most, but my sister was affected too."

"Where was your mother when this happened?"

"Out of it."

"Out of it on alcohol or on drugs?"

"Alcohol."

"How long did this go on for?"

"Five years, four months and fifteen days."

"And how did it stop?"

"We killed him."

Anna regretted her confession the second after she told Libby what she had said. Her sister had bustled in from the supermarket just minutes after Marie left with the photographer, and had been happily setting about putting the shopping away when Anna reached out and touched her arm. "I told her, Libby."

"Told her what?" Libby turned to face her sister, her eyes wide as she clutched a tin of baked beans she was about to place in the cupboard.

"That we killed him."

"What? How could you do that, Anna? We'd put it behind us – it was finished." Libby's head was tilted like a confused child's, all her adult mannerisms stripped away by the revelation. She turned away from Anna and clutched on to the edges of the kitchen surface for support. "What am I supposed to do now? Did you think about that? Did you think about what would happen to my children when their friends find out? No one will want to play with them because their mother is a killer. We'll be social pariahs."

"No, Libby." Anna moved forward to comfort her sister, reaching out to put a hand on her shoulder which was abruptly pushed away as Libby turned back to face her.

"You get the hell out of this house, Anna. You've just ruined my life in two selfish fucking hours. You'll get wall-to-wall publicity for this, but what about me? I have a family. This isn't a game for me."

Tears started to stream down Libby's face and she gathered her arms to her waist in an attempt to console herself.

"We swore we'd never tell anyone what happened," she sobbed. "We left our past behind the day we left Wellinghurst. Now some shabby little tabloid is going to tell the world." Libby shook her head and jabbed her finger towards the front door. "You go now, Anna. Go."

6

LLOYD'S INTERVIEW BOMBSHELL FOR SOCIAL
DEMOCRATS' CAMPAIGN

MONDAY, APRIL 6TH, 2009, UK NEWSWIRE

The Social Democrats' election campaign was said to be in disarray last night following the publication of an explosive interview with leader Richard Williams' wife in a Sunday newspaper.

Anna Lloyd told the *Sunday Echo* that Williams had jilted her over claims she previously worked as an escort girl, despite having already been fully aware of her past, including a troubled childhood in which she was convicted of the manslaughter of her abusive stepfather.

The actress revealed she had killed her stepfather at the age of 14 following years of verbal, physical and sexual abuse of both her and her then 16-year-old sister, Libby Howarth, now 39. The pair spent two years at Wellinghurst Juvenile Centre before being released.

Lloyd described spending years in poverty trying to support

herself through drama school and her early years as an actress. During this period she admitted to working for the Mademoiselles escort agency for just six months. Lloyd told the *Sunday Echo* that she never had sexual intercourse with her clients and felt "deeply ashamed" of her past employment.

Most damaging to the SDP is the actress's claim that Williams had been aware of her work for the escort agency and had been fully sympathetic to her plight until the allegations interfered with his political career.

Prime Minister Kelvin Davis last night said he was "disturbed" by the way in which Williams had treated his wife and called for the Social Democrats leader to "do the right thing and stand down to support Anna at this distressing time".

Last night Williams refused to comment to reporters waiting outside his Highgate home.

"I feel like I'm finished here, Henry. We've backed ourselves into a corner we can't get out of." Richard sighed deeply as he looked around the meeting table into the faces of his closest colleagues. Once again, another Monday morning planning meeting had been completely dominated by the negative headlines over his marriage. But today's front pages were beyond anything they had previously feared. Even in their worst nightmares.

"She's certainly left us with egg on our faces, that's for sure," Henry replied, with typical understatement.

"I thought you said Joy had briefed her before the interview?" Sandra snapped at Henry. "Just what exactly is your wife telling Anna these days? Surely allowing her to plaster her darkest secrets all over the front pages isn't good PR – even in showbiz terms." Sandra shook her head to emphasise her dismay.

"Look, all I know is that Joy spoke to Anna before the interview but had no idea what she was intending to say. Until today, none of us knew Anna even had a conviction for manslaughter. Well, none of us except Richard." Henry pointedly turned his gaze on his boss.

"There's no point in us sitting arguing over the facts here," Bob said, wiping a large bead of sweat from the side of his forehead. "We need to work out what we do next. I've felt very uncomfortable right from the start about Richard being advised to distance himself from Anna and I think now justifiably so. We have absolutely no chance of influencing her actions now. We've cut our noses off to spite our faces."

"Well, thanks for the 'I told you so', Bob," sniped Henry, "but, actually, it's not too common to have escort girls for first ladies at Number 10. A little voice inside tells me that, were Richard to get back with Anna, the public might just have a little wobble about that one too." Henry presented a self-satisfied smile in the direction of Sandra who gave a small nod in non-committal agreement, neither noticing Richard's face turn ashen with anger.

"You talk about Anna like she's someone I barely know, Henry. She does actually happen to be my wife so I'd thank you to have a bit of bloody respect if it's not too much to ask." Richard eyeballed each of his colleagues in turn. "What Anna suffered in her childhood is unimaginable to the rest of us and I never, ever want to hear another bad word said against her. I have fucked up very, very badly, and right now I have to live with what has happened and I need each of your support."

"Can I suggest that we see what the next couple of days brings?" Ray volunteered. "Things may well have calmed down by then. This could just be a little bounce for the Alliance Party in the immediate wake of the furore so let's not be hasty. Are we agreed?"

"It's certainly the most sensible statement to come out of your mouth in recent memory so, on that basis alone, I'll agree," said Sandra before breaking into her half smile, half grimace that had become the stuff of political legend.

"All right," Richard agreed. "Let's sit tight for another couple of days and try and get on with business. Maybe if people see us keeping a level head then they'll be able to get past the headlines."

"And maybe they won't," said Bob, folding his arms to signal his dismay.

Sitting alone in her hotel room, Anna was reminded of her early days when she was just breaking into the more successful phase of her acting career. Her first major TV role saw her take the part of a young lawyer in a sitcom called *Eagles*, filmed in Manchester. She was on set five days a week, meaning she spent an equal number of nights staying in the nearby Sheraton. When she first landed the part, Anna thought the hotel stay was one of the perks of the job. She could order from room service, never had to cook a meal and didn't have to wash her sheets. Within about three weeks, however, the shine began to fade and she longed to be back in her Clapham flat where she could make her own meals and spread out on a comfortable sofa in front of the television surrounded by her own familiar belongings which gave her the closest thing to security she'd ever had. She quickly began to associate her hotel room with the loneliness she had been trying to escape since childhood. Now here she was again, left alone to feel the despair of the fourteen-year-old girl whose mother didn't love her enough to stop Dennis, her pathetic excuse for a stepfather, from mercilessly abusing her. By the age of fourteen she had come to believe that in some way she must have done something to deserve the pain and humiliation inflicted on her so regularly. But one thing Dennis hadn't reckoned on was Libby's inbuilt sense of justice. It was the uppermost trait that Anna had come to admire in human beings – and thus her enduring attraction to Richard.

She had told him about her troubled past just six months into their relationship. They had taken their first weekend break together to a hotel in Cornwall and, after a long and intimate dinner, they had ordered a nightcap to be sent to their room. Once settled into the sofa, clutching their cognacs, Anna had known the moment was right to bare her soul. He had listened silently, holding her hand as she poured out the full story. From her mother Linda's depression and decline into alcoholism after their father left when Anna was just eight, to her unforgivable betrayal when she turned a blind eye to the abuse faced by her daughters by the second husband she married two years later. Sadly, for Anna, she was Dennis's "favourite". In a hushed voice, sometimes crying, sometimes numb, she told Richard how her stepfather would wait until he thought everyone was asleep before sneaking into her and Libby's bedroom to abuse her. He had told the sisters he would kill them if they made any sound or dared tell anyone. But they knew it would be futile telling their mother anyway – because on one of his late-night visits Libby had seen her pass their bedroom door, obviously wondering where Dennis had got to. She stopped just a few feet outside, turned on her heels when she realised where he was and walked quickly back to her bedroom. Her mother, Anna had explained to Richard, couldn't bear to be alone.

"Yet she sentenced her innocent daughters to the loneliest ordeal of all," he had replied.

"That was my mother," she mumbled.

"What happened to her?" Richard had asked, sweeping her hair back from her tear-streaked face.

"She drank herself to death when I was fourteen. Libby found her, face up, covered in vomit. She'd choked on it."

"Anna," he'd said, shaking his head in disbelief. "Then you were left with him."

"Not for long." Anna had continued matter-of-factly as she worked through the story she had been desperate to tell for years. "Two days after my mother's funeral, he visited our bedroom, but Libby and I were waiting for him. We had vowed on the day our mother died that he would never hurt us again. Before he had even reached my bed Libby stabbed him in the back. He swung round and lunged for her but I hit him over the head with the bottle of vodka we had found by our mother's body. Then we ran. Our plan wasn't really to kill him, we just had to make it stop. But he died, and we were found two days later. We had nowhere to go and hadn't even left Bristol, so the police picked us up by the bus station where we'd been begging for money to get away. The most amazing thing was how kind these officers were to us. When we were sentenced to the young offender unit, one of them said he felt so bad about it he had thought about leaving the force. He couldn't get over the injustice of our being punished after everything we'd gone through. But Libby and I didn't care where we were sent. We were finally free. Nowhere could ever have been as bad as the place we had called home. Wellinghurst was like *Fantasy Island* compared to where we'd come from. Cooked meals, clean clothes – and no need to sleep with your eyes open."

"Anna," Richard whispered, folding her into his arms. "I'm so, so sorry. I can't believe what you've been through." He held her so tightly it almost hurt. "I don't want you to ever feel frightened again."

She had felt so safe in that moment. So accepted. But sitting in her hotel room, now with only herself for company, she had been transported right back to those dark days. Betrayed by her husband now as well as her mother. She was frightened and she was alone. The ocean of life had spat her onto the rocks where she would have to wait and hope for rescue.

The phone rang in Kelvin's office just as he was helping himself to another cherry which he gobbled quickly before spitting the stone into the bin and picking up the receiver.

"Yup," Kelvin said, still processing the remnants of the fruit skin.

"Reggie Caldwell for you, sir," said the operator.

"Go ahead." Kelvin reached for another cherry as he waited the few seconds it took to connect Reggie. "I thought you were supposed to be at a family wedding?" Kelvin asked teasingly. "Don't tell me you've run off with the groom."

"Very funny, Kelvin. I just thought you'd like to know that the murderess's husband is getting a further kicking in the polls following this weekend's revelations."

"Fantastic. We in front yet?"

"Not quite, but the *Daily Echo* are running a poll tomorrow which gives only a three-point lead to the Democrats. That's back from ten points two weeks ago."

"Well, that's moving in the right direction," said Kelvin. "How do we get on top now, Reg?"

"We've got to keep homing in on Williams' heartlessness. That's got to be the focus of the interview tomorrow on *Today with Michelle and Paul*. You need to appear genuinely shocked and upset by his behaviour. I'll have a full briefing with you before nine am."

"What time's the interview?"

"You're on at quarter past eleven and we'll be at the studios for ten forty-five, so plenty of time to go through it in the morning."

"And how do I play it with Anna? I mean, do I want to be seen to be sympathising with a murderess?"

"She was sexually abused, Kelvin," Reggie said dramatically as if announcing it for the first time. "The media have been pretty united in their support for her. In fact, most are painting her as a heroine of our time. One editorial I read this morning compared her to Evita. So, I think you need to be sympathising with her big time."

"Fine. Now get back to your wedding – and make sure you let them know that it's been bloody inconvenient letting you off on a Monday. Hope they appreciate the sacrifice." Kelvin smiled at his own joke.

"See you in the morning then, if I don't speak to you before." Reggie hung up and Kelvin got back to his cherries.

Richard slumped down onto the sofa and took a large gulp of wine. It had been a long day and he knew he should try and get to bed before midnight but he was savouring a few moments of normality in his own home. He turned to look at Anna's empty armchair and felt the now familiar lurch of his stomach whenever he thought about her. He had been an absolute fool to announce a separation so quickly, that much he knew. It had been the act of a desperate and confused man who had his eyes so firmly fixed on the finish line he hadn't noticed the large foot sticking out from the sidelines waiting to trip him up. Right until the moment he had made the announcement outside of the college, he had trusted Henry implicitly. Now, he couldn't help but hold him more than partially responsible for all that had gone wrong. Shouldn't Henry have known to try and ride out the first few days to see how things were panning out before making the rash decision of cutting Anna off? With his supposed wealth of PR and press experience, did he not realise such a move would play badly with the voting public?

Worst of all though, Richard realised Henry had treated both he and Anna as little more than political commodities. He hadn't stopped to think for even a moment about the carnage it would cause in their personal lives. Henry was only interested in coming up with fast solutions and soundbites.

As he had stood before the press and Bristol students that day, Richard had known almost as soon as the words left his mouth, that he was doing the wrong thing. And when, on the journey home, Henry had revealed he hadn't even had time to warn Anna about the announcement, Richard had felt sick to his stomach. But there was no going back. In politics, only the weak and vulnerable are forced to make U-turns – or obvious ones anyway. He knew he would be eaten alive if he tried to go back to Anna now.

Richard took another long slug from his glass, this time to finish it. His head was swimming with politics, pain and confusion. He missed Anna more than he could have ever imagined. He realised now that she was part of his internal fibre. He had only loved her more for her past, and how she had survived it, and yet it was now the very thing that separated them. He had a duty to his country to win this election and rid them of the hapless Alliance Party. But he knew, too, that he had a duty to his wife to make amends for his wrongdoing and to try to win her back. He didn't know which way to turn.

As he rose from the sofa to switch off the lamp and head upstairs to bed, Richard decided the best he could do was keep going. If he tried to choose which way to turn now, he knew he would only end up more lost.

7

"I SHARE ANNA'S PAIN," PM TELLS CHAT SHOW HOSTS

TUESDAY APRIL 7TH, 2009, UK NEWSWIRE

Prime Minister Kelvin Davis today opened his heart on national television to reveal he, too, had been forced into marital separation, comparing his situation to that of the actress Anna Lloyd.

In an interview on the *Today with Michelle and Paul* programme, Davis said he knew "the pain of an enforced marriage split", adding that he felt "devastated" for Lloyd, who recently separated from SDP leader Richard Williams.

The PM also went on to launch a scathing attack on Williams saying he was "deeply shocked" over his decision to leave his wife following revelations of her past as an escort girl and conviction for the manslaughter of her stepfather who had abused her during her early teens.

He said: "What Anna suffered is unimaginable. And I'm just so dismayed that, at a time when she needed Richard most, he walked away from her. I know the pain of an enforced marriage split. I know the devastation it causes the one left behind."

The TV interview was the first time Davis has opened up about his divorce five years ago from his then wife, Trish. The split came three years into his first term as PM and there were rumours at the time that his wife had felt pushed out because of her frumpy image.

But Davis told presenters Michelle Pelling and Paul Stoddart that it had been his wife's decision to leave because she "no longer wanted to live life in the public eye". When questioned by Pelling on his motivation for publicly supporting Lloyd, Davis replied: "This isn't about politics. This is about human decency – something which I believe Richard Williams lacks."

A spokesperson for the opposition leader said Davis was "once again blatantly capitalising on a private matter" between Williams and his wife.

Anna pushed back the covers on the hotel bed and reached for her mobile. It had buzzed three times in the last hour, but only the third one managed to rouse her enough to make her actually sit up. It was 10.20am, much later than Anna usually rose, but then she didn't exactly have much on at the moment. Her heart skipped a beat when she saw one of the texts was from Libby. She quickly opened it.

I'm still too angry to speak to you but need to know where you are and that you're okay. L.

Anna tapped out a quick reply.

Staying at The Metropole. Am fine. So sorry I've made things difficult for you. Couldn't live a lie any longer. Press would find out soon enough anyway now they're digging. Have things been awful? Love you. Xxx

Anna opened the remaining two texts from Joy. The first received at 8am.

We need to talk. J.

Then the second at 9.15.

Can you at least confirm you're still alive!?

She thought about how things had been left with Joy and wondered where it had all gone wrong. They used to be so close but that had changed over the last few weeks. Anna wondered if Libby had been right all along when she said Henry had only recommended that Joy work for her so she could act as his spy – and secret messenger. They had got along so well to begin with, and enjoyed mocking the sanctimonious self-importance their husbands often displayed. But once the political stakes got higher, the ground had shifted between them and the seeds of doubt within Anna had grown.

She stared at the message on her mobile and was just about to reply to Joy when another text came in from Libby.

House still surrounded by photographers now taking pics of kids. Not been out since you left. So yes, awful.

Anna put her head in her hands. The last thing she had ever wanted was to hurt Libby and her family. She hadn't intended to tell the reporter the full story, but the truth took her over and came flooding out. It had been hanging over her for twenty years and there had been nowhere left to hide. She hated that Libby was so angry, but once the press had twigged that she had dark secrets in her past, it was only a matter of time before they uncovered the manslaughter conviction. They had changed their surnames to Lloyd when they left the detention centre, but Anna had always thought it miraculous that none of their old school friends had ever gone to the press. Her looks had changed radically since childhood when she had been slightly chubby with mouse-brown, usually greasy hair seeing as they were rarely allowed to bathe or shower, in stark contrast to her now trim figure and glossy blonde tresses. Her accent was much crisper than before, something she had mastered at drama school, and she realised they must simply never have recognised her. After all, who could have imagined that the wretched little abused creature who skulked around the school corridors could have re-emerged as a successful actress and politician's wife? Sometimes, that was even too much for Anna to believe.

Having successfully managed to balance two tubs of pad thai noodles on her left arm, Joy freed up the right to rummage in her bag for the house keys. For the neighbours overlooking the home she shared with Henry in Battersea, this must have been a familiar sight as, in the four years they'd lived there, she'd not once remembered to take her keys out of her bag before she lifted the cartons from the takeaway every Tuesday night.

One of the tubs would usually sit out on the kitchen surface waiting for Henry to return later in the evening, while Joy would make light work of the second one – rarely stopping to tip it out onto a plate and usually eating it whilst standing.

Food – and her desire to eat lots of it – had become a

significant issue in Joy's life. As Henry became more and more busy, and they saw each other less and less, eating had filled the growing void in her life. But as she made her way through to the kitchen and slapped the cartons down onto the surface, she decided tonight would be different. Tonight she would eat slowly off a plate, sitting down. Tonight she needed to think.

Her phone hadn't stopped ringing since the story about Anna first broke – mainly from reporters looking for interviews or information, yet she had barely spoken to her client herself. Things had changed between them in the last few weeks. There used to be a lot of trust, but the people around them had cut into that. Now, Joy suspected it would be difficult for them to carry on working together. She could tell almost instantly that Anna's hawk-eyed sister was a force to be reckoned with and wouldn't make life easy for her. Joy was used to dealing with intimidating people with big personalities, but it was the way Libby hung back and simply stared that had unnerved her so much. She didn't have to say anything – the way she had looked at her said it all. Her eyes screamed, *'I don't trust you.'* And Joy had known that she would soon lose her most high-profile client, because Anna would always follow her sister's advice.

"You've got ten seconds to get yourselves down here or there's no screen time tonight," Libby hollered up the stairs to the three kids. She had been dreading this morning since teatime yesterday when Dan had announced that he had a breakfast meeting and she'd need to take the children to school. Libby hadn't left the house since Anna had revealed they'd killed their stepfather, her fear of the looks she'd be met with at the school gate rendering her too terrified to go out. She had imagined the mothers hustling their children away from her and urging them to run into their classrooms so they could escape the violent beast in their midst. Dan, who would remain unfazed if a tornado was headed straight for him, had obviously failed to hear the whispering that must have been going on behind his back for the last few days when he'd been taking the children in. And Ollie had never even mentioned the newspaper story since Libby had been forced to sit them down the previous Sunday to explain what had happened. She hadn't told them she'd been sexually abused, just that her stepfather had been an extremely violent man who would have really hurt her and Anna had they not fought back. When she asked the children what the kids at school were saying, Ollie had simply replied: "They're cool."

Jasmine, who never missed an opportunity to tell a dramatic story, had said: "Oh my God, the girls at school were just like soooo amazed that Anna's been staying with us – and that the paparazzi totally know my name. Can I have a sleepover party on Friday after school so my friends can see the photographers?"

Libby hadn't been able to contain herself in response: "Has no one mentioned the fact your mother committed a crime?"

"Oh yeah," Jasmine had replied. "They think you and Anna are so brave. Gabby thinks I look like Anna, do you, Mum?"

Dan had chuckled while Libby tutted at the children's flippancy. In her view, even if people were on the surface being quite PC about it all, their true feelings would soon come out when the murderess turned up in person at the school. And today was that day.

Libby heard the familiar sound of feet hitting the upstairs landing and watched in silence as her three children appeared in front of her one by one.

"Right then." She swallowed hard. "I guess we'd better get going."

Libby took a deep breath then opened the front door. The handful of snappers waiting outside – by now convinced she was never coming out – suddenly leapt into action, bulbs relentlessly flashing as Libby guided her children along the path. A few of the photographers walked ahead of them. Libby stopped for a moment, realising she'd have to make a split-second decision on whether to keep going or flee back to the relative safety of her home. She turned to find Jasmine beaming for the cameras, striking a variety of ridiculous poses, which were quickly copied by her brothers. Soon the three of them were sticking their tongues out, then forcing their mouths wide with their fingers.

"Come on," Libby said firmly, pushing the children forward. "I'd really rather you didn't take pictures of the kids," she said to the photographers.

"We've got our shots now. We'll not show their faces," one of them replied, backing away to stand at the side where he started looking over what he'd taken.

Libby walked on purposefully, while the children chattered excitedly about what all their friends would say when they got into the papers. Jasmine was desperately hoping she'd make *Heat* magazine, which Libby suspected was doubtful.

She couldn't believe the continued interest in her and her family. She understood why Anna was still splashed across the front pages – but not herself.

They cut across the park, before turning onto the street leading to the school. Libby could feel her heart racing as the familiar faces started to appear in front of her. First, she spotted the mother of a girl in Jasmine's class climbing out of her enormous Land Rover. She kept her head down, desperately hoping to avoid her gaze.

"Libby," she heard the woman call loudly.

Everything inside of Libby screamed *'noooooo'*, but she turned to face the mother who was by now bounding over to her from her car. Ironically, Libby thought, they'd never even exchanged names. But this woman had no doubt of Libby's.

"How are you?" she was asking, with the most sincere look of concern Libby had ever seen. "I read all about your terrible ordeal – and I had no idea that you are Anna Lloyd's sister. I just think she's the most wonderful woman. I feel so connected to your plight. Pippa's just desperate to have Jasmine for a sleepover, but I'd love to talk to you properly. Would you like to bring her over next Friday night and come in for a glass of wine?"

Libby was suddenly aware that she was expected to reply. Until that point she had simply stood with her eyes wide open and mouth slightly ajar as the woman spoke.

"That sounds lovely, yes," was all she could manage.

"Fantastic," the woman shrieked victoriously. "Pippa can give Jasmine our address. See you next week." She waved casually as her daughter, who had been standing meekly by her side throughout, turned to smile at Jasmine before trotting off behind her mother towards the school gates.

"Yuck," Jasmine said in a loud whisper. "I don't want to have a sleepover at Pippa's. She's a total swot."

"Oh, sorry," Libby replied vaguely.

As they neared the school, Libby caught sight of the woman she was dreading seeing most – Franchesca Carruthers, mother of four and queen bee at the school. She had appeared judgemental towards Libby even before she discovered she was a murderess so the thought of how she would treat her now, armed with this knowledge, was almost inconceivable. Typically, Franchesca had already delivered all four children to their classrooms – she was never late – and was now heading straight for Libby who smiled fraily in her direction before pushing the children forward. But before she could take another step Franchesca had come to an abrupt stop in front of her where she now stood with arms outstretched. At first, Libby thought she was trying to wave them off the premises, but within seconds of being folded into a tight bear hug, she realised they were actually embracing.

"God," Franchesca was saying loudly. "You've been through hell." She let go of Libby, only to then cup her face between her large, matronly hands. "I have been fundraising for the NSPCC for the last thirteen years and not for one minute did I ever stop to think whether someone I knew might have actually been abused themselves." Tears were now welling up in Franchesca's eyes while Libby just prayed that she would let go of her face. Fortunately, she obliged, opting now just to rest her hand proprietarily on Libby's shoulder.

"I want you to know that you can talk to me *any* time, okay? If you need space, I can take the kids. If you need support, I can listen. I'm here, all right?"

Libby nodded, afraid to glance left or right over Franchesca's shoulder in case she caught the eye of the small crowd of parents assembled around them, each one trying to appear as though they were doing anything other than staring.

"Thank you, Franchesca. I appreciate your support," Libby finally replied in stunned monotone, before setting off towards the school entrance again – mortified, but rather buoyed by her new-found status as a local heroine.

8

DAVIS TO COMFORT LLOYD OVER LUNCH AT NUMBER 10

THURSDAY, APRIL 9TH, 2009, UK NEWSWIRE

Prime Minister Kelvin Davis will today meet with Anna Lloyd, the actress wife of opposition leader Richard Williams, as part of an official reception to celebrate Women of Courage.

Sources close to the Prime Minister admitted Lloyd was a late addition to the guest list, but added that Mr Davis had felt "compelled and inspired" after reading of the actress's suffering during her youth at the hands of her stepfather.

Lloyd revealed in a recent newspaper interview that, following years of abuse, she and her sister had killed their stepfather shortly after their mother's death from alcoholism.

Lloyd will join eight other women who have overcome extreme adversity, including 43-year-old dinner lady, Maggie Rae, who fought off armed attackers at a school in Manchester in July last year.

Mrs Rae barricaded herself along with one hundred children into the school dining room, forcing the mob – who were looking for a rival gang member – to give up their search and leave without harming anyone.

Davis's hand of friendship to Lloyd follows a remarkable turnaround in political fortunes in the polls, which now puts his Alliance Party just a few points behind the SDP. Williams has been unable to stave off an Alliance onslaught following his decision to separate from Lloyd in the aftermath of tabloid claims that she previously worked as a professional escort.

But the Prime Minister's decision to invite Lloyd to the lunch at Number 10 did not win the support of all his parliamentary colleagues. Alliance backbencher Lizzie Ancroft said the actress was "not worthy of a place at a table honouring courageous women".

She added: "The sordid allegations about Anna Lloyd's past along with the revelation that she has a previous conviction for the manslaughter of her stepfather, have only added fuel to the publicity juggernaut surrounding this attention-seeking actress.

"I am disappointed that the Prime Minister has chosen to join the circus, turning what should have been a celebration of bravery into little more than a charade."

"Do you want me to run through everyone's names one more time?" Reggie asked, as he broke into a trot in an attempt to keep up with Kelvin's trademark brisk walk through the halls of Number 10.

"No, I think I've got it, thank you. Where's Lloyd sitting in relation to me?"

"You're at the top of the table and she'll be sitting to your left. You'll have Anita Blaine on your right – the woman who..."

"Rescued a drunk from a drain, I remember."

"Well, it was more of a flooded ditch than a drain..."

"I've got it, Reggie. Where's Alfie sitting?"

"The Home Secretary's in the middle of the table and the Minister for Women is at the opposite end to you."

Kelvin paused briefly just before they reached the door to the reception room.

"Well, I hope they've put the knives away," he said with a wry smile.

"Knives?"

"I'll be sitting next to a convicted killer, Reggie. You can't be too careful."

"Oh," said Reggie, looking concerned.

"Don't worry, Reg. I'm used to fighting women off." Kelvin winked at his press secretary before making his grand entrance into the room.

Anna tried to remain focused on the very broad Mancunian dinner lady who had accosted her as soon as she'd walked into the reception room, but she couldn't help but steal a long glance at Kelvin as he walked in. She hadn't seen him up close in at least four months and she thought he'd lost a bit of weight around his midriff. His hair was slicked back as usual, and he'd chosen a bright pink tie for the occasion – clearly to show he was in touch with women, Anna thought. She had never known quite what to make of Kelvin. While he was a hugely charismatic and engaging character, there was more than a small element of slime around him and it was clear he had an eye for the ladies. He especially enjoyed giving long, lingering glances – of which Anna had been at the receiving end of more than a few. And within a few seconds of entering the room, his eyes had found her out and he was, indeed, staring at her. Anna focused intently on the dinner lady again, who was enjoying a long rant along the lines of "don't worry, love, all men are shits". Anna nodded appreciatively and hoped the next two hours would pass quickly.

Kelvin, who had already greeted a couple of courageous women, quickly side-stepped his way towards Anna.

"My dear," he said, in the tone of a long-lost uncle. "So nice to see you here." He lunged forward and planted a lingering kiss on her left cheek.

"Thanks for inviting me," said Anna. "It's actually my first engagement since the whole marriage saga kicked off – in fact, it's pretty much my first time out anywhere since then."

"Well, you're among friends here today," Kelvin said earnestly. Anna smiled politely but decided to move Kelvin's attentions on before he said something that would really make her regret her decision to join him for this event. She was beginning to sense that the talk about this being "a non-political celebration, focused entirely on the women whose courage it sought to highlight" had actually just been a line to hook her into boosting Kelvin's campaign. The thought made her stomach lurch and she turned quickly to the lady standing expectantly between them.

"This is Maggie Rae," Anna said, touching her new acquaintance on the arm.

"Hiya, Mr Davis. Thanks ever so much for inviting me," Maggie gushed.

"You are most welcome, Maggie. I've heard so much about you." Kelvin's eyes darted around the room as he searched out an advisor or PA who would keep him right on timing.

"If I could encourage you ladies to move towards the far side of the room, we are going to gather for a small photo."

"Oooh, lovely," Maggie said, heading quickly in the direction Kelvin was pointing.

The Prime Minister leaned in towards Anna. "Might I say, you look particularly beautiful today, Anna. Your recent upset has done nothing to harm your looks."

"You're very kind, Kelvin. Thank you," replied Anna curtly in order not to further encourage him. But Kelvin hadn't finished.

"You just stick to your guns – metaphorically, of course – and stay as far away as you can from Richard, because I've always known he's all front and no substance. Frankly, you need a better man than that. I know how it feels to be publicly dumped and if you ever need someone to talk to, do not hesitate to call me here. Do you understand?" With this he gave Anna a conspiratorial nod, before marching off in the direction of Reggie.

Anna raised her eyes to the ceiling and sighed at the naivety of her decision to attend. With or without Richard, she was still a political pawn and realised she would have to be more careful in future about the events she chose to support. It was clear Kelvin was still living up to his reputation as a womaniser. Anna couldn't help but wonder what he would have planned for next week's visit from the Italian Prime Minister, with whom he famously enjoyed "socialising", but she had no doubt he would be looking forward to it.

"Well, the headlines are clearly not going away," Richard said, making sure he caught Henry's eye as he made this point, "So we've got to look at how we can turn things around. I have my own ideas on what needs to be done, but first I'd like to hear from each of you." Richard looked around his inner circle expectantly.

"If I could just say," Bob jumped in. "It was clear to me from the start that public opinion would not change whilst Richard remained estranged from Anna. People are firmly on her side and, right now, she appears to be a woman in need of support from the husband she clearly still loves. I was never in favour of the separation in the first place..."

Sandra groaned and raised her eyes to the ceiling.

"... but, it's time to look forward, not back. Richard needs to make amends for his wrongdoing."

"Are you seriously saying he should go back to Anna after all that's been said?" Sandra asked, her mouth hanging open with incredulity. "She has just spent the afternoon with Kelvin Davis after all. Talk about kicking sand in our faces."

"And maybe we asked for that," Ray piped in. "I'm with Bob one hundred per cent. I don't believe we can win this election without Anna back in the fold. The biggest question is going to be whether she'll have him back and whether the public are going to be willing to forgive him before May 7th."

"But how are we going to announce this spectacular U-turn?" Sandra demanded. "It's going to look like Richard has been forced to go back grovelling. That does nothing to improve our standing..."

Richard allowed the voices of his colleagues to fade away as he thought about the last couple of weeks. He had been swept into a whirlwind of press conferences, speeches and briefings which had left him doubting whether he would ever remember who he actually was as a human being. He only knew what he had become. A man who would ditch his wife, a woman he truly loved, at the first sign of a bad poll rating.

"I know this might come as a shock to some of you," Henry was talking directly to him now, "but I think I need to start by making an apology today. While I still think Anna needed some time away from the cameras, I fully accept that in not consulting with her first we made a mistake for which I am substantially responsible." He cleared his throat nervously before turning to

Richard. "I am prepared to tender my resignation if it would help this situation."

A brief stunned silence followed before Richard finally spoke. "I appreciate that offer, Henry, and I agree that we got this wrong, but I think it is more than just you who owes the apologies around here. What happens between my wife and I should never have been about politics and I was absolutely wrong to mix the two things together. It is me who owes her the biggest apology of all and I want to try and do that today. If it doesn't work out, there's nothing we can do to change the situation. If I have to fall on my sword over this one I will. So let's not discuss how it is handled or who gets to know what. All I ask is that you give me a couple of hours to do what I have to."

"What about the prison visit at three?" Henry asked.

"I can be a little late, can't I? My marriage comes first."

"Understood," said Henry meekly.

The doorman at Number 10 nodded to Anna before setting her loose to face the huge press pack waiting outside. The cameras started flashing just as soon as the door opened and Anna had to momentarily shield her eyes before stepping out. She felt her legs shaking and worried that her movement would seem awkward, such was her tension. She remembered the early years of her career when she would suffer terrible stage fright and would have to force herself to walk out in front of the audience. Today, that level of fear had returned. She took a deep breath and walked towards the sea of cameras and reporters all readily hovering behind the barrier on the other side of the street.

She could hear them calling her name over and over.

"Anna, Anna. Give us a smile. Look this way, Anna. That's it, love," the photographers were saying. The reporters, on the other hand, always stuck to the more formal "Ms Lloyd". "When was the last time you spoke to your husband?" a female voice shouted. "What did the Prime Minister say to you, Ms Lloyd?" a male reporter cut in.

Anna knew she had two choices: stay and talk to them or smile and walk away quickly. She thought the latter would be the most sensible option, but there was something about the cameras flashing and the way they were all beckoning her that she just couldn't resist. She moved closer to the pack and waited as the reporters jostled to get right in front of her.

"I spoke only briefly with the Prime Minister," Anna began. "This was not a political visit, but rather a chance to celebrate and acknowledge women who have displayed enormous courage in their lives..."

"Have you spoken to your husband?" another reporter interjected.

"I've not spoken to my husband since he made the announcement that we were to separate."

"Are you going to divorce?" a male voice rang out.

"I'm just taking one day at a time right now, thanks. I've only just started to get back on my feet after everything that's gone on and I'm obviously very concerned about the effect all this is having on my sister and her family, since some of the recent reports have involved her."

"Will you be voting Alliance on May 7th now?" a young male reporter cheekily asked.

"No, I'll be voting SDP as I always have." Anna smiled. "I may not like my husband very much right now, but I do still believe he's the right man to lead this country."

Suddenly there was a rush of questions that all merged into one loud roar and Anna decided it was time to move. She could see her driver waiting for her a little further up the street so she thanked the reporters then turned around swiftly. They were still calling for her even as she closed the door of the car and when she turned to see what the clattering sound was to her right, she realised the photographers were chasing the vehicle down the street, pressing their lenses against the window to catch whatever shot they could. Anna knew she should be finding this experience deeply, deeply unsettling, but instead, she felt totally numb; the camera flashes providing a comforting break from reality. She wondered if that was why she had craved fame so much all these years? Because the world of celebrity had seemed to provide a perfect refuge from the past.

Except now she could see that shelter was built on sand and its walls made of paper.

Once they had cleared Downing Street and were making their way back towards the hotel, Anna checked her mobile phone. She had two missed calls; one from Libby and one from Richard. Anna quickly dialled the person she most needed to talk to.

It took several rings before Libby finally answered.

"Hi Anna," she said in a tone that was neither warm nor cold.

"Libby, I'm so sorry. I've felt so awful these last few days. I really, really hope I haven't ruined everything for you. I hadn't planned on telling that reporter about what we did, but once I started talking I just couldn't stop myself. It had to come out."

"It's okay, Anna. You were right when you said it was only a matter of time before the press got onto it. We've been lucky to keep it secret for this long."

"How are Dan and the kids? Is everything all right?"

"All right? They're all bloody delighted. We've never been so popular. I'm now some kind of local hero, while the kids have had more play-date requests in the last week than they have since the beginning of the year."

Anna laughed with relief. "So I haven't ruined your life?"

"No, but I have you to blame for the fact I've now been asked to sit on countless boards for women's refuges, not to mention the events I've been asked to speak at. I'm already booked for the Women's Institute next month. Dan's finding the whole thing hilarious. He just loves the fact that I suddenly have to be nice to everyone."

"Have the photographers gone?"

"They packed up yesterday. They must have got sick of looking at my crumpled face and bird's-nest hair every morning."

"I'm sorry, Libby. For everything I've put you through. And not just these last couple of weeks, but all the times I've been too busy to talk. I realise now what I've missed and I just felt so devastated when I thought we might never speak again. I really need you, Libs."

"Don't be silly, Noo-Noo," she replied softly, Anna's heart swelling with the warmth of hearing her sister call her the pet name she used in childhood. "I couldn't turn my back on you. Why don't you come over and have dinner with us?"

"I'd love to. I'm meeting Joy at four but I could be with you by six."

"Great. I'll see you then."

Anna stared back down at her phone as she tried to figure out whether it would be a good idea to call Richard back or not. She was still badly hurting from their split, but she was also incredibly curious as to what he would have to say. In the end, her decision was made for her when her mobile rang again.

"Hello Richard," she answered tersely.

"Anna." His voice broke. "I'm so, so sorry. I allowed myself to be talked into something I knew wasn't right. I've hurt you and I've humiliated you and I'm so damn sorry. I told the campaign team today that our marriage could no longer be based on politics but what is best for the two of us. I need you back, Anna. Can you please forgive me and come back to me?"

Anna sat in silence for a few moments, absorbing what her husband had just said.

"Anna?" His voice was full of insecurity.

"I'm still here, Richard. You dumped me on national television without even the slightest warning and then, when you've taken a kicking in the polls for it, you call me out of the blue and ask me to come back. Do you think I'm completely stupid or something?" Anna's voice was picking up in both pace and volume. "Do you think I'm such a sad excuse for a human being that I would allow you to shit all over me in front of the whole world and then just hold the door open for you to do it all over again – as and when the political need takes it?"

"Anna, please..."

"You can forget your apologies. In fact, you can forget you were ever bloody married to me. You hurt me more than I can ever, ever tell you. I loved you... I loved you and you cast me out like a leper. Now you must live with the consequences and you deserve every bit of bad press that you get. I hate that the Alliance Party have a chance of winning now, but I'm not prepared to live a lie just to get you votes. Goodbye."

Anna cut off the call and hurled the phone into her bag before letting out a frustrated cry. Her heart was racing and her head pounding with the force of blood pumping around her body. Nothing stung more than the pain of betrayal. Yet she had been betrayed by nearly every person she had ever loved. Everyone but Libby.

"You still want me to take you to Crouch End?" her driver asked cautiously.

"Yes please, John. I'm fine. Just putting Richard straight on a couple of things."

"Quite right." He smiled.

As she reached the top step of the stairway, Anna could see Joy already sitting on their favourite sofa in the coffee house where they had been holding their meetings for years. It had a downstairs section with only a couple of tables which were invariably empty so it was perfect for them to hold a private conversation – and for Anna to go unnoticed. Only, whereas before their coffee sessions would have involved a considerable amount of bitching, gossip and laughter, today's meeting would be a lot more formal. As she made her way down the stairs, Anna noticed the tension on Joy's face, her mouth set in a grimace as she sipped her coffee, seemingly lost in thought.

"Hello Joy," Anna said as she reached the last step. Joy got to her feet and stepped forward to kiss her on each cheek, though Anna noticed the broad smile with which she usually greeted her was missing.

"You look good, Anna," she said distantly. "You'd never know you'd been through a life crisis."

"I don't feel I'm quite through that crisis yet," Anna replied, trying to keep things upbeat even though she felt decidedly shaken by her phone call with Richard. "It's more Libby I've been worried about lately," she continued. "This whole thing has had a huge impact on her."

"It must have been tough."

"Yes. It's been bloody awful, but in a strange sort of way I think we both feel a big burden has been lifted from our shoulders. After all, I have nothing left to hide – and I can't tell you how good that feels."

"I'm glad you're finding some peace in all this. I wish I could say the same for myself." Joy sighed.

Anna sensed an uncomfortable shift in the conversation. "What's on your mind?"

"I've had to ask a lot of questions of myself these last couple of weeks. Being married to Henry and working for you has not been without its complications."

"I can imagine." Anna smiled.

"Since Henry took on the communications job for the Democrats, he became almost obsessed by your influence over Richard. He would ask me on a daily basis who you were meeting with, what you were saying, what jobs you were considering. It became impossible to separate work from our marriage and, I'm afraid, I feel like I've been too influenced by Henry in the last couple of years."

"What do you mean?"

"I mean I knew he was going to tell Richard to cut you off and I didn't warn you."

Anna sat back in her chair, taking a few moments to let what Joy had just told her sink in. "I'm shocked on both counts here, Joy. First, that you seem to be inferring Henry instructed Richard to leave me rather than it being Richard's decision, and secondly, that you had the chance to help me out in a bad situation and you didn't. Isn't that what I employ you for?"

Joy stared at her feet, the two women staying silent as the waitress arrived with the peppermint tea Anna had ordered upstairs. She looked between them as she set the cup and teapot down, trying to work out what was going on before deciding to make a hasty retreat.

"Actually, I'm not sure quite what it is you employ me for now, Anna. You haven't listened to a word of advice I've given you in months. Regardless of what I'd say, you'd just do your own thing anyway. I guess that's what fame and power do to a person."

Anna studied Joy's face for signs of irony, but there were none. She was absolutely serious.

"Where is this all coming from?" Anna asked, still stunned

by the sudden outburst. "We've always got along so well. I had no idea you felt like this."

"And when is the last time you stopped to consider how anyone else actually felt? There's only one star on the Anna Lloyd show. No one else gets a look-in." Joy's eyes were blazing, betraying what looked like years of pent-up anger.

"Well, you're showing your true colours now, aren't you?" Anna said, reaching for her handbag which she then clutched defensively to her stomach as she prepared to leave. "To think I trusted you, Joy, when all along you just resented me."

"I don't resent you. I pity you," Joy replied defiantly, her flushed cheeks the only indicator of her discomfort.

"I don't understand this, Joy. But, I think it goes without saying that we can't work together anymore after what you've just told me."

"Well, I'll just have to deal with that." Joy turned and looked away from Anna who was by now fighting back tears as she sprung to her feet and made her way up the stairs, all the time trying to work out what had caused Joy to feel so bitter. She had thought they got along so well and, although Anna knew she could be a bit self-centred sometimes, she always believed they had a balanced friendship in which they could both confide their secrets. But then, perhaps Joy was angry that Anna hadn't shared her biggest secret of all – which she'd had to read in a Sunday newspaper like everyone else. Whatever it was, Anna knew there was no going back. She just hoped things between them wouldn't turn uglier.

Libby was lowering the heat on the bolognese sauce when the doorbell rang. She laid her wooden mixing spoon down and was about to head to the front door when she heard Dan in the hallway, ushering Anna in.

"So we've got you to blame for our new-found local fame, have we?" he joked.

"Libby told me you were loving the celebrity, Dan, so don't try and tell me otherwise," Anna replied, laughing.

The kitchen door opened and Libby turned to greet her sister. She marvelled at how effortlessly glamorous Anna looked in her figure-hugging wool dress and knee-length black boots. It had always seemed to Libby that Anna managed to look good in anything while, in contrast, she was a lost cause on the fashion front and had long since given up trying.

"You look sickeningly good as ever," she said to Anna, planting a kiss on her cheek.

"I applied extra war paint this morning before going for lunch at Number 10. Turns out I needed it."

"Why?" Libby smiled. "Was Kelvin harassing you?"

"Not really. Kelvin was just Kelvin. It was Joy who ruined my day."

"Is that your PR woman?" Dan chipped in from the kitchen table behind them, where he'd now seated himself.

"It was my PR woman, yes." Anna sat down beside Dan who proceeded to pour her a large glass of red wine.

"What's happened?" Libby asked.

"She told me today that she knew Richard was going to announce a separation but didn't warn me. She then went on to pretty much call me a selfish cow who only cared about myself."

"What?" Libby shrieked in outrage.

"I never liked her," Dan added.

"You've never even met her," said Libby.

"Yeah, but I didn't like the sound of her, and I've seen her on TV and she's got a really dodgy American-English accent going on. I just thought she was a bit up herself."

"Well," Anna continued, fuelled by her first few gulps of wine, "I think she's been feeding me Henry's lines as well. She as good as admitted it. When she was telling me to watch what I said to that *Echo* reporter, it wasn't because she was worried about my reputation – she was too busy worrying about Richard's."

"What a stupid cow," Libby raged before turning back to strain the spaghetti.

"The problem is I'm now left without a PR agent when I need one the most. I haven't a clue where to start looking because Richard always helped me with that before."

"What did she do exactly then? What do you need?" Libby asked as she slopped the spaghetti onto the six plates laid out on the kitchen surface.

"I need to find someone who can answer press enquiries for me, and help arrange TV interviews and appearances. That kind of thing."

"Well, I can do that," Libby said.

"She needs a professional, Libs." Dan chuckled. "You can't just suddenly call yourself a PR agent just because you've seen off a few photographers on the school run."

"It was just a suggestion." Libby shrugged her shoulders and continued plating up, before Anna cut in.

"I think that's a wonderful idea. Why pay a stranger who I don't even know I can trust when I can work with my own sister? You can consider yourself hired, Libby."

"You hear that, Dan." Libby spun around to look at her husband, jabbing the spoon she'd been using to serve up the bolognese sauce in his direction. "You're now married to a PR agent for a famous actress, so eat that." She winked.

"Oh God," Dan droned to Anna. "You've only just given her the job and already she's turned into a media monster. I'd better have another drink."

9

WILLIAMS HINTS AT MARRIAGE RECONCILIATION

FRIDAY, APRIL 10TH, 2009, UK NEWSWIRE

Opposition leader Richard Williams has hinted his marriage to the actress Anna Lloyd is not over, despite her apparent anger at the way he handled their recent separation.

Following a visit yesterday to Pentonville Prison in London, Williams told reporters that he was "still very much a married man".

The SDP leader's marriage was rocked following claims in a Sunday newspaper that Lloyd had previously worked as an escort girl. Shortly after, Williams publicly announced their separation in a move rumoured to have been advised by party spin doctors who were keen for Lloyd to be taken out of the political picture as quickly as possible.

Sources close to Williams revealed he has had "second thoughts" about the separation in recent days but denied this was down to a sudden fall in support for the Democrats in the polls.

Lloyd's recent disclosure that she and her sister, Libby Howarth, killed their stepfather as teenagers following years of abuse, has led to a huge outpouring of public sympathy for the actress.

Williams is later today due to give a TV interview to the *AllNews24* channel in which it is expected he will discuss his marriage amid speculation that he may be attempting to bring his wife back into the party fold.

R ichard straightened his tie and allowed the make-up girl to apply a light dusting of face powder while he waited for Esther Yarleth to arrive for the interview. From the corner of his eye he could see Henry nervously shuffling from foot to foot. The interview had been organised as an opportunity for Richard "to reconnect with the public" but, as the SDP leader had informed his campaign team earlier that morning, he actually intended to use the chance to send an appeal to Anna – an idea that had been warmly welcomed by Bob and Ray whilst Sandra and Henry's response had been slightly more muted. "This is your call," was all his head of communications had said.

But Richard's mind was firmly made up. He needed Anna back and he knew it. Not just to improve his chances of winning the election, but because without her he felt weak, inept and unable to lead a nation. Today, he would do what he should have done right from the start. He would tell the truth – and he would be honest about the situation he and Anna had found themselves in. Henry, who was paying penance for his sins, would just have to go along with it.

Richard heard Esther before he saw her. She was chattering loudly to an assistant in the corridor, complaining about the way her hair had been styled. "She's not done it how I asked her. It's all curled up at the ends. I look like a bloody bridesmaid."

Richard smiled in Henry's direction and, for the first time that day, he had managed to return one, raising his eyebrows in response to the commotion in the hallway.

"I think the curls look great," Richard said cheekily as Esther entered the studio, catching her completely by surprise as she was seemingly unaware of the long distances her voice could travel.

"Thank you, Richard," she answered stiffly, before extending her right hand. "Glad to see you're still finding your sense of humour at this difficult time."

Richard smiled again, but remembered why Henry frequently warned him against getting up Esther's nose: "Just be straight and act like you fancy her. She'll warm to that," he'd been advised.

"I only meant that you look stunning, as always," Richard replied in an attempt at reconciliation.

"Thank you." She eyed him suspiciously before gesturing to him to sit back down. "We'd better crack on because we've only got thirty seconds before we're live."

"Of course," Richard said, feeling the anxiety beginning to crank up another couple of levels.

He sat silently as Esther was counted in and watched her breeze through her introduction in which she mastered the art of colluding with the audience. "We've all been shocked by the twists and turns in Richard Williams' political and private life over the last couple of weeks. Now, for the first time since his separation from Anna Lloyd, he is telling his side of the story."

She turned now to look at Richard, an intensely patronising smile fixed to her face. Although attractive, he thought she was the kind of woman you could only ever fantasise about rather than actually fancy. In person, she was just way too controlled and way too false.

"It's been quite a shocking couple of weeks, hasn't it?" Esther began. "Had there been problems in your marriage prior to the allegations that your wife had worked as a professional escort?"

Nice start, Richard thought to himself. Nothing quite like getting to the point. He shifted in his seat slightly. "I don't really want to go down the line of talking in depth about my marriage, because I think that's personal, but what I will say is that I didn't feel there were any significant problems in our relationship."

"That does rather beg the question then why you announced a separation from Anna almost as soon as a newspaper printed claims about her?"

"All I announced was the fact that Anna would be stepping out of the public eye for a while, allowing me to focus on the very important task of winning the election. The events that transpired after that spun way beyond either of our control."

"In what way?" Esther demanded.

Richard cleared his throat. "I mean the way it was construed by the media. That Anna and I then never really had the opportunity to talk to each other about what was happening. She left home almost as soon as I'd made the announcement."

"Have you spoken since?"

"Briefly."

"And what was said?"

"Well, again, I'm not going to go into detail about private conversations. I admitted to Anna that I had made mistakes." Richard shuffled in his seat and prayed the interview wasn't going to get any more difficult. He could feel the vein in his right temple throbbing away and hoped it wasn't noticeable. Henry was scratching his head and ambling around in the corner, making it even more difficult to concentrate.

"Were you aware of your wife's suffering at the hands of her stepfather and of her conviction for his manslaughter?"

"Yes, of course I was."

"She has said since your separation that you were previously very sympathetic about the difficulties she had faced in her youth. Difficulties which must have contributed to her life choices in her early twenties."

"That's right, yes. I feel very strongly that people who have been failed by society as badly as Anna and her sister were, deserve all the help the state can offer. It's part of the reason I went into politics – to try and fight for a more just society."

"So how 'just' do you think it was to abandon your own wife in her hour of greatest need?"

Richard had seen it coming, but it still didn't soften the blow. He and Henry had even prepared for this question in the car on the way to the studios. But no matter how he phrased the answer, there was no way to dress up betraying the woman you love. So, he decided not to stick to the planned answer, but to say what he really felt.

"When I announced my separation from Anna, I did what I thought was right for the Social Democratic Party. Both Anna and I shared a vision of an SDP government. Neither of us wanted to see anything get in the way of that and so, stupidly I guess now, I thought I was doing what was best all round. I genuinely thought I was protecting Anna by keeping her out of the spotlight."

"But, according to your wife, you didn't agree this with her before you made the announcement." Esther, by this point, was perched on the edge of her seat, clearly enjoying what Richard was sure would be one of her career highlights.

"The announcement was rushed. I have many regrets about the way it all happened. The last couple of weeks have been as bewildering as they've been painful and I will have to live with my mistakes for the rest of my life. But I am determined to help this nation find its feet again. This country needs an SDP government – we cannot afford another eight years of Alliance rule or those truly in need will be left to suffer without end. And it was this fear that led me to act as hastily as I did and for that I'm truly sorry."

"Have you apologised to your wife?"

"Yes. Unreservedly."

"Has she accepted that apology?"

"No. And she has every right to be angry."

"Do you want your wife back, Mr Williams?"

"Absolutely, without question. I miss her terribly and I want Anna to be by my side when we defeat an Alliance government and win back the chance for the British people to turn this country around again, but that is a decision for her."

Richard cast his eyes to the floor and fought to control the unexpected emotion that was welling up inside of him. He wanted Esther to jump in and move the interview on but, instead, she seemed to be savouring every moment knowing it would likely make headlines around the world. But whilst the media got on with picking over his every facial expression and turn of phrase, Richard prayed his interview would have the desired impact on his target audience: Anna.

Libby switched the TV off using the remote control and turned to look at her sister. Anna had watched the entire interview, seated on the edge of the bed in her hotel room, in absolute silence. It was sheer chance they had caught it because Libby had come over to help Anna move her stuff back to their house, and had switched the TV news on to watch the one o'clock headlines and there it was. *Lunchtime*

Live with Esther Yarleth and an exclusive interview to end all exclusives.

"You all right, Anna?" Libby asked, resting her arm on her sister's shoulder.

"I think so," Anna said wearily. "I don't quite know what to make of that."

Libby had been expecting this – the moment Anna would finally waver, beaten down by the pressure of the last few weeks.

"What's upset you?"

"I believe him, Libs. I believe he genuinely wants me back." Anna was starting to cry now, first in small gasps which soon turned into heavy sobs.

"And what do you want, Anna?"

"I think I want him back too," she gasped. "I hate being alone with no home to go back to."

"Oh, Noo-Noo." Libby threw her arms around her sister. "You're coming to stay with us – you know that my home is your home."

"I know that, and I'm so incredibly glad to have you and Dan and the kids, but I want to be back in my own bed, with my own belongings around me. I just want my old life back."

Libby clenched her sister's face between her hands so she could fix her fully in the eyes. "It's a big decision you're making, Anna. And it might not work. You will still feel a lot of anger towards Richard even if you go back and make up."

"You're right, I know. I still love Richard, though, and I really want him to win this election. Meeting Kelvin again this week just reminded me what a slime-bucket he is and I genuinely believe Richard can make a difference. Will you support me if I go back?"

"Anna, I will support you, of course, but if he hurts you again I will never forgive him. And if it doesn't work out, our door is open for you to come back and stay again."

"Thank you, Libby." Anna reached out to embrace her sister. "I'd be so lost without you."

~

Richard stared intently out of the car window as Henry, sitting to his left, continued his rant about the interview with Esther Yarleth.

"I mean you *never, never* admit to a mistake in politics," he raged. "You can say you have regrets but to just blatantly come out and say you ballsed it up is taking such a risk with the voters. I don't know what I'm to do with you, Dickie, I really don't."

Richard smiled at the familiarity of Henry toying with him again as he had before the fall-out over Anna had threatened to blow their working relationship apart. "Well, we can't do much worse than we have been doing, Henry, so I wouldn't worry about it too much," he replied.

Henry swung around in his seat to look at Richard. "We've got to get back to business now. Whatever Anna decides to do, we can't go losing our focus. We have everything to fight for..."

To Richard's great relief he was spared the rest of the lecture when Henry's mobile started ringing, as it did every few minutes. While Henry barked instructions down the phone, Richard sank into his chair and reached for his mobile. He cast his eyes over the usual array of briefing notes and updates in his inbox, then sat up quickly when a text from Anna flashed up. *Can we talk?* was all she had written.

Yes! Richard hastily replied. *Can you come over tonight? I should be home by nine.*

I'm heading back to the house now. Will wait for you, came the answer within minutes.

Richard took a deep breath and allowed himself to genuinely smile for the first time in days. He turned to look at

Henry who appeared distinctly less happy as he glared at his own phone.

"What's wrong, Henry? It looks like you've had bad news?"

"Joy has asked me to meet her at the flat in an hour. Would you mind if I duck out of tonight's meeting?"

"No. I'm sure we'll manage," Richard replied, aware that he was enjoying Henry's sudden gloominess a little too much. He observed it so rarely. "Is there a problem?"

"Well, she's never asked me to meet her at home urgently before so I can only assume there's one bloody great big problem."

"Good luck then, mate."

Henry eyed Richard with suspicion and wondered why his mood had picked up so notably. But his mind soon wandered back to Joy's phone call. Her tone sounded terminal – and Henry could well imagine what was coming.

Joy was waiting for Henry in the living room of the three-bedroom apartment in Chelsea they had chosen together four years ago. It had suited their lifestyles perfectly and he thought they'd been happy in it. Until this moment, when he found her sitting silently with her coat on, staring into space.

"What's all this about?" he asked cautiously, taking a seat opposite her.

"I'm leaving you," she said, still staring at the same spot on the wall.

"What? Why? I mean, I know we've both been busy lately and things have been a bit stressful and chaotic, but I thought we were okay."

"Okay?" Joy asked, turning towards him to reveal her intense anger. "You've done nothing but bully and harass me for the last five years, turning what should have been a dream job into a nightmare, and you think that's okay? That's not okay, Henry. Nothing about you is okay. You are a manipulative, selfish man and I am finished with this." She stood up quickly.

"Joy," Henry gasped, standing in an attempt to block her way. "I don't know what to say. I just didn't know things had got this bad. Why didn't you say something earlier?"

"Because I couldn't get a word in edgeways. You were too busy telling me what to do to listen to what I had to say. So hear this; my bags are packed, and I'm heading out of the door."

"Where will you stay?"

"I'm moving in with a friend, but you won't be needing my contact details. My lawyer will be in touch soon enough. Goodbye Henry."

He watched helplessly as Joy walked briskly to the front door, then listened to the sound of her footsteps growing more distant in the corridor before she got into the lift which would carry her from his life.

Anna felt her troubles melt away as she stepped over the threshold of her front door. She breathed in the familiar smell of her scented candles and the beeswax polish Joanna used on their wooden surfaces. She walked through into the living area and paused for a moment to appreciate the sight of perfectly plumped cushions – Joanna hadn't slackened in her absence – before curling up on the sofa she had been longing to relax into for the last two weeks. She mentally recorded the moment that she finally slumped back into its glorious softness and knew she was home to stay.

A few minutes later she went up to the bedroom and unpacked her clothes, throwing the majority of them into the laundry basket. How good it was to be able to use her own washing machine without first either having to ask, or pay for it. She took a long, leisurely bath and smiled as she wrapped herself in her favourite Egyptian cotton bath sheet. She felt her soul refuel after a long bout of loneliness and displacement.

Just as she was brushing her hair, she heard Richard's key in the lock and pulled on her robe before going downstairs to meet him. By the time she had made it into the living area, he was standing in front of the fireplace waiting for her. He looked as she felt; terrified.

"It's good to see you," he said softly.

"And you," Anna said, leaning against the door.

"Are you staying?" Richard asked, nodding towards her robe.

"Yes. I'm staying."

Richard walked cautiously towards Anna and came to a stop just inches from her.

"I'm so, so sorry, Anna." He rested his forehead against hers and allowed his tears to fall. She reached for his hands and held them behind her back, before leaning into his chest and whispering, "I believe you."

10

REUNITED: LLOYD AND WILLIAMS HIT CAMPAIGN TRAIL TOGETHER

MONDAY, APRIL 13TH, 2009, UK NEWSWIRE

Opposition leader Richard Williams will today be accompanied by his actress wife, Anna Lloyd, as they hit the campaign trail together just three days after their reconciliation.

The couple are set to visit a care home in Derby this morning before embarking on a walkabout in the town centre. The Social Democrats leader is expected to use the visit to promote the party's Free Care for the Elderly policy – a key manifesto pledge.

Williams announced their marital separation two weeks ago following claims in a Sunday newspaper that Lloyd had previously worked as a professional escort.

But, after a sharp fall in the polls and an apparent change of heart by Williams, the two were reunited on Friday evening.

The couple appeared briefly outside their Highgate home

on Saturday morning to pause for pictures before heading off to Williams' Bristol South constituency for the weekend.

Neither made a formal statement, but Williams told reporters: "I am delighted to have my wife back by my side again, where she belongs".

When asked what plans they had for the weekend, Williams said: "We're going to meet my constituents and get on with campaigning for the people of this country. It's business as usual for both of us, and we're more determined than ever to fight for Britain".

The couple were set to be joined on the campaign trail today by film director Don Monteith, a major party donor, who was raised in Derby.

A nna could barely conceal her disappointment as she boarded the Democrats' battle bus. She had imagined it would be decked out rather like a large motorhome, with small kitchen area, couched seating and dining tables. In reality, it was just a coach – and a slightly shabby one at that – with a couple of table areas and a tiny loo. Anna turned to look at Richard who smiled encouragingly as he guided her towards one of the tables.

She dusted some crumbs off the inside chair, and patted down the back of her blue pencil skirt to avoid it getting crushed, before sitting down. She and Camilla had gone to great lengths to choose the perfect suit for her first day's campaigning and she was already concerned about how it would look by the time they'd finished the cramped coach trip.

"I feel like we should have brought some sandwiches and a flask of tea with us." Anna laughed as Richard took his seat beside her.

"Might not have been a bad idea," said Richard, only half-jokingly. "But I'm told the canteen food at Derby General is worth holding out for."

"Is that where we're eating?" Anna asked in disbelief.

"This is the reality of life as a Social Democrat leader's wife, Anna." Richard winked.

Anna raised her eyes to the ceiling as she thought about the many hours she would have to spend on this bus over the next few weeks in the run-up to the election. But she had made Richard a promise and, in actual fact, it was one she was more than happy to fulfill. She now felt totally committed to helping her husband become the next Prime Minister because, despite the mistakes he had made in their marriage, she had absolutely no doubt that he was the best man for the job. Anna's spirits were soon further lifted when she spotted Ray Molsley boarding the bus – her firm favourite among Richard's colleagues. She waved animatedly at him then stopped suddenly when she realised he was being followed by Don Monteith.

"You didn't tell me Don Monteith was coming today," Anna said, turning sharply on Richard.

"Didn't I? Sorry. Things have just been so chaotic lately."

"I'd have liked to have prepared myself a bit better before meeting him." Anna tutted. She couldn't sulk for long, though, because the two men were now standing by her side.

Anna got to her feet quickly.

"Good morning, Ray," she said breezily, kissing him on both cheeks. She then looked towards Don who quickly stepped forward.

"Don Monteith. Pleasure to meet you, Anna," the film director said, flashing her a tobacco-stained smile before leaning in to kiss her. He smelled of a mix of strong aftershave and cigarettes which combined to create a heady, almost sensual fragrance, Anna thought. He was shorter than she'd expected, but his lined and tanned face was attractive in an unusual sense.

"A pleasure to meet you too, Don," said Anna. "I'm delighted you're joining us today. Will you sit with us for the journey?"

"I'd love to," said the director as he squeezed himself into the seat across from her at the window. He was quickly followed by Ray who sat opposite Richard. As the two politicians immediately started to discuss the day's schedule, Don leaned forward towards Anna.

"I have a lot of admiration for you after hearing about your upbringing and what you've come through."

"Thanks, Don." Anna smiled. "I really appreciate that."

"We have a lot in common actually," Don added.

"You mean you're a stressed-out actress married to a politician too?" She laughed.

"No, I mean I was physically abused by my father as a child."

Anna's face dropped. "Oh," she whispered, leaning in towards him so they could speak quietly.

"He was a very angry man, and me and my two brothers were regularly leathered and locked in our rooms all day and night without a scrap of food. He also drank himself to death, which was a blessing really."

"I'm sorry. I didn't know that about you," Anna said, immediately sensing that the brash and intimidating persona Don liked to portray through the media, was actually far from who he was. He spoke in a very matter-of-fact way, despite the subject, but she thought his eyes told a different story.

"Well, it's not something I've talked about in the press to any great extent, but it's still a big part of my life in a way. And I spent a lot of time thinking about it again when I read about you. I know where you've come from and I know how hard you must have fought to get out of it. I just wanted you to know that I really admire you for it."

Anna looked down at her lap and blinked back the tears she was struggling to fight off because of Don's unexpected kindness.

"I didn't mean to upset you," he said, his eyes full of concern.

"No, it's fine," Anna replied, taking a deep breath. "It's just been a crazy couple of weeks and people have been so lovely to me."

"I'll be honest with you," Don said, leaning sharply forward again. "I always thought you were a bit shallow or something – just because of the kind of parts you've chosen in the past."

"They were all I was offered," Anna promptly interjected.

"I see you in a totally different light now. You've got a lot to offer – politically, but also creatively."

"Thank you," she said, beaming inside and out as she accepted the compliment paid to her by one of the UK's best directors.

"Where do you see your career going from here?" he asked, leaning in to show his interest.

"I'm looking to take on more challenging roles," she said confidently.

"I want to break out of the stereotyped 'bitch' parts and take on something that requires subtlety and vulnerability." Don nodded sagely, encouraging her to continue. "And, if I'm honest, I would like to try Hollywood in the future. I think it's a natural progression for me."

"Of course," he agreed. "And I'd be happy to help you."

Anna smiled casually as she tried to conceal her excitement. But, sitting on board that shabby battle bus about to set off for Derby, she realised, ironically, that by disclosing the pain of her childhood she had altered her image with both the public and industry. She was no longer seen as a one-dimensional glamour puss, but a serious actress on the brink of the kind of stratospheric stardom she had so longed for since her youth when she dreamed of being someone completely different. Someone loved and adored. Someone who mattered.

It was a beautiful spring day and, as the sunlight beamed into Marie's dockside apartment, exposing more than a slight build-up of dust around the surfaces, she decided it was time she gave the place a serious clean. Working for a Sunday paper meant you got Sundays and Mondays off; also meaning at least one of your *weekend* days would typically be spent alone. Usually, Marie would take herself off to the gym or go to the supermarket, but she'd done both yesterday so she couldn't put off the now unavoidable housework.

She had lived a surreal existence these last few weeks, working almost every available hour – and most of that on the Anna Lloyd story. Now things had slowed down slightly she knew she would have Damian on her back pushing for her to come up with another blinding exclusive.

When she joined the *Echo* she had expected to at least enjoy the thrill of the chase, but soon discovered there was very little thrill involved when you worked under constant pressure. It was do or die. You either had a scoop or you didn't.

Marie was also finding it tougher and tougher to work for Damian who seemed to be relentlessly focusing in on her, expecting a major exclusive every single week. She couldn't decide whether he liked her or loathed her, but there was no in-between. She was definitely getting undue attention from him and she didn't know how to handle it.

She found him quite an intriguing character, and there was something about him that made her feel a bit sorry for him. She liked his boyish qualities but really disliked his bullying streak. And just when she was on the verge of deciding she absolutely loathed him, he would reveal a very different side to his character. Like the previous Thursday when he had slipped out at lunchtime and returned with a huge beam on his face as he showed the picture editor the huge plastic truck he had bought his nephew for his fourth birthday. Marie had been gobsmacked by the way he spoke about the child. He had gone on for about ten minutes about how his nephew knew everything there was to know about building sites and construction. And once he'd got started on the little boy, Charlie, it was like he couldn't stop. Marie couldn't help but gawp as he then launched into how clever his nephew was, detailing when he began to talk, walk, potty train. The lot.

"He's unbelievable with numbers. He counts to a hundred, and he's already adding up. I mean, he's just such a bright kid and he's never got his nose out of a book."

Only when Damian realised the picture editor was agitated to get back to work, did he finally move off. As he turned to walk back to his desk, Marie had caught the mix of embarrassment and loneliness on his face as he obviously realised he'd been rambling on about his nephew to someone who just wasn't interested.

Marie found her Marigold gloves under the kitchen sink and pulled them on firmly as a sign of her intent to get the cleaning done. She then hunted out everything she needed to get through the whole flat. As she made her way towards the bathroom, where she was planning to start, she heard her mobile ringing. She ran back through to the kitchen and grabbed the phone from her bag – then groaned as she saw the name Damian Blunt flashing on the screen.

"It's my bloody day off," she shouted aloud before answering the call. "Hi Damian," she said flatly.

"Marie, hi. Sorry to call on your day off..."

No you're not, Marie thought, or you would have waited till Tuesday.

"...but it's a big week for us and I've got a tip-off that I want you to get onto first thing in the morning."

"Right." She rolled her eyes.

"I'm told Joy Gooding has left Henry Morton. Now, the fact that's happened right after the whole Anna Lloyd thing means I think there's a good story in there. So I'm giving you this one, Marie, but I need you to deliver on it because we've got to keep coming out on top over this election campaign. The dailies will be onto it soon enough, so we need to find a good angle. You up for it?"

"Yes, I'll start making calls as soon as I get in," she assured him without enthusiasm.

"Right. Good." Damian paused awkwardly. "You up to much today then?"

"Yeah, er, just heading out for lunch with some friends actually," she lied. Marie didn't want Damian to know her life was as lonely and increasingly meaningless as she suspected his was.

"Great. Well, you have a good time then and I'll see you in the morning."

"Yes... thanks. Bye." Marie ended the call and sat down for a moment on a breakfast stool next to her kitchen counter. Now she felt even more confused about where she stood with Damian. Was he testing her? Was he trying to give her a helping hand or setting her up for a fall? Either way, she knew already she was in for another tough week. She wondered when she would ever start to feel the sense of expectation and excitement with which she used to wake every morning of her early career. These days she increasingly seemed to begin – and end – each day with a sense of impending doom. Worse still, she was having trouble sleeping as she wrestled with both her conscience and the unending anxiety of producing the kind of exclusives that could and probably would destroy lives. She had no doubt Joy Gooding wouldn't just hand her a story as soon as she put a call in, so, as usual, she was going to have to bully it out of her.

She shook her head and almost laughed at the bitter irony that saw her now play the role of the aggressor when she had spent much of her childhood cowering from a crowd of angry playground tormentors who hated her for being smart and pretty – a seemingly unforgivable combination. She had promised herself then that she would never make another human being feel as shit about themselves as they made her, but she suspected she'd already broken that promise in the last few weeks.

Marie let out a long sigh of despair as she set her mobile phone down on the kitchen counter and stared at it as if searching for answers. She was dreading tomorrow already.

As much as she desperately wanted to, Anna couldn't put off facing Henry for much longer. He had looked distinctly huffy when he boarded the bus and saw Ray and Don sitting with Richard, so he'd sat himself down a few rows away and began barking orders noisily into his mobile phone to make his presence – and importance – known. Thirty minutes later he appeared by Richard's side and told him he needed a word to which Richard had responded that he'd go to the loo first and then they'd talk.

Henry had stepped back to let Richard past and had then loitered around the table again, looking sheepishly in Anna's direction.

"Can I sit down a minute, Anna?" he finally asked.

"Yes," she'd replied sharply.

Once he'd awkwardly manoeuvred his long limbs into the nearest thing he could find to a comfortable position, Henry cleared his throat, making it known he was about to embark on a speech. He quickly glanced over at Don and Ray just to check they were still safely tied up in animated conversation before turning to Anna.

"Look, Anna. These past few weeks have been tough on all of us..."

"Some more than others," she quipped.

"Well, that may be true, but I've paid a heavy price for what's gone on too."

"If you're talking about you and Joy then you only have yourself to blame."

"There are two sides to every story," he corrected. "Life with Joy could be extremely frustrating – and she's certainly not the victim she likes to portray herself as. She was quite jealous of you, you know. She felt your good looks had granted you a very easy passage in life – which I must say, had tainted my view of you at times. She couldn't have been more wrong, of course." He leaned in closer to Anna, looking for a reaction, but opted to move on quickly when he found none. "That's all irrelevant now, I suppose. For her part, she said she found me way too domineering – particularly over her relationship with you." Henry was staring forlornly at his shoes, like a recently chastised schoolboy.

"And is that true, Henry?"

"I suppose it is, Anna. I've just been so determined to let nothing slip and to make sure we're all in tune, as it were, that I put her under more pressure than was right."

Against her better judgement, Anna allowed in a small amount of sympathy which, once implanted, became difficult to suppress.

"I'm sorry she left, Henry. It must be tough. But you have to know that you have caused both Richard and I a great deal of pain lately – and I think you're lucky to have kept your job."

"I know, I know," he said, shaking his head. "I've thought of little else these last couple of days and I can only apologise. I also know that you will find it hard to trust me now, but all I can say is I have only ever had both Richard's and the Social Democrats' best interests at heart. I don't always get it right, but I am not selfishly motivated – and I can assure you that I will never interfere in your marriage again. You have my word."

Henry was looking directly at Anna now and she realised she was going to have to jump one way or the other.

"Well, I've not always behaved perfectly myself, Henry. And Joy had quite a bit to say to me about the way I treated her. Maybe we should all put the last few weeks down to a learning experience and wipe the slate clean. Do you know Joy resigned as my PR agent?"

"Yes, Richard told me. I can't think what she's going to do next. Maybe head to Thailand or something to 'find herself'. I wouldn't put anything past Joy." He smiled.

"She's certainly unpredictable," Anna agreed.

Henry's face suddenly tightened again as he worked his way up to another serious note.

"I'm grateful that you can try and put everything behind you. But I need to acknowledge that I shouldn't have pushed you out. I was utterly wrong and I know I'm lucky to still be here after what happened."

He held out his hand and Anna extended hers in return before they shook firmly.

"Thank you, Anna," Henry said, his face visibly relaxing. "I've been a bloody arse, but I just want this win so badly – for Richard, the party, and for the country. I think I've learned my lesson, but you just let me know if I step over the mark again, will you?"

"That's one thing I can guarantee, Henry." Anna smiled.

Reggie felt sick to his stomach as he waited for Kelvin to make his grand entrance for the manifesto launch. Having worked with the Prime Minister for the last three years, Reggie was used to his late starts but, today of all days, he particularly didn't appreciate the torture of having to stand beside an impatient press pack all growing increasingly frustrated at the delay. When he'd texted the Deputy PM to ask what the hold-up was he'd received the brief and cryptic reply: *Last-minute tweaking.*

Just as Reggie was about to burst from the room to personally hunt Kelvin down, the door opened and the PM entered wearing a broad smile that suggested he was completely oblivious to the half-hour wait he had subjected his audience to.

He strutted casually to the platform, before stopping in front of the large screen that carried their election slogan: *Better for Britain.*

He launched quickly into some of the Alliance Party's more familiar pledges before hitting on the new income tax cut. Reggie knew this would be seen as a desperate attempt to win over voters, but it was the best card in their pack right now.

Reggie watched the smirking faces of the reporters as Kelvin banged on about a better-off Britain and just knew tomorrow's headlines would be merciless. He decided it was better to switch off, rather than mentally record the agony, so he allowed his thoughts to roam and his eyes to wander around the room.

He looked over the row of cameramen squashed together at the back and wondered what job satisfaction they could possibly get out of a press conference like this where all they had to do was stand like dodos, mindlessly recording the moment. Then, a glint of red hair caught his eye and he realised there was a woman standing on her own just to the side of the cameras.

Reggie racked his brain as to who this woman could be. He thought there was something familiar about her, but he felt pretty sure she wasn't a journalist and certain she hadn't been authorised by him to attend. So if he hadn't authorised it, who had?

Then Reggie looked at her more closely and started working through a few possibilities, his mind hovering around make-up artist or civil servant when an alarm bell suddenly sounded within. He knew exactly who this was. It was Joy Gooding. And before he could even start to question why she might be there, he arrived at the answer. He'd heard she'd left Henry Morton and was no longer looking after Anna Lloyd so he bet she'd come knocking on Kelvin's door – probably with the suggestion of insider information – and he'd fallen for it. That moron, Reggie thought. He couldn't imagine what a showbiz PR agent could possibly have to offer a Prime Minister, other than advice on where he should have his teeth whitened. But then, Reggie realised, that was exactly the type of information that would impress Kelvin who he believed should never be left on his own, even for a minute, to make a decision. Joy Gooding, he was quite certain, would spell nothing but trouble.

Both the hospital tour and walkabout in Derby had gone to plan and Anna sensed a quiet confidence growing once again in the SDP camp. Richard seemed happy and relaxed and even Henry had started joking again. When a hospital consultant had talked them through a new cosmetic surgery technique they had been successfully using on burns patients, Henry had teased Anna about the rumours that had circulated in the press a year ago that she'd had a slight facelift. "Is that the same procedure you had?" he'd cheekily whispered, prompting Anna to dig him sharply in the ribs with her elbow. And later, when they were back on the bus heading towards their next stop, Leicester, she'd heard Henry calling Richard "Dicky" again, when they were talking privately. It felt good to Anna to be back on familiar territory after so much uncertainty. And whether Henry's apology had been genuine or not, there was no denying the great sense of camaraderie on the battle bus, with the events of the last couple of weeks only serving to motivate the SDP leadership even further in their quest for power.

They'd parted with Don Monteith in Derby as he'd had to catch a train back down to London, but he'd spent the best part of the day with them and had provided a real boost to the campaign when he told reporters outside Derby General that there was "no one else for the job but Richard Williams".

"If the Social Democrats don't win this election then we've only got ourselves to blame for the mess this country will end up in with four more years of an Alliance government," he'd said.

"The last eight years of Alliance rule have brought us back to the same shameful class divide that has been the scourge of this nation. It's time for change and it's time we put stupid gossip and headlines to one side and voted for a true leader, not some jumped-up twit, who's only interested in lining his own pockets and those of his rich friends."

Anna and Henry had watched in great amusement as Richard, who was standing next to Don outside the hospital, desperately tried to stifle a laugh. Only someone who didn't work in politics could get away with such a direct hit. But they all knew that Don Monteith had landed a real blow to the Alliance Party – and to Kelvin in particular.

Anna had chosen to sit on her own towards the back of the bus while Henry and Richard worked on the next speech to be made in Leicester where they were to visit a new police station. It had been a very long day so she rolled up her cardigan, propped it against the window and attempted to get some rest.

She thought about Joy and wondered what she'd be doing now – and which new actress or presenter she would be pursuing for a contract. She felt a little wrench inside at the thought they would never work together again. Her ex-PR agent would surely have enjoyed the cut and thrust of life on the campaign trail – and Anna thought her experience of managing a large horde of press would have come in very handy at times. Still, she comforted herself with the thought that Joy would soon have tired of all the policy speak and petty in-fighting and would probably be better off as far away from politics as she could get.

Typically, just as Anna was drifting off she heard her mobile phone ringing. Her first thought was to leave it, but curiosity got the better of her and she reached into her bag. It was Libby.

"Hi Libs," she said, a little woozily.

"You sound knackered. Has the election trail got to you already?"

"It's only my first day of campaigning and, yes, I'm already exhausted."

"Oh well, just another twenty-three blistering days to go," Libby joked. "Anyway," she continued. "I thought you should know I've been very active on your behalf today. I sent an email out to all your media contacts letting them know I'm handling the press side of things for you and the phone's not stopped ringing since. I've had lots of offers and requests for interviews – including loads of TV stuff." Anna laughed at Libby's breathless excitement.

"Sounds great, Libs. No interviews until after the election now though."

"I know, I know. I told them that. What a few of them did say, though, was that Joy stopped returning their calls two weeks ago. So I don't know what she's been up to, but she's clearly not been doing the job you were paying her to."

Anna sighed. "I don't know what to think about Joy anymore. She made out it was all Henry's doing, and that she was bullied into this and that, but I'm beginning to doubt that now. I think she had her own agenda going on."

"Well, if you've already arrived at that conclusion then that makes what I'm about to tell you a bit easier."

"Oh no, what?" Anna demanded anxiously.

"I was watching the launch of the Alliance manifesto on TV earlier and I could swear I spotted Joy there at the back of the press conference."

"But, what would she be doing there?"

"Well, what do you think, Anna? She's not a reporter, she's a so-called PR expert."

"You think she's working for Kelvin?"

"Looks like it, I'm afraid."

"Shit," Anna said, reeling from the implications. "That back-stabbing bitch." She looked over to where Henry and Richard were sitting and saw Henry locked in conversation on his mobile phone. She studied the way his face had fallen, the confusion registering in his eyes. "Looks like Henry already knows," she told Libby.

"Poor sod. He may have his faults but he didn't deserve that."

"No," Anna replied. "None of us did."

11

DEMOCRATS RIDING HIGH IN THE POLLS AGAIN

TUESDAY, APRIL 14TH, 2009, UK NEWSWIRE

The Social Democrats today regained a 10-point lead over the Alliance Party after the opposition leader, Richard Williams, enjoyed a major upturn in public support following his reunion with wife Anna Lloyd.

The latest poll results also follow a high-profile day of campaigning for Williams and his wife in Derby, where they were joined by the Oscar-winning film director, Don Monteith.

The group visited Derby General Hospital where they met staff and patients. Monteith and Williams then spoke to reporters outside, where the film director launched a ferocious attack on the Prime Minister, Kelvin Davis.

Monteith accused the PM of "lining his own pockets", an accusation that infuriated the Alliance leadership.

An Alliance Party spokesperson said Monteith had "overstepped the mark by a clear mile" and should publicly apologise for his "totally unfair comments".

Davis was yesterday in Cardiff where he visited a new waterside housing development. He used the visit to pledge Alliance support to the beleaguered construction industry and vowed to reinject confidence into Britain's ailing property market.

He also launched a veiled attack on Williams' reunion with Anna Lloyd, after the two were briefly separated following newspaper claims about the actress's past.

Davis said: "When you vote Alliance, you vote for a party of courage, a party of change and a party of commitment. We won't chop and change our minds at the drop of a hat – or according to what the latest opinion polls suggest about our private and professional lives. We are a party of integrity and a party of clear vision".

R ichard worked hard to steady his breathing as he took his final steps towards the conference room at the Victoria Street HQ. He knew once the door was opened all eyes would be on him and that he would have to give a confident and controlled performance in order to maintain their lead in the polls. Anna had shown him the breathing exercises several months ago after criticism of his "wooden" presentation skills in the press. He'd since worked very hard with Anna on speaking with conviction, taking his time to set out his case clearly and passionately, yet he still found it hard to suppress his nerves – especially in moments like this. He had doubted that such a simple thing as taking deep breaths from the stomach could make any significant impact on a career-long problem, but it had actually worked a treat, and he was now frequently described as a "polished performer" when he gave important speeches.

Henry walked by his side chattering away in his right ear, trying to give him a last-minute pep talk. The odd words: "sincerity", "conviction", "humility" would creep through, but otherwise Richard remained silently focused on the task ahead. With all that had gone on over the last two weeks, he could not afford to slip up on any level. He felt the adrenaline start to course through him and he fought desperately to hold his nerve. If he let fear take hold, it could finish him. Henry opened the side door to the conference room and they parted ways as Richard headed towards the podium and his head of communications slipped off to join Anna, Ray and Bob at the back.

Richard continued to breathe deeply before swallowing hard as he took up his position behind the glass stand. He had taken the decision on the bus from Derby the day before to speak without notes. He and Henry had felt it would provide a sharp contrast to Kelvin's highly-scripted speech the day before.

He glanced around the room and found Anna's eyes staring intently back at him. The photographers snapped away, capturing the look that said, *'I support you'*. Richard smiled and remembered his purpose, with the Democrats' election slogan, *"The Courage for Change"* ringing in his ears. He was there to bring hope to a nation that had become despondent in the face of a fierce recession and an inept government who didn't want to rock the boat by taking some of the tough decisions that were necessary to fight back.

"If anyone is in any doubt," Richard began, "I'm here to fight." He locked the audience in a determined stare.

"I am here to fight for a country that has been sold promises of wealth and prosperity for all, then dropped from the greatest of heights when the house that had been built on sand crumbled to the ground.

"I'm here to fight for the tough economic and taxation

changes that must be put into place if we are to rise to be a proud nation again.

"And I'm here to fight for those of you who have worked hard only to find that your pensions have been diminished, or your jobs have been lost or are now unstable.

"There is a choice – and that is change."

Richard paused briefly and looked across the room, the audience partially obscured by the camera lights that gave him a sense of remoteness from those he was addressing. What effect his words were having on them he didn't know, but he was being guided by a stronger force now: belief. He no longer feared forgetting his words – because they had been etched into his mind over years of planning and preparation for the job he believed he was destined to do. He didn't know why, but it was a belief he had possessed from a young age watching a succession of governments and leaders and thinking, *I can do better.*

So, as he carefully set out the Democrats' plans to raise the higher level of taxation, whilst increasing spending on health, policing and schools and a pensions insurance scheme for all, he knew that his speech would be part of history.

When he had covered their key policy pledges he stopped for a few seconds just to savour the moment. He looked across to the film crews perched at the back of the room, then the rows of reporters, leading to the pool of photographers at the front. The cameras continued to flash, but the place was otherwise completely silent.

He took another deep breath and spoke his remaining few lines slowly, emphasising every word. "I am here to make sure we fulfill our promises. To deliver for Britain. Sometimes there will be difficult decisions to make and challenges to overcome, but... together, we have the courage for change."

Richard smiled graciously as his colleagues, and a good contingent of the press, applauded his speech. He looked across towards Henry and Anna who were grinning and clapping enthusiastically and he knew it had gone as well as he thought. Now all they needed to do was cross the finish line, and pray no one would throw any other obstacles in their way.

~

Joy could tell Reggie hated her from the first moment they locked horns. The confrontation had come during a debriefing in Kelvin's office after Monday's manifesto launch. Joy had thought Kelvin came over as a little "stiff and rehearsed" while Reggie seemingly thought the whole thing had gone fabulously. Joy soon gathered that Reggie was the ultimate "yes" man, and would nod along enthusiastically with anything Kelvin said, even when his ideas and requests were patently ridiculous.

He had quickly seized on the opportunity to try and assert himself over her in front of their boss, saying: "Joy, I know you're keen to make an impact on your first day, but politics is very different from showbusiness. When you stand up as an actor, you simply want people to like you, but when you stand up as a politician they need to trust and respect you."

"Well, thank you for that wonderful insight," Joy had sarcastically replied. "But you know, I had actually worked that one out for myself and, even with that in mind, I still think we need to get Kelvin looking more natural so that the audience can focus entirely on what he's saying, rather than how he's saying it."

Reggie had simply sneered in response but Joy had felt very unsettled when she noticed Kelvin scowling from the other side of the desk. Clearly, she hadn't been appointed to tell him the truth. She was only there to inflict as much damage as possible on the other side. And even Joy had to admit she was the perfect candidate for that job. Henry had caused her nothing but anxiety and self-doubt over the last few years and this was her chance to pay him back and regain some respect for herself. If it hurt Anna and Richard too – as it inevitably would – she wasn't going to lose any sleep. Neither of them had actually cared about her. They had both been way too self-absorbed to worry about the welfare of those around them.

Today, she had been given the task of analysing Richard's manifesto speech and reporting back on any chinks in his armour. Trouble was, despite studying the footage three times, she couldn't really find much. Since his reunion with Anna, it was clear Richard had got back into his stride and was now sprinting to the finish.

Joy watched closely as the cameras then panned across to Anna laughing happily in the crowd with Henry. She couldn't believe those two had become pally again so quickly. She felt so rejected as she sat alone watching the three people she had once really loved and cared about. The pain of seeing them all emerging victorious on May the 7th was just too much for Joy to bear. So if there were no chinks in Richard's armour right now they were going to have to create some.

Joy's mobile started ringing and she sighed loudly when she recognised Reggie's number.

"Where are you, Joy?" he demanded as though she was an errant teenager.

"I'm just finishing up dissecting Richard Williams' manifesto speech like you

asked me to."

"So what are your thoughts?"

Joy's mind raced. She couldn't tell him she'd just sat watching TV for the last two hours without reaching a conclusion so she stalled for time.

"I think his confidence is peaking and we need to do something about it."

"And what do you suggest?" Reggie had asked sceptically.

"Let's have coffee and I'll talk you through what I have in mind."

Joy ended the call as quickly as possible. She only had fifteen minutes in which to come up with an idea that would help win Reggie and Kelvin's trust and establish her as part of the team. She knew she had one fallback plan but she wasn't sure whether she had the guts to put it into action. Because if she did, she would become public enemy number one with the three people she had once been closest to.

Marie had been actively avoiding Damian all morning. The truth was she had been too scared to call Joy Gooding because she hadn't yet worked out her approach. *Hi. I hear you've split up from your husband, want to tell the* Sunday Echo *why?* Somehow, she couldn't see her falling for that one. So her only other option was to come up with a veiled threat. *A very trustworthy source has given us details of your acrimonious split with Henry Morton – do you want to tell the story from your side?*

Marie decided that was definitely the best line to take and, once she'd settled on it, she knew the only thing to do was to take the plunge. She reached for the handset on her desk phone and had just started to punch in Joy's number when her own mobile rang. She checked the screen on the handset and could hardly believe her eyes when she realised the number displayed was the very one she had been about to call.

"Hello," Marie answered cautiously.

"Hello, Marie, it's Joy Gooding here," she announced confidently. "We've spoken several times in the past when I represented Anna Lloyd."

"Yes, I remember, Joy. Have you been speaking to Damian?

Did he ask you to call me?" Marie enquired, still baffled over the timing of Joy's call.

"Damian? No, I haven't spoken to him in years, thank God." The two laughed. "No, I called because I have a story for you."

"Oh?" Things were looking up, thought Marie.

"Yes, but first I must tell you this isn't going to come from me but a very well-placed source, do you understand?"

"Of course."

"Well," Joy began in hushed, conspiratorial tones. "As you know, until a few days ago I worked very closely with Anna Lloyd and was never far from her side in the weeks leading to her separation from Richard Williams."

"I can imagine," said Marie expectantly.

"Yes, and I thought you'd be interested to know that I witnessed several nasty rows between them which will shed new light on what really caused their separation."

"Do you have time to meet this afternoon, Joy?"

"I'd rather do this by phone."

"No problem," Marie replied. She needed to check Damian would be happy with the alternative story before she stepped down from pursuing the line he'd asked her to follow about Joy's own marriage. "I'll call you back within an hour."

She strode over to Damian's office and tapped on his door, and from the way he quickly closed down a couple of pages on his computer as he beckoned her in, she could tell he hadn't been looking at anything connected to work.

"How's the Gooding story coming along then? You got my splash yet?"

"Yes," said Marie casually. "But the splash won't be on the break-up between Joy Gooding and Henry Morton. It'll be about a much, much bigger couple."

"You got something else on Lloyd and Williams?" Damian asked, eyes bulging.

"Joy's offered me the inside track on the rows leading to their separation."

"How did you swing that one?"

"We just had a conversation, that's all." Marie raised her eyebrows teasingly. "I'll send you the copy by the end of tomorrow."

With that, she breezed back out of his office, privately celebrating the fact that, for once, she'd been handed an easy exclusive without having to spend another week harassing people in the name of the *Sunday Echo*.

Libby smiled as she heard the front door open and Dan bellow "hello" through the hallway as he did every night. He dropped his bag and started to make his way towards the kitchen. Listening to his approaching footsteps, Libby imagined what would be running through his mind as, for the first time in years, he had arrived home to a house empty of kids. Usually, by this time in the evening they'd be climbing the walls – literally in Ollie's case – while they waited for Libby to serve them tea. Tonight there was only absolute silence. Dan pushed open the kitchen door and looked around suspiciously.

"Where's the kids?" Dan asked.

"At your mother's." Libby smiled, glancing up only momentarily before she resumed typing.

"My mother's?"

"Yes." Libby fixed him with a challenging glare. "At your mother's while I finish my work. She's going to take them three afternoons a week."

"I see," Dan said.

"She's dropping them back here in ten minutes so I'm just finishing this email and then I'll put their tea on."

"Right," he replied, but didn't move away.

"Is there something wrong, Dan?" She turned to face him.

"No. I'm just a bit surprised that you've taken this so far."

"Taken what so far?"

"This working for Anna thing?"

"It's not a thing, Dan. It's a job. And we need the money don't we?"

"Yes, but..."

"But your nose is out of joint because I'm no longer just little wifey, who looks after the kids, washes your underpants and cooks the tea. Is that it?"

"No, Libby." Dan crossed the room to stand closer to his wife. "I just want to make sure this is right for you, not just Anna."

"I volunteered to do this job, Dan. Until now, I've been moping around on my fat arse most of the day wishing something exciting would happen to me. Now something exciting finally is happening to me. I have a job I love, and I've spoken to people today who are all desperate to talk to me. And do you know what, Dan? I feel good. I feel bloody good."

"Right." Dan raised his eyebrows passively. "That's me told."

Libby got to her feet and threw her arms around Dan's neck.

"Don't worry, darling. I still love you. And I'll still wash your undies."

"Good," Dan said, kissing her firmly on the lips. "I might be able to afford some bloody new ones now you've finally shifted yourself."

"Out," Libby joked, slapping him on the backside before pointing dramatically to the front door. "I've got work to do."

Dan chuckled happily as he walked out of the kitchen, leaving Libby to wonder why she hadn't gone back to work earlier. She had feared losing control of her family if she wasn't there for them every second but, in reality, she'd lost control of her own life. With what Anna had agreed to pay her they were no longer under constant financial pressure and could even take a couple of foreign holidays a year, or maybe redecorate. But it was more than the money that was driving Libby. She was good at this. The press contacts she had spoken to were all warming to her which would come in very useful for when she needed to try and dig Anna out of a spot. And it also meant she got to spend more time with her sister who, until recently, had been starting to feel like a bit of a stranger to her.

Richard and Anna could hear the screams from the crowd half a mile away as they inched slowly closer to the Leicester Square Odeon, huddled together in the back seat of the chauffeur-driven car. Anna's stomach lurched at the thought of making her first major appearance before the public since being outed as a former escort girl – and killer. The more contained campaign outings, where they were surrounded by aides and police, just hadn't seemed as daunting as stepping out in front of a large crowd like this. She'd had a nightmare the previous night that the onlookers had been chanting *"murderer"* at her as she walked along the red carpet and Richard had had to rush her indoors. And all she could think once they'd got inside was: *Is he going to leave me again?*

Now she had to face that nightmare. Henry had told her over and over again that the public were firmly behind her but still, she feared that could change at any minute.

Richard was talking to her about that day's campaigning but all Anna could do was watch the row of cars in front slowly start to clear until it was their turn to get out and face the crowd.

Richard's chauffeur leapt out of the driving seat and soon appeared to Anna's left. Before she had a chance to stop him, the door was open and Anna went into autopilot, swinging her legs around to face the pavement before stepping out. The screams were overwhelming and Anna stood stock still in panic. She thought she could hear them hurling abuse at her. She couldn't catch her breath and reached for the car door to steady herself. Richard was now at her side and had folded his arm through hers, unaware of her torment.

"Let me back in the car," she said frantically. "I need to get back in the car."

"What's the problem, Anna?" Richard asked in confusion.

"They're screaming at me, Richard. They hate me."

Richard pulled Anna close to his side and whispered loudly in her ear. "Anna, they're screaming *for* you. Listen, they're chanting your name."

She tried to pull herself together just long enough to hear what they were actually saying. The chants were in perfect rhythm, with not a single voice out of step. And, just as Richard had told her, it was her name they were calling over and over again. She clutched his arm tightly and they began to walk forward, pausing for a few moments to smile for the photographers who were shouting for them to kiss. Richard moved in awkwardly and pecked her on the lips. He probably shouldn't have done that, Anna thought. The papers would have the body language experts all over the pictures tomorrow, but they could worry about that later. Right now she was just savouring the moment. Her darkest secrets were out and the public still loved her. It was the ultimate acceptance.

She separated from Richard to greet some of the well-wishers who were holding their arms out to her. She saw a young girl of what she guessed to be around thirteen standing next to her mother and screaming her name. Anna reached out to shake her hand but the girl lurched forward and pulled her into an embrace. "Oh my God. You're amazing," the girl shrieked, tears tumbling down her face. Anna swallowed hard, trying not to show her shock. She thanked the girl, kissing her on the cheek before pulling away to walk towards the cinema, still shaking as many hands as possible. Soon one of the film PR agents was pulling at Anna's arm and telling her to walk with her. "Your husband's waiting for you," she said in a tone that was a bit too schoolmarmish for Anna's liking.

She turned to see Richard standing in the foyer of the cinema smiling broadly in her direction as he chatted to Don. The PR agent led her quickly to where they were standing.

"Sweetheart," Don said, his Derby accent turned up particularly thickly for the evening. Anna could see he was in a different mode to the more sombre and attentive director she had met on the bus and so warmed to.

"You look absolutely divine, but you've completely overshadowed my film premiere." He laughed.

"Yes, sorry about that," Richard said jovially. "Henry's going to be absolutely ecstatic though."

"He'll have me at every film premiere going now," Anna chipped in.

"Well, you two get on in there and enjoy the film. Will I see you after for a drink?"

"We could use a drink, couldn't we, Anna?" Richard said, giving her a comforting hug around the waist. "We're living like nuns at the moment."

"And a good thing too." Don winked cheekily in Anna's direction, making her jolt slightly as she realised he was probably referring to her past.

She turned with Richard to walk towards the cinema theatre and, once out of earshot, whispered: "Was he just having a dig about the escort work?"

"Who knows and who cares, Anna. He's just a big-headed oink."

"I thought you liked him?"

"There's a difference between tolerating for the sake of the election and actually liking," Richard whispered, careful to keep smiling so the photographers wouldn't pick up on the more serious turn in the conversation. He signalled for Anna to go into the cinema in front of him and, as she stepped into the darkness, she couldn't help but wonder whether Richard was just tolerating her for the sake of the election too.

12

DAVIS "BUCKLING UNDER PRESSURE" ON TAX REFORM

Thursday, April 16th, 2009, UK Newswire

Prime Minister Kelvin Davis was today accused by opposition parties of carrying out a major policy U-turn after announcing a surprise round of tax cuts if the Alliance Party wins the General Election next month.

Davis yesterday pledged his government would raise the special personal tax allowance for the over-75s by £2,000 a year to enable them to "keep more of their hard-earned money".

The Social Democrats immediately seized on the move, calling it "an act of desperation" and arguing that the cut would primarily benefit better-off pensioners rather than those in real need.

The announcement by Kelvin Davis came on the same day that several polls placed the SDP 12 points clear of the Alliance.

Today, SDP officials said the government's pensions policy was now "in chaos". A party spokesman added: "Alliance Party credibility on taxation and pensions is now in absolute tatters as they flail around looking for ways to endear themselves to voters who gave up on them years ago."

D amian pounced on Marie's email as soon as he spotted it in his inbox. It was eight-thirty in the morning and he usually liked to start his day in the office by going through the papers, but, as soon as he saw the subject line *Lloyd/Williams Copy*, he threw his routine out of the window. He double clicked and leaned forward to read the full contents. Almost the day Damian hit forty he noticed his reading vision starting to go but, more than a year on, he still hadn't been able to bring himself to buy a pair of glasses. He squinted slightly at the screen, first noting the time the message was sent last night, 2216. Marie had started her email with a brief note:

```
Hi   Damian.   Story   on   background   to
Lloyd/Williams   split   follows.   Couldn't
resist  adding  the  headline.  I  think  it's
the splash — don't you? Marie.
```

I'll be the judge of that, Damian thought to himself, at the same time knowing he would never actually say that to Marie. Any other reporter would have got it in the neck for a cheeky comment like that, but she was different.

He quickly read on, a smile lighting his face as soon as he saw her headline.

I'M NOT A NUN, LLOYD TOLD WILLIAMS BEFORE SPLIT

By Marie Simpson

Today, the Sunday Echo *lifts the lid on a string of rows between Social Democrat leader Richard Williams and his actress wife Anna Lloyd that led to their sensational split just days into the General Election campaign.*

The revelations throw into serious doubt the newly reunited couple's claims that their marriage is now rock solid.

A friend of the couple, who witnessed the rows first hand, has told the Sunday Echo *how Lloyd once screamed down the phone, "I am not a nun", in a row with Williams over her role as a lap dancer in a TV drama.*

The friend said the couple regularly argued as the SDP leader struggled to control his wife's insatiable desire to grow her acting career, regardless of the controversy caused by her choice of roles.

During the same telephone row, Lloyd also told Williams: "I'll never be Barbara Bush. I am an actress".

Damian sat back in his chair and allowed himself a moment's break from reading the story just to relish what was proving to be a run of amazing front-page exclusives on Lloyd and Williams. They had demolished the competition over the course of the campaign, pushed up sales by another 100,000 and – the icing on the cake – delighted Viktor Nemov, the billionaire media mogul and owner of the *Echo* titles. Damian smiled again to himself as he thought how an executive role in the Nemov News Group must now almost certainly be in the bag. Nemov was a big pal of Kelvin's and had pledged his unfailing support to the Alliance leader before the election campaign. He had all but promised Damian a long shelf life with the group if he delivered on this pledge – and Damian knew he had done that and more. Just one more sensational splash right before Britain heads to the polls and his career would be secure. Even better, for Damian, was the thought that he didn't have to come up with it.

He looked through the glass divide to his office and saw Marie walk into the newsroom to begin her day's work. He chuckled to himself as he watched her fumble around her pockets and then her handbag looking for her mobile, only to realise she had already laid it down on the side of her desk. In her he saw a kindred spirit; a loner, driven by a sense of inadequacy and the desire to prove others wrong.

He studied her a moment longer and frowned as he detected more than a hint of sadness settle across Marie's face as she sat down at her computer to start her day's work. She was a confusing mix of motivated and reluctant all at once – some days up, some days down. All part of her complex but engaging personality, he guessed. He wondered if it would be deeply unprofessional to ask her on a date. Then he decided he would leave it until after the election – when they would hopefully be out celebrating together – to raise that prospect.

"God, I'd forgotten how grubby this city looks," Kelvin whispered to Reggie as they made their way through the centre of Leeds on their luxury battle bus. Joy, sitting opposite, shook her head in dismay when she overheard his comment. If only the people of Leeds could hear what he actually thought. At the time she had accepted Kelvin's offer of working on his campaign team, she believed it would be the perfect tonic to get herself over her break-up with Henry – and Anna. But within a few days she realised she should have just made a clean break and taken her time before deciding what to do next. Now, she was forced to study on a daily basis footage of her husband and her former close friend storming the country with what was clearly a winning campaign.

She could tell Henry and Anna had put their differences

aside, and she shivered every time she watched them laughing gaily as they strolled behind Richard on some tour or walkabout. Not only had they mended bridges, but Joy could see they were now really getting on. It was as though they had forgotten her completely. And that, more than anything, was what made her want to wipe the smiles off their smug faces.

She hoped desperately that Kelvin's tour of a housing project in Woodhouse would go without a hitch and they could get back to London as soon as possible. Kelvin had to chair a cabinet meeting later that afternoon so Joy was fully intending going home and getting an early night. The last few weeks had left her completely drained and she needed to get some serious rest if she was going to be able to withstand another two weeks of being bossed around by a grossly insecure Reggie.

The bus pulled in near the estate and Joy looked out of the window to see a large group of housing officials, along with the local Alliance candidate – who clearly didn't stand a chance – all nervously waiting to greet Kelvin. Behind them were gathered a rather bewildered-looking group of local residents who had come to get a look at the Prime Minister. And to the side were the usual assortment of photographers and film crews, who had already begun to capture the PM's arrival.

"My tie straight, Joy?" Kelvin asked casually.

"Yes, Kelvin," she replied robotically, wondering if he had begun to regret employing her as much as she regretted choosing to work for him.

She trotted dutifully down the bus, taking care not to get too close to Reggie who had made it clear very early on that he was to walk immediately behind the PM, making Joy feel like the second bridesmaid.

Kelvin bounced off of the coach, sweeping his foppish fringe back as he stepped onto the pavement. He thrust out his hand to enthusiastically greet the local candidate, Eric Maitlin, but his perma-smile was almost instantly wiped from his face when he felt the crack of an egg hitting the back of his head. His face froze as he first registered the impact and then the obvious consequences of a broken egg shedding its contents down the back of your neck and jacket. The special branch team were quick to act and wrestled the perpetrator – a spotty, teenage local – from the scene. The crowd jeered at the sight of the boy being led away, and suddenly the atmosphere turned ugly.

Police officers moved in to control the local residents, while Reggie led Kelvin back on the bus so he could change his jacket. As Joy followed them up the steps she could hear Kelvin ranting. "What does that say about my bloody security when I'm pelted with an egg at close range, five seconds after stepping off the bus? There needs to be a serious rethink on security if I'm going to do any more of these sodding walkabouts. I'm not going to stand there like a mug and let some little turd take a pop at me. God knows, in this area, I'm lucky I wasn't shot."

Reggie started furiously wiping at the back of the Prime Minister's head before helping him remove his jacket. Kelvin turned momentarily towards the window and realised that the ungainly scene was being filmed and photographed by the assembled media on the street outside.

"Shut the fucking blinds will you, Joy," he barked.

She quickly reached to pull the shade down over the window before stepping back into the shadows. Even counting her first job working as a waitress, Joy had never felt so disrespected by an employer. She was clearly becoming surplus to requirement as Kelvin realised she didn't have the insider information on the SDP that he at first hoped. Her only chance of making it through the campaign with her professional esteem intact was what would surely be the splash in this Sunday's *Echo* about Richard and Anna's rows before the split. Maybe then Kelvin would see her worth – and Henry would finally realise that he couldn't just walk away scot-free from his years of bullying without paying for it.

Trying to get five minutes alone in a bathroom to do a pregnancy test proved to be no easy feat for Anna. She had joined Richard on a whistle-stop tour of Wales and they were running to an extremely tight schedule which was seriously stressing Henry out. Using the toilet on the bus was a non-starter, both because of its gut-churning acrid smell and the constant motion, therefore she had to wait until they stopped at a campaign venue. Even then, each time Anna asked to go to the toilet, Henry would say, "Okay, but please make it quick," and she'd have to scuttle off while he hovered outside the door waiting for her. It had been difficult enough to get hold of a pregnancy test in the first place. It wasn't as if she could just stroll into her local Boots and ask for a kit, so Libby had picked one up for her and slipped it to Anna under the table on the bus earlier that morning. Libby had decided to join them for the day on the campaign trail as it was her only chance to catch up properly with Anna to discuss offers of work, which had been piling in.

Henry's mood eased towards the end of the afternoon and Anna saw her moment to do the test when she passed the ladies' loos as they toured a biscuit factory outside Cardiff. While the others listened to the factory manager prattling on about top-of-the-range equipment, Anna snuck off and quickly found herself alone in a toilet cubicle with no one timing her visit. She pulled the test stick out of the box and followed the instructions to the letter. This was not Anna's first test in the last few years, but rather her fifth. Three of her previous tests had been negative and one positive. Eighteen months ago she had got so far as receiving an appointment date for the twelve-week scan but lost the pregnancy two weeks beforehand. Months later she still found herself crying every day in grief and anger that the child she so wanted had been taken from her. So they had opted to hold off for a while with Anna instead choosing to busy herself with work projects – until today, where she found herself standing in a toilet cubicle, waiting and hoping.

She had been feeling sick and a bit hormonal for the last week and, when things didn't change, she allowed herself to feel just a little bit of excitement.

Libby had bought a digital test so she didn't even have the option of delaying the disappointment by holding the stick up to the light to examine the lines more closely in search of something faint but wonderful. Instead, the test would flash up either *Pregnant* or *Not Pregnant*. As blunt as that. Something began to flash at the end of the stick and, just like waiting for a photo booth to spill its pictures, she knew the test was about to deliver the news – good or bad. Anna felt her stomach lurch, and she looked away momentarily, bracing herself for the result. When she looked back down at the tiny screen it carried only one word: *Pregnant.*

Anna stumbled backwards in shock and heard herself give a little yelp of glee. She put the test back in her bag and headed out of the cubicle. She stopped to wash her hands and check her face in the mirror. Her cheeks were flushed bright red with excitement. *Please let me keep this pregnancy*, she called out silently to the heavens.

She found Libby and Henry waiting outside the toilets for her; Libby clearly aware why Anna had been in the loo for over ten minutes, while Henry looked confused and impatient.

"This is quite a reception party," Anna joked.

"Everything all right?" Henry asked.

"Absolutely fine. I've just got a bit of a headache, so I took a few moments out, that's all."

"It's been a bloody manic day, that's for sure. I've got some paracetamol in my jacket on the bus if you want some?" he offered helpfully.

"That would be great, thanks."

Anna winked at Libby as Henry walked in front, leading them back to join the rest of the pack.

"Well?" Libby whispered, impatiently.

"Well." Anna giggled. "This is one trip to a biscuit factory I'm going to remember for the rest of my life."

Ray made it over to Bob's Victoria flat just after seven-thirty in the evening to join him for the drink they'd been promising to have for the last two weeks. This was the one day in the entire campaign that their schedules had actually allowed for them to meet in London without being accompanied by an entourage of some kind. Both men were extremely loyal to Richard, but absolutely devoted to the party, and they had wanted to sit down over a drink to analyse the events of the past fortnight and what they meant for the SDP.

Bob gave Ray his usual back-slapping, cheery welcome when he arrived and quickly showed him through to the sparsely furnished living room where his cleaner/housekeeper had laid out a selection of nibbles for them, ranging from crisps to stuffed vol-au-vents and warmed quiche. Bob had often told Ray he couldn't possibly survive without Babs – a fifty-eight-year-old divorcee who had started out doing a few hours cleaning for him each week, and now practically organised all his domestic arrangements. Beyond its tidiness, however, Bob's flat represented the ultimate bachelor's pad, with only the most basic of furniture and carpets and wallpaper dating back to the early nineties. Even Ray, who didn't count himself as a particular expert in interior design, could see the place was badly in need of updating.

"Tuck in," Bob instructed Ray as he gestured towards the food.

Ray helped himself to a plate and a couple of pieces of quiche before grabbing a handful of crisps. He and Bob were due to attend a function in the City later that evening and they had arranged for a driver to collect them both shortly after 8pm so they could continue talking in the car. With little time, Ray got straight to the point.

"What do you reckon then, Bob? Are we gonna walk it or do you think Kelvin could do some damage yet?"

"Well," Bob replied, hastily trying to finish chewing a prawn vol-au-vent, "I think based on where we are now, we could win a good majority. But my biggest worry is that, wherever I go, the main thing people want to ask about is Anna Lloyd. Not unemployment, not housing, not health, Anna bloody Lloyd. That just can't be a good thing."

"I know," Ray said, shaking his head. "It's nice that she's back and I even think she's good for the party. She's young and fresh and helps take us away from the hardline socialist image of the past. As far as women go, she has cross-party appeal – especially after what came out about her past. But, right now, when a voter thinks about Richard Williams and the Social Democrats, they think Anna Lloyd. That means if she starts getting up to some of her old tricks or, unthinkably, if she actually decides to walk, then we could suffer big time."

"What does Sandra think?" asked Bob.

"She thinks he should have married a wallflower and then we wouldn't be in this bloody mess." Both men chuckled at the head of policy's typically severe assessment.

"Well, Anna seems to have fallen into line for the moment," Bob optimistically suggested, "so I think we just try to keep things steady, not take any major risks, and go for the finish line."

"I agree," said Ray. "The worst has got to be behind us, so we just need to keep the ship steady."

"Do we know of any more skeletons lurking behind Anna or Richard?"

Ray raised his eyebrows as he considered Bob's pertinent question. "Henry says no. He said he'd grilled them both straight after Anna came back. So, as long as they're telling the truth, we've got nothing to worry about."

"As long as they're telling the truth," Bob echoed.

The rest of the afternoon had passed painfully slowly as Anna patiently waited to find the right moment to tell Richard her news. That time finally came after they had finished eating dinner with the local MP and party chairman in Cardiff, and – rather than taking the battle bus back to London – were to be chauffeured home by Richard's driver, Les, because of the lateness of the hour. Libby had already left by train earlier in the afternoon so she could make it back home in time to put the kids to bed. Anna had almost burst into tears when she'd said goodbye to her sister, overcome by a wave of tiredness and emotion. She had barely touched any dinner, and just yearned to be settled into the back of the car with Richard and heading home to Highgate.

It was after eight-thirty in the evening and, after they had bid farewell to their Cardiff hosts, Anna and Richard finally climbed into the Prius, where they would be sheltered from politics for just a couple of hours. As soon as she sat down, Anna took off her shoes and undid the top button on her trousers which she noticed were already beginning to feel tight. Then she curled her legs up onto the seat and tilted her head back. Richard loosened his tie and tossed his papers onto the floor, mumbling, "I'll read these in the morning." He very rarely conceded to being tired, but the fact he couldn't face reading any more briefing documents told Anna that Richard must have been exhausted. She leaned into her husband's side, stroking his arm as Les skillfully whisked them through the city centre and out towards the M4 back to London. For the first twenty minutes they sat mainly in silence, unwinding from the intensity of the day. Finally, his senses slightly restored, Richard turned to look at Anna. "You okay, darling? You're awfully quiet."

"I'm just very tired," Anna said wearily, "but happy." She looked up at her husband and smiled. "I've been feeling a little off colour the last few days which made me decide to take a pregnancy test."

Richard turned his whole body now to face Anna, eyes wide with expectation. "You didn't say you were feeling unwell, Anna. What was the result of the test?"

"Positive." Anna smiled again, tears starting to spill over with relief at finally being able to tell him.

"Oh, Anna," Richard whispered into her ear. "That's wonderful news. Just imagine a baby in Downing Street. That's going to shake the place up." He smiled to himself before taking her hand in his and stroking it as he spoke. "You must take so much care now. You can't go pushing yourself like this."

"I'm fine, Richard, honestly. I'll make sure I rest when I'm feeling tired, but I'm happy to keep campaigning with you. I wouldn't be anywhere else right now."

"This could turn out to be quite a year," Richard said, eyes gleaming. "When would the baby be due?"

"Sometime late November/early December, I think."

"It's too much to take in, isn't it?" He beamed, the schoolboy excitement that Anna loved to see so much in him, coming shining through. "We could be having our first Christmas at Number 10 with a newborn baby. It's unbelievable."

"Well, we've some way to go to achieve either," said Anna, with a note of caution. "But that's the dream."

Richard leaned in closer to his wife and kissed her softly on the forehead. "We'll make it a reality, Anna. I know we will."

13

LLOYD AND WILLIAMS FACING NEW CLAIMS OVER
MARRIAGE

MONDAY, APRIL 20TH, 2009, UK NEWSWIRE

Richard Williams' bid to reach Downing Street was once again
rocked by claims over his private life when a Sunday
newspaper published details of the alleged rows between the
SDP leader and his actress wife in the run-up to their recent
marital split.

The *Sunday Echo* claimed Anna Lloyd had told her
husband she was no "Barbara Bush", in a barbed reference to
her image, during an alleged row with him over her role as a
lap dancer in an ITV drama.

The newspaper quoted an unnamed friend as saying the
couple regularly argued over Lloyd's choice of acting roles,
along with her public image which has often courted
controversy, leading Lloyd to allegedly tell her husband she
was "not a nun".

A spokesman for the Social Democrats was quick to

condemn the claims as "absolute nonsense, fabricated by a coward who dare not speak her name".

There has been much speculation within the media about who the source of the article could be, with one radio show host this morning claiming the details were passed to the paper by a former PR agent to Anna Lloyd.

TalkLive host Clive Farrell, a former Alliance Party communications chief, claimed on his show that he had been told "at first hand, from someone within the party" that Joy Gooding – who recently separated from Social Democrat press chief, Henry Morton, and who subsequently joined the Alliance Party as a communications officer – was the source behind the *Sunday Echo* story.

Farrell's claims were immediately denied by the Alliance Party in a statement released last night.

The statement added that the party "is not interested in idle gossip, but is resolutely focused on the real issues that matter to the people of Britain".

J oy could tell just by the smugness spreading across Reggie's face and the anger over Kelvin's that her little briefing with Marie Simpson at the *Sunday Echo* hadn't gone down well. Emotionally, this created some turmoil for her as, on one hand, she simply didn't care what they thought but, on the other, she really didn't want to lose face in front of Henry and word would soon spread that Kelvin had seen it as a complete cock-up.

"I must say, Joy, that even by Reggie's standards this is a cheap stunt," Kelvin said, whilst pointing randomly at the newspaper front pages spread across his desk. Joy switched her eyes to Reggie for a moment – who was propped up like a little meerkat in front of the Prime Minister, hanging on his every word and looking distinctly hurt that he had been put down in this way, even as a joke.

"Well," Joy began, "I'm sorry if you feel it has in some way embarrassed you but, even though I agree it's a fairly low blow, I do believe the article in the *Sunday Echo* had the desired effect in demonstrating the cracks in Williams' marriage again. After all, the polls show that voters wouldn't tolerate another separation and so I feel it's in the public interest to expose the problems that still exist."

"How do you know they still exist?" Reggie asked sulkily, furious that Joy hadn't been cowed by Kelvin's jibe.

"The thing that goes against your argument, Joy," the Prime Minister said, flashing a false smile, "is that it was completely bloody obvious that the story came from you – and therefore the Alliance Party. That, my dear, makes us look like a bunch of desperate, nasty morons."

Reggie then took his turn to stick the boot in. "I had also clearly briefed you that we were not to continue a personal assault on the Williams' marriage because it would ultimately reflect badly on us."

"You had done no such thing," Joy replied indignantly.

"Let's not bicker about it," Kelvin cut in. "We're twelve points behind in the polls, so we'd better come up with something bloody good if we're going to stop the Social Democrat juggernaut. Lloyd has a lot of public sympathy on her side so I want to make sure we turn all our attention on Williams without being seen to have planted anything. So the two of you need to put your heads together and come up with something good, do you hear? We're entering the final straight and we need to pull something out of the bag or we're sunk. No amateur jobs this time," he added, directing his gaze at Joy.

She wanted to lean across his desk and slap him but, in spite of his smug attitude, she knew Kelvin had a point. Either they delivered one last cruel and devastating blow to Richard Williams' reputation or the Alliance Party would be decimated for years to come. And even worse, so would her career.

Anna paced slowly around the living room looking for a distraction before eventually deciding to take a seat on the sofa and read the papers. Despite the fact her absence from campaigning – and on a day when the media spotlight would be firmly on their relationship – would surely whip up speculation of a rift, she and Richard had taken the difficult decision the night before that Anna should stay at home. She had been deeply upset by the article in the *Sunday Echo*, which she instantly knew had come from Joy. She recalled clearly the mobile conversation she'd had with Richard a few weeks ago in which she'd made the comment about not being a nun, and Joy had been the only person to overhear apart from her driver, John, whose loyalty she would never even pause to question. While she and Joy had parted professional ways on fairly strained terms, Anna had still cared about her former friend. She had cried bitterly with Richard the night before at the thought of Joy making the call to the journalist and quite happily spilling Anna's personal comments for nothing more than political gain. Even worse, Anna knew that Joy wasn't even an Alliance Party supporter. The only reason she had joined them was for revenge. By nine in the evening Anna had felt so tired and emotional it had become clear she was in no state to travel to Portsmouth with the rest of them. She had instead agreed to travel to Edinburgh with Richard the following day.

What made her absence from the campaign trail worse, was that they weren't even in a position to say she was pregnant –

which would have helped both the situation, and the entire campaign, enormously. Rather, she would now have to mask the waves of nausea with a false smile, and regularly apply blusher to her increasingly pale pallor, which the press would no doubt interpret as a sign of deep misery.

Anna cast her eyes over the front page of *Today*, but threw the paper back onto the coffee table as soon as she spotted the lead story, questioning the status of her and Richard's relationship.

She reached for the house phone and dialled Richard's mobile number. It was ten am and she seemed to remember him saying he would be on the bus until at least half past.

He answered after three rings.

"Hi, darling," he said breezily. "How you feeling?"

"Okay," Anna replied. "I still feel a bit shaken by the whole Joy thing. It just feels a bit surreal. Is Henry worried about the coverage?"

"Not really. We've taken a bit of a knock in the papers today but he thinks they'll move on soon enough, especially once they see us out and about again tomorrow. We've already put out a statement saying you won't be campaigning today due to other work commitments, but will be back on the road with us on Tuesday. I think it would be good if you could say a brief few words tomorrow as well, just countering what Joy has put out there."

Anna raised her eyes at the thought of it, but outwardly agreed. "Of course."

"Oh, and Anna..." Richard broke into a whisper. "I wondered if you would mind Henry staying with us for the last couple of weeks of the campaign. It would make sense from a planning perspective... but, also, he seems pretty down."

"Right," Anna said, taken aback. "Is he upset about the *Sunday Echo* thing?"

"I think that's brought it to a head, yes. He was just saying this morning that it's very difficult going back to an empty house every night, knowing that the woman he used to share it with is now actively plotting his and our downfall. When you think about it, it must be bloody awful. Thing is, we need Henry to be strong and focused and I just think he could use a bit of support right now."

"Okay," Anna said. She did sympathise with Henry's plight. After all, it was not so long ago that she was in a very similar position, but she equally felt a bit uncomfortable about the man who had nearly ruined their marriage now coming to live with them – even if it was just for a couple of weeks.

"Great. Thanks, Anna. I'll bring him back this evening then."

"Okay."

"I love you," Richard said, about to end the call.

"Do you think I'm selfish?" Anna suddenly asked.

"What? Where did that come from?"

"Joy said I was selfish. I wondered if that's what you thought too?"

"Don't even think about what that woman said. She clearly has issues if she can just turn her back on the people she was supposed to care about and flounce off with the opposition. She obviously has no principles whatsoever, so is in no position to judge others."

"I know," Anna replied distantly. "But I think maybe she told me the truth. I have been selfish. Reading what I said to you in the *Echo* really shocked me. I just wasn't supporting you, Richard, and I want you to know I'm sorry. I don't want to be like that anymore."

"I love you the way you are," Richard said softly, "but life is so much easier for me when I know you're by my side. So thank you."

Libby physically deflated as she looked around the majestic vision that was Franchesca Carruthers' home. It was beyond tasteful; lavish enough to let you know a lot of money had been spent, without being in any way gauche – a period property in its truest sense, with elaborate cornicing, solid oak doors and real fireplaces. Libby was dropping Jasmine in for a play date but Franchesca had immediately offered her a cup of tea – and almost certainly so she could get the low-down on Anna and Richard. Ollie and Rupert hadn't complained as it meant they got to go and play upstairs for a few minutes too, in what, Libby had heard, was the most amazing playroom packed solid with toys and games.

As the kids played, Libby had been left to peruse the living room while Franchesca made the tea. Having taken in the furnishings, she moved on to the sea of family photos resting on top of the grand piano by the window. Libby noticed they were mainly of the kids, a couple of them including Franchesca – her blonde hair, tanned, glowing skin and ridiculously long legs showcased in each – and there were also a few very aged pictures of what looked like Franchesca's parents' wedding. Weirdly, thought Libby, there were none of Franchesca's husband.

She leaned closer to double-check, when the door suddenly swung open and Franchesca arrived carrying a large tray with teapot, cups and biscuits laid out on top. She set it down carefully on the coffee table before turning her attention to Libby.

"Come and have a seat," she said, gesturing towards the sofa. "We just don't get the chance to have a proper chat in the morning so it's lovely to get a few minutes to catch up."

"Yes, it's great," Libby answered in what she hoped was an

enthusiastic tone, all the while awaiting the inquisition. She watched Franchesca carefully pour the tea into the cups, placing a little teaspoon on the saucers before handing one over to Libby.

"So, how's Dan?" Franchesca asked.

"He's good," said Libby, unsure of what she could add to her reply to make their lives sound more interesting. "He's busy at work – they've landed a big entertainment client – so it means he has to stay on a bit later some evenings, but he still usually makes it back to help put the kids to bed."

"That must be nice," Franchesca said wistfully.

Libby had heard Franchesca's husband was a big shot in the City so she assumed he probably worked late most evenings.

"Does Will put in long hours then?" Libby asked whilst reaching forward to pick up her cup of tea.

"Long hours with other women," Franchesca snarled. Libby slammed the cup back onto the saucer in a fruitless attempt to catch some of the tea that had sloshed over the top when her hand jolted with the shock of what she had just heard.

"You didn't know?" Franchesca asked sceptically.

"No," Libby heard herself whisper meekly.

"I threw him out because he's a philandering bastard, so I'm now officially a single mother. I can't believe you hadn't heard. It spread around the school in five minutes."

"Sorry, I didn't know. I've been a bit distracted lately."

"It's rather refreshing to know you're out of the gossip circle," Franchesca said, relaxing again. "And of course you've been distracted. What a time of it you must be having. Someone told me you were working with your sister now."

"Yes, I'm handling her PR," Libby said proudly.

"Gosh, what fun. You must be fighting the media off at the moment, she's so much in the spotlight."

"It definitely has its moments," Libby answered, suddenly

feeling the urge to check her mobile in case she'd missed any calls.

"Well, I hope you get that little shit Kelvin Davis out of office," said Franchesca, her face contorting as though she were sucking on limes.

"You're not an Alliance voter then." Libby laughed.

"Actually, I've voted Alliance all my adult life, but not this time. My protest is on principle not politics. He behaved in a deplorable manner towards a very good friend of mine."

Libby had not been involved in the world of politics for long, but the little she'd learned in the past couple of weeks had taught her that any information on the opposition is useful information, particularly where there's a hint of scandal.

"How awful," she replied cautiously, making sure her voice carried just the right note of concern. "What..." she started quietly. "What was it that he did?"

Anna didn't know whether it was pregnancy or a slight mellowing with age, but as soon as she saw Henry walk in the door behind Richard – his head bowed, and his face pale and drawn – she immediately felt a maternal urge to comfort and shelter him. As Richard walked nonchalantly into the living room, Henry had hung by the door, clutching a holdall bag in his left hand and looking as apprehensive as a little evacuee in the Blitz. Anna rushed over to take his bag and guided him into the room. She knew she should still hate him but, right now, that seemed akin to kicking a puppy.

"Come in and sit down, Henry. Just relax and treat the place as your own. Would you like a glass of wine?"

Henry's eyes lit up. "I'd kill for one, thanks Anna. It's been a bloody long day."

"How did Portsmouth go?" Anna said, throwing the question to either man.

"Not bad," Richard replied while he scoured the kitchen drawers for a bottle opener. Once retrieved, he was able to give a fuller account. "Obviously, we were there to push our benefit reforms, but as soon as we opened the floor to journalists' questions, the only thing tabled for discussion was our marriage." Richard shook his head in dismay as he began to fill three wine glasses.

"None for me," Anna reminded him, before adding for Henry's benefit. "I've got a bit of a headache."

He nodded then said: "We just need to use your presence tomorrow, Anna, to put an end to the gossip and let us get back to focusing on the real campaign. Richard said you'd be willing to say a few words to reporters and I think that would really help – as long as you're comfortable with that?"

"Of course." Anna smiled and couldn't help but note the difference in Henry's approach. Just a few weeks ago he would have been much more aggressive when asking her to help out and there would always be more than just a slight hint of emotional blackmail involved along the lines of, *"Richard is under a lot of pressure right now, Anna, and it is your role as leader's wife to..."*

She also noticed the change in her own attitude as to how she would have taken Henry's input a few weeks ago, and how she was taking it now. She wondered if it was him or her that had changed more. Or had Joy's absence somehow altered the dynamic between them? As she began to get to know Henry better, she was beginning to understand his frustration over her past behaviour. And the more she thought about it, the more she realised that Joy had done nothing to broker a truce between them; instead, she had added fuel to Anna's fire by encouraging her to rebel against Richard and Henry's requests. Anna guessed that in some way this little game had given Joy a sense of power among a group of people by whom she felt dominated. After all, Henry had been very much a star appointment within the Social Democrats and attracted many column inches in his own right.

Anna listened as the two men chatted through the plan for Edinburgh the following day. She marvelled at their raw determination. They really wanted to win this election – and not just for themselves.

"I want to try and squeeze that visit in if we possibly can," Richard told Henry. "I've read a lot about this specialist learning unit and I'd like to see for myself what they're doing so right. It could be very important for our support-in-education plan."

"It'll push the rally back then, which will mean we're very late home." Henry looked in Anna's direction.

"That's fine. I can sleep on the plane." She nodded at Richard to reassure him, before settling back in the sofa to watch the two men at work again.

She could see why Richard had forgiven Henry now. The two of them had become inseparable in the last year as the momentum behind their cause intensified. At times in their conversation they were almost seamless in picking up on each other's thoughts which she found spellbinding to watch.

Seeing their commitment at first hand, she couldn't help but feel ashamed of the controversy she had stirred for them along the way. She wished she could take her selfish actions back. Instead, she would focus on what she could offer now. Whatever they asked of her, she would do. All her life she had craved fame and attention and, when it came, it did nothing to ease the pain of her past. That was a void that could never be filled. It was time to focus on others now. And she knew she would never have to completely leave her acting skills behind. After all, the performances she gave over the coming weeks would have to be the best of her career. There would be no dress rehearsal.

14

"OUR MARRIAGE IS STRONGER THAN EVER," INSISTS DEFIANT LLOYD

WEDNESDAY, APRIL 22ND, 2009, UK NEWSWIRE

The actress Anna Lloyd yesterday launched a staunch defence of her marriage to Social Democrats leader Richard Williams as she campaigned with her husband in Edinburgh.

She told reporters that she and Williams were now "an unbreakable force" following their recent marital turmoil in the wake of claims Lloyd had once worked as a professional escort.

Speaking as she and her husband greeted crowds of well-wishers along the Scottish capital's Princes Street, she said: "Our recent separation only proved to us how much our marriage means. Our reconciliation is no publicity stunt, as the *Sunday Echo's* cowardly, anonymous source will be well aware.

"Richard and I are firmly committed to each other and to winning the General Election for the long-suffering people of this country. We are totally united in our marriage and our desire for change".

The couple's walkabout followed a speech by Williams outside the Scottish Parliament in which he pledged to strengthen devolution and "work with Holyrood for the benefit of the people of Scotland".

The pair were well received by the Scottish public and politicians alike with many people presenting flowers and gifts to Ms Lloyd.

Meanwhile, the Alliance MP, Lizzie Ancroft, poured cold water on the opposition leader's reunion with his wife, calling it a "cynical ploy".

Speaking to *AllNews 24*, Ancroft said: "Richard Williams and Anna Lloyd take the British public for complete fools if they think they can convince us all that they have genuinely put their differences behind them and are now a happy and committed couple.

"Anna Lloyd continues to act out her little soap opera – and though her acting may at times seem convincing – no one is fooled by the plot".

A nna smiled as she watched herself – for what seemed like the one hundredth time – making her statement in Edinburgh. In Henry's debriefing he had told her she "convincingly engaged with voters, showing both loyalty and love in her defence of Richard". In other words, it went well. The clip had topped every TV news bulletin and the presenters on *AllNews 24* were now about to lead a discussion on "RiAnnagate" as the press had dubbed the ongoing saga. Anna couldn't help but laugh as they rolled out the same old "relationship expert" who had been making a small fortune in the last few weeks pontificating on a marriage she knew absolutely nothing about. She had to hand it to this woman though, she could keep the material coming. She never ran out of hand signals, gestures, looks and expressions to flag up as "significant". Picking over yesterday's outing she noted how Anna had leaned in towards Richard as he spoke, "even stopping to touch his hand gently at one point and whisper a few words of encouragement". In fact, what Anna had actually whispered was that she needed the toilet again and was going to have to make a run for it into Jenners department store. However, the upshot from this relationship expert was that she did believe Richard and Anna were still in love. So that was all right then. Anna switched off the television and made her way slowly towards the bathroom. She had another long and busy day ahead so Richard had allowed her to lie in until eight. She was due to meet Don Monteith for a late breakfast at ten, before joining Richard on the campaign trail again at a car plant in Essex. She had been very excited when Don called on Monday evening to suggest they meet. He had even hinted that he might have a project in mind for her. But Anna also knew that now was not the time to be focusing on her career – both because of the election and the baby. Richard had encouraged her to go ahead and meet with Don anyway as he was a good contact – and they needed to keep him on side for the duration of the campaign. Henry had looked a little concerned at the mention of a possible film role – clearly imagining Anna about to embark on something akin to an *Eyes Wide Shut* sequel – but had managed to stay quiet which was the greatest sign to her yet that he was making a serious effort to maintain the now easy truce between them.

Libby's fingers trembled as they hovered over the telephone keypad. She knew all she had to do was dial Franchesca Carruthers' number and ask her a straightforward question, but the thought was still terrifying. Would she take it the wrong way and just think Libby was using her connections for political gain? Or would she be able to see the bigger picture? As she began to punch the number into the pad, she hoped with all her heart that Franchesca was now a Social Democrat supporter.

It took a few long rings before she answered: "Franchesca Carruthers, hello?"

"Oh, hi, Franchesca, this is Libby," she began shakily. "I hope I haven't disturbed you. I was looking for you at drop-off this morning but you're too punctual for me..." Libby laughed awkwardly and, realising she was starting to stray off course, decided just to cut to the point. "Look, I hope you don't mind me asking you this, but... you may have noticed that the Alliance Party are running a bit of a smear campaign against Anna and Richard."

"That had come to my attention, yes." Franchesca sighed in what Libby hoped was a supportive gesture.

"Well, I remember you told me you had a friend that had been treated very badly by Kelvin Davis and..." Libby took an involuntary breath, which turned into an audible gulp. "I wondered if you would mind asking her if she'd be willing to go public with it."

"What do you mean 'public'?" Franchesa asked.

"I mean, whether she would be willing to talk to the press." Libby tensed again, shutting her eyes as she waited for the answer.

"Well..." Franchesca's voice sounded unusually slight. "It's not as easy as just calling my friend, I'm afraid."

"Why not?"

"Because it was me who had an affair with Kelvin. I guess

you could say it was a counter-attack for the many times Will had cheated on me."

"Oh," was all Libby could muster.

"Look, Libby," Franchesca continued. "I've been following everything that's been said about your sister, and I think it's completely disgraceful. Kelvin Davis is a conman and a liar who should be exposed, but I can't put my children through a public scandal like that. It just wouldn't be fair to them."

Libby could tell the window of opportunity she had with Franchesca was closing fast, so she tried the only shot she had.

"How about if we didn't reveal details of the affair, but simply said you went on a couple of dates together? It would still allow us to make the point that he tends to treat women badly. I think that would still be enough to weaken his stance and bring him down from the moral high ground he's been trying to stand on."

The phone line went quiet for a few agonising moments as Franchesca thought the suggestion through.

"I'm going to need time to think about this," she said finally. "I don't care about what people think of me, but I don't want my children to feel ashamed of me."

"You wouldn't need to give much detail, Franchesca. I think simply talking about the way he spoke to you would be enough, because there's been rumours of his womanising circulating for years, but this will be the first time someone actually talks about his attitude to women publicly. We are concerned that Kelvin is willing to stop at nothing to win this election, so we have to try and arm ourselves in any way we can. By doing this, you will genuinely be helping the Social Democrats to try and oust that man from power and undo the damage he's been inflicting on us all for so long."

"I hear what you're saying, Libby. And I would love to help, I really would, but this is a very big ask."

"I know, Franchesca. It's not something I'm enjoying doing,

but I've watched my sister and brother-in-law get dragged through the mud these last few weeks and I can't just sit around and do nothing. I hope you understand that I just had to make this call."

"I do understand, but I need time to think it over. I will call you this afternoon, either way."

Libby thanked Franchesca before ending the call. This would go one of two ways, she thought. Either Franchesca would accept that Libby had good reason to ask her and, hopefully, agree to help, or she would put the phone down, call some other mothers at the school and, between them, turn her into a complete social pariah. Libby was just beginning to realise that, in politics, the stakes were always high.

From the moment Anna stepped out of the car, she realised the Soho café had been a very poor choice of venue for meeting Don Monteith. Although her driver had managed to shake off two photographers on the way over, reinforcements surrounded her as soon as her feet hit the pavement. Where they had come from, she didn't know, but already Anna had a creeping suspicion that Don might have tipped them off in an effort to promote himself and his new film. She walked briskly inside the café and found him already waiting at a corner table. He waved breezily and Anna, not wishing to cause a scene, decided not to mention the photographers and instead behave as though nothing was wrong.

"How are you my darling?" he said, kissing her on both cheeks before flagging down a passing waiter to take her coat. "Sit down, please." He gestured towards the seat across from him.

"Thanks." She placed her handbag at her feet and loosened

her silk neck scarf before turning her attention back to the director. "So, Don, I must congratulate you. I see you're number one at the box office this week. You must be thrilled."

"Yeah, it's going really well, thanks. We open in the US next week so that's gonna be a big one. We've got premieres in New York and LA."

"You're a busy man then." Anna smiled. "I'm very fortunate to steal some of your time."

He nodded. "Well, this is a rare day off for me so I thought I'd make the most of it by meeting a very beautiful actress for brunch."

Anna felt herself wince at Don's crude attempt at charm, and instead of responding to him she browsed the breakfast menu until she'd made her choice. When the waiter came to take their order, Anna asked for poached egg on toast while Don just ordered another coffee.

"Are you not having anything to eat?" Anna asked.

"No, I'm not a big eater in the mornings."

"You should have said," Anna replied, confused at his suggestion of brunch when he wasn't going to eat anything himself.

"Well, coffee seems so meagre compared to brunch, doesn't it." He smiled. "Anyway, you need to relax and eat properly when you're not on the road, cos there was nothing worth eating on that battle bus."

"That's true." Anna laughed. "Sadly, it's like a second home right now as well."

"But just you wait until you land the big prize." Don winked. "You'll never have to face a soggy ploughman's sandwich again."

"Even if we do make it, we'll still have to get out on that road in another few years' time. There's no escaping that battle bus."

"You'll be too busy with your film career by then, Anna."

Don winked again, causing Anna to wonder if it had become something of an involuntary movement around women.

She smiled, a little embarrassed. "We'll see. Right now I feel very committed to supporting Richard and getting involved more in social campaigning."

"Very good for you. Now..." he announced dramatically. "I wanna talk to you about a little project I've got coming up on the horizon. Stay right there and I'll be back in a minute." Don suddenly rose to his feet and headed off to the toilets. Fortunately for Anna, her order arrived just at that point so she was saved from having to sit alone with only a glass of water to occupy her time. Watching Don swagger off in the direction of the mens' toilets, she couldn't help but think how agitated he had seemed recently compared to the day they had first met on the bus. Today his eyes darted around the room as he spoke, his smile a little forced. Perhaps he'd been celebrating his latest film's success a little too hard? Whatever the reason, she had begun to feel tired at the thought of trying to sustain a long conversation with Don so she texted John and asked him to park nearby so she could keep their meeting brief. She could tell Don there'd been a change of campaigning schedule and she now had to meet Richard a little earlier.

She heard Don's footsteps behind her again and looked up to see him passing her chair. He turned his head to smile at her and she noticed a cluster of white powder tucked under his right nostril. Anna immediately knew what it was – in her early twenties she'd dated a guy who told her he was an investment broker but who actually turned out to be dealing cocaine. And although he had been a good deal more discreet that Don, Anna had on more than one occasion, spotted that same white powder up his nose. It turned her stomach to think she was spending time alone with a man who publicly professed to care about society and the welfare of others, but who was quite happy to perpetuate the misery of thousands of innocent people caught in the middle of drug wars. Not to mention the fact that if it got out she'd been spending time with a cocaine user it could derail the campaign all over again. She looked at him in his designer T-shirt and jacket, the smell of his expensive aftershave invading her breakfast, and she saw in an instant what this man really was – a shallow, insecure product of an even shallower and insecure industry. It was an industry over which she'd fretted in recent years whether she was thin or young enough to continue in, wondering whether she'd require cosmetic surgery to keep winning even semi-decent roles. And sitting across from Don Monteith in the restaurant that day, she made a decision that it was an industry she no longer wanted anything to do with. She had been handed an opportunity to do some good in the world, and she was going to make the most of it.

Don was smiling across at her as he chattered on about the "amazing" project he had in mind for her.

"It's a sort of British *Sex in the City* meets *Beaches*," he continued in a loud, over-animated voice. "Your character would be very similar to Samantha, but you would encounter real struggles that allow the audience to totally relate."

Anna reached for her wallet and placed a twenty pound note on the table.

"What you doing?" Don asked, perplexed.

"I'm leaving," Anna replied, smiling.

"Why?"

"Because meeting you today, Don, has made me realise everything that's wrong with this business. You said we were alike. You were right. You are like the self-indulgent, mixed-up person I was. But that's not who I want to be now."

Don was staring at her as if she had just lost her mind – unable to even comprehend how she could insult someone of his stature and turn down the chance of starring in one of his films. Taking advantage of his stunned silence, Anna stood up to leave.

"Good luck with the project." She smiled.

With that she turned her back on Don Monteith, and all those like him.

Richard and Henry were so transfixed by the lunchtime news that they didn't even hear Anna coming in the office door. It was only when she perched herself on the table behind them that Richard turned and smiled to acknowledge her presence.

She could just make out the strapline running across the bottom of the screen.

CAPTURED MISSIONARIES RELEASED – PM TO MAKE STATEMENT.

Anna instantly knew the story they were referring to was that of the two British missionaries who had been taken hostage in Manila three years ago. Their families had been calling on Kelvin Davis ever since they were taken to help secure their release by putting pressure on the Philippine government to intervene. Kelvin had seemed reluctant to get involved until the last few weeks when, as the third anniversary of their capture approached and the media coverage around it increased, he had clearly spotted the opportunity to win points with the voting public. Unsurprisingly, he was about to milk every possible popularity-boosting second out of the situation. The picture cut away from the studio and brought the TV audience live to the Downing Street press conference where Kelvin was just approaching the podium wearing a bright pink tie and a look that, to Anna, seemed infuriatingly smug.

As he stood to address the assembled press, pictures of the two missionaries appeared on a plasma screen behind him, just to ensure there could be no doubt in any viewer's mind as to Kelvin's involvement in this diplomatic triumph.

"Debbie Cartwright and Lorraine McGann were, one hour ago, released from the hell that has been their lives for the last three years." Kelvin pursed his lip at the end of the sentence as if stifling a personal pain before continuing. "For their families, who never stopped fighting, the nightmare is finally over. This government has been working tirelessly with the Philippine authorities to secure their release and, in the last few days, I personally spoke with the Philippine president regarding this matter..."

"Give us a break," Henry shouted at the screen, shaking his head in frustration.

"... I am overjoyed," continued Kelvin, "that our efforts have now paid off and that these two missionaries are returning home to the love of their friends and families. I have spoken with them both by telephone within the last twenty minutes and they are very tired, but very happy."

Richard grabbed for the remote and cut Kelvin off in his prime.

"I can't watch any more," he said, folding his arms across his chest in a gesture Anna saw as half-protective, half-defeatist.

"Look, he may win a couple of points from this, but any bounce won't last more than a couple of days," Henry declared convincingly.

"The guy is a complete charlatan," Richard vented. "And he keeps getting away with it." Anna watched the vein on her husband's forehead start to pulsate as he raged against his political adversary. "I mean, who's he trying to bloody well kid when he says his government have been working on this tirelessly? He barely knew these women's names until a couple of days ago when it was patently obvious they were about to be released. And there's *AllNews 24* blindly attributing their freedom to Kelvin Davis. It's sickening."

"Let it go, Richard," Anna said, putting a firm hand on his back. "Henry's right. This can only buy him a few decent headlines for a couple of days max. Then it's back to where he belongs."

"Sometimes, I just don't understand why we're even having to fight this election. Isn't it obvious to anyone with half a brain that Davis has sold this country out. Why are we even having to debate it, for God's sake? It's just so fucking tiring." Richard shook his head.

Anna could see the dark circles setting more deeply under his eyes as he sat himself down on the desk edge and swept his hand over his forehead. She wanted to reach out and hold him, but it wouldn't have been appropriate with Henry in the room. Instead, she moved to sit beside him, in the most basic display of solidarity.

"Just a couple more weeks, Richard," she said quietly. "Then this will all be over and Kelvin will just be another name on the speakers' circuit."

Anna could hear her mobile ringing in her bag. She wondered whether it would seem selfish to pick up now, but Richard hated to hear phones ringing out so she answered to find it was Libby.

"Hi, Libs," she said in a muted tone. "How's it going?"

"Rather well, actually," Libby replied smugly. "I've been doing a little muck-raking on Kelvin Davis and I seem to have unearthed a rather large skeleton."

Anna listened in total silence as her sister filled her in on Franchesca's joyless dalliance with Davis before proudly announcing that she had convinced the woman to talk to the press about the shabby way in which she had been treated by the Prime Minister.

Richard and Henry could only look on in bemusement as Anna took the call. But before she could even tell them what had happened, they were smiling too. The sheer unadulterated pleasure on Anna's face told them Christmas had come early.

She ended the call before turning to look at them. "Seems like Kelvin's bounce will be shorter-lived than he thinks..."

The four large glasses of Sauvignon Blanc Marie had just finished drinking in the pub had left her feeling almost numb as she drifted down Oxford Street towards Marble Arch Tube. It was only ten when she had decided to tell her friends she was calling it a night. They had tried their best to get her to stay, but she had nothing more to give. She felt drunk and tired and empty. The black cloud that liked to hang over her sometimes was back with a vengeance – and rather than just staying for a few hours, it had been hanging around for over a week now blocking any light she had left in her life.

It was a lovely, mild London evening; the kind that would usually have given Marie a little spring in her step as she walked, but instead, her feet hit the pavement heavily, drumming their own solemn beat with each step. She studied the faces of the homeless people who filled the shop doorways along the street. Some appeared suitably haunted, but others seemed merrily resigned to their feral existence; at least one even displaying some signs of contentment, propped up under his blankets, reading a book. Could it be, Marie wondered, that some of these wretched souls were actually happier than she was?

Her career was going from strength to strength, and her recent run of front-page scoops had made her the talk of

Hackland, but she was significantly less happy than she had been six months ago as a general news reporter on a daily paper. She had enjoyed her busy days out covering press conferences, talking to people who were part of major events. She may have been deluding herself, but Marie really believed then that she was actually making a difference in the world; fuelling democracy and throwing light on issues that needed to be exposed. Her parents had been proud. And so had she.

The *Sunday Echo* was one of the world's biggest-selling papers so when Damian had actually headhunted her to offer her a job, it had been too tempting an offer to turn down. He'd added ten thousand to her former salary too. He'd promised her she could steer clear of kiss and tells and focus more on political and social issues. What the job had now turned into though, was more like political mud-slinging. Worst of all, she was slinging the mud at the party she wanted to win the election, whilst giving Kelvin Davis – a man she despised – a leg up.

And Marie sensed there were more claims and counter-claims to come from the Alliance Party and the SDP in what was turning out to be one of the dirtiest campaigns ever. Meanwhile, she had, somewhat unwittingly, found herself as the main catalyst in the whole sorry affair.

Her humble and dignified parents had preferred to say as little as possible about her recent run of headline-grabbing articles, her father simply commenting: "Well, you always said you wanted to see your stories on the front pages." That had only depressed Marie even further as she remembered how she would sit with him until late in the evenings, even on school nights, discussing weighty issues like the Middle East and social inequality. He'd always laughed when she got fired up and would tell her it was only a matter of time before she could put the world to rights in print.

She guessed that kiss and tells about politicians wasn't quite what he'd had in mind.

But there was no getting out of it. She was weighed down by an enormous mortgage and she needed the money. Her dance with the devil would have to continue for now. Endless days of shovelling shit stretched out ahead. And to top it all off, she would turn thirty next week still single. Still desperately lonely and still feeling like a worthless piece of nothing.

Marie tutted aloud at the sheer self-indulgence of her thoughts. She should pick herself up and get on with it, just as her father had every morning in life that he'd walked into the pen-pushing job he'd hated so much.

She saw the lights of the underground station on the other side of the road and stepped off the pavement to cross. She heard the blare of the bus's horn first before turning to see the look of shock and anger across the driver's face. She leapt back, hitting the pavement edge with a thud. The base of her back ached where she'd taken the impact. She rolled on her side to catch her breath and eased herself backwards so her legs were no longer on the road.

"You okay, love?" a friendly passer-by asked with a booze-induced slur. "You nearly got yourself killed there."

"I'm fine," Marie replied, hastily standing up to avoid a further scene.

The pain in her back twisted with every step, forcing her to slowly hobble towards the station. *What was I thinking stepping out like that?* she asked herself. *I could have died.* And then that nasty, unrelenting voice in her head came back at her. *And what a loss to the world that would have been,* it sneered.

15

FORMER LOVER ACCUSES PM OF SEXISM AND CALLING HER "A TYPICAL WOMAN"

MONDAY, APRIL 27TH, 2009, UK NEWSWIRE

Prime Minister Kelvin Davis was today fighting claims of sexism after a former lover accused him of humiliating her in front of male aides and making disparaging remarks about a female Alliance MP.

Davis, who separated from his wife Trish five years ago, admitted to seeing 43-year-old single mother, Franchesca Carruthers, "several times" at his Downing Street flat. But he vehemently denied calling her a "typical bloody woman" or MP Lizzie Ancroft "a prime example of why women should not be allowed in politics".

Carruthers told the *News on Sunday* newspaper that she first met Davis at a charity function where he had invited her to share dinner with him at Number 10. But she claimed that on the third occasion she visited him Davis had humiliated her in front of staff.

She said: "It was obvious that Kelvin regularly had women to stay at Downing Street and that he had no interest in female company other than for his own gratification. Once he got what he wanted I was dispatched pretty quickly with him instructing me in front of a male aide to 'pop off home now'."

Carruthers also told the newspaper that Davis made no secret of his dislike of fellow Alliance MP Lizzie Ancroft.

"He said he found her [Ancroft] way too outspoken for a woman and that he saw her as an embarrassment to the party", Carruthers alleged.

An Alliance Party spokesperson conceded Mr Davis had shared several dates at Downing Street with Franchesca Carruthers, but denied claims of sexism.

He said: "The Prime Minister is entitled to a private life, just like any other human being. He is not, however, a sexist and has nothing but admiration for Lizzie Ancroft and the great work she does on behalf of her constituency and the Alliance party".

The allegations came as the Social Democrats maintained a healthy lead in the polls, despite Davis's recent bounce following the release of the two missionaries kidnapped in Manila.

The SDP is nine points ahead of the Alliance Party with ten days to go until Britain votes.

J oy found herself a nice, dim corner in the coffee shop and sat down. She savoured every second as she laid her cup in front of her before lifting the book out of her bag, opening it and placing it on her lap. She was going to enjoy this twenty-minute break from Alliance HQ. The pressure of working in the press office was becoming unbearable. There was hardly a second where someone was not demanding something of you. She felt she had to be across absolutely every media comment or Reggie and Kelvin would be down on her like a ton of bricks. Her working life now was in sharp contrast to the days when she was her own boss, handling Anna's publicity. She wondered where it had all gone wrong. She had spent her career in communications and yet there had been a total breakdown on that front between her and the two people she had once been closest too.

She blamed Henry, she blamed herself, she blamed the shitty existences called the worlds of showbusiness and politics. Within these worlds there was no reality, only illusions.

Her mobile started ringing. She thought she had turned the damn thing off, but she clearly hadn't and it was Downing Street – and almost certainly Kelvin. She wavered before plucking up the courage to answer.

"Hello. Joy Gooding speaking."

"I have the Prime Minister for you."

Joy raised her eyebrows at the pomp and ceremony surrounding the man she now knew to be totally unworthy of it.

"Hi, Kelvin," she said, certain her casual greeting would piss him off.

"Joy," he started tersely. "It appears that your decision to place the exposé on the Williams' marriage with the *Sunday Echo* has now triggered some kind of tit for tat, just as I feared."

"Well, they will be looking to gain some ground, yes."

"Yes," Kelvin echoed sneeringly. "In my view they're not only gaining ground, they're absolutely trouncing us when it comes to press coverage."

"I can understand that you're angry about the Carruthers story, Kelvin. But, of course, legal action is still an option if the claims she made against you are untrue. I mentioned that to

Reggie last night." Joy smirked to herself, knowing that legal action would be out of the question in this instance.

"Let's just worry about winning the damned election, rather than pissing around with lawyers, shall we? You agreed to turn your attentions to Williams and deliver a highly damaging story about him that can't be traced back to me so please just get on and do your job so I can keep mine."

The line went dead as did any pleasure Joy had managed to reap from her two minutes of solitude. By now she hated Kelvin with a vengeance. But she also couldn't bear to see Richard, Anna and Henry celebrating at Downing Street without her. So she would finish what she had started. Then figure out what the hell she was going to do with the rest of her life.

The air was thick with tension as the three women travelled in silence, squashed together in the back of the chauffeur-driven car like schoolgirls waiting outside the headmistress's office. They were to be at the Women's Refuge in Kent for nine-thirty in the morning, so it had been an early start. The car had collected Anna first before travelling south of the river to collect Sandra and Libby. Aware that Sandra viewed her as nothing more than a frivolous liability, Anna hadn't even attempted to make an effort with her. Henry had insisted she joined them on the visit "just in case the press interest gets out of hand" and simply wouldn't take no for an answer when Anna protested. Her only defence had been to invite her sister along for moral support. Sandra had openly sneered when Anna told her they would be picking up Libby, making it clear she found the thought of accompanying the two of them even more laughable.

"It'll be a family affair then," she'd said, raising her eyebrows in what Anna had found to be a very dismissive manner.

Libby had tried to break the ice by offering her two fellow passengers a ginger-nut biscuit, but this gesture had only seemed all the more bizarre to Sandra who'd openly guffawed, turning her down with a wave of the hand and a "not for me". She'd then sat glued to her mobile in silence while Anna and Libby nibbled on the biscuits and exchanged a few self-conscious sentences, aware Sandra would be paying far more attention to what they were saying than she was letting on.

Ten minutes later Sandra laid down her phone and started to give the women a quick briefing on both the refuge and the SDP's planned policy of creating one hundred more centres like them in the UK to offer sanctuary to those affected by domestic violence. She spoke slowly as though addressing children, taking care to emphasise important points whilst looking at each of them to make sure they had understood.

Anna, she explained, was to meet the staff first before having morning tea in the lounge with the residents. "Don't worry though," she'd added, "they usually make sure the complete nutters are kept well away from important visitors – though you always have to be prepared for anything. Just try not to look shocked if something strange happens. Keep your cool as though you're used to dealing with such situations."

Afterwards, Anna would be expected to say a few words to the press outside. "Keep it simple and don't get emotional," Sandra advised. "And don't make any statements or answer questions about policy. In fact, don't answer any questions at all. We all comfortable with that?" she asked, her tone clearly inferring there would be no room for disagreement.

Anna and Libby had dutifully nodded their heads before deciding the best course of action for surviving the journey unscathed was to say as little as possible – which seemed to suit their travelling companion more than adequately.

Though his caller ID always flashed up as unknown, Viktor Nemov's thick Russian accent allowed the person he was contacting to establish his identity well before he'd finished uttering his first word.

"Damian," he said, pronouncing it Demien.

"Good morning, Viktor," Damian replied with a shrill he knew gave away his anxiety but he couldn't seem to stop himself doing it.

"How are we doing on election coverage? Are we knocking competition for six?"

It always amused Damian to hear Viktor's pidgin English which he had failed to improve on despite the countless private tutors he had employed to help him crack the language. It was the only chink in his armour Damian could find, so he regularly used it to his own psychological advantage to uphold what little bit of confidence he could retain in Viktor's presence.

"More than six, Viktor. We've stolen the show in this campaign with a set of absolutely cracking exclusives."

"Okay, okay," Viktor said in an impatient tone that was designed to remind Damian he was rarely impressed with what had already happened. "I had discussion with Kelvin Davis yesterday."

"Oh, yes," said Damian, holding his breath.

"Yes, he didn't feel our front page was strong compared with *News on Sunday* and the Social Democrats is gaining ground."

Damian raised his eyes to the ceiling with the realisation that Kelvin had likely got Viktor worked up into a panic that the knighthood he'd no doubt been promised if the Alliance won, was fast sailing down the river. Now he would be asked to come up with an exclusive that would ensure the SDP was well and truly crushed at the polls.

"We need to finish this on top, Damian. What have we got for Sunday?"

"Well, we've got a great celebrity kiss and tell and…"

"I'm not interested in celebrities right now," Viktor shouted.

"I know, Viktor. I was just about to say we're also working on something huge about Richard Williams."

"What huge?" Viktor asked, his English fast deserting him now he was worked up.

"Something that will undermine everything Richard Williams has said about his reunion with Anna Lloyd." The second the words had left his mouth, Damian regretted them. They didn't have a story about one of the Williams having an affair, or anything even close – but now he was going to have to come up with one.

"You've got someone who says they have affair with Richard Williams?"

"Not quite, but we've got a very big lead which I can talk you through in the next couple of days once we've fully checked it out."

"Okay. You let me know when you've come up with goods. We need big story; big sales."

"Got it, Viktor. I'll call you soon." Damian ended the call and put his head in his hands.

The staff at the refuge were warm and welcoming and Anna immediately felt at ease as she was led, along with Libby and a sullen Sandra, into the reception room where several residents were waiting to meet them. The room was large and bright and not at all the shabby, dingy dwellings that Anna had imagined. Against her wishes, but very much in line with Sandra's, television cameras had been allowed to film some of their visit. The TV crews would not be allowed to capture what they were saying, but they would be able to use footage of Anna greeting the women who had agreed to appear on camera. The first of those was a young single mother called Jessica who Anna thought looked a lot like Libby when she was younger, with her naturally curly hair and warm, open face, free of make-up. She smiled encouragingly as Jessica was led over to meet her. Anna immediately noticed the young woman was shaking so she took her hand as they exchanged hellos, then leaned forward and whispered: "Don't worry. I'm nervous too."

Jessica smiled shyly, tears filling her eyes. "I asked if I could meet you today," she told Anna, "because I wanted to thank you for saying what you did about abuse. When I saw that someone as beautiful and successful as you had been through the same as me it gave me a bit of hope that maybe I could have a future too."

Anna's hormones surged and she battled not to burst into tears herself. She knew she would be accused of acting if she dared lose her composure. Instead, she gave Jessica a friendly rub on the arm and said: "Of course you have every chance of a bright future. It means a lot to me to hear that my story touched you. Thank you for meeting me today. How are you finding the hostel?"

"Really good," the young woman replied. "The counselling here has helped me a lot and I'm feeling better about being able to get a job and make something of myself."

Anna studied Jessica's face for a moment, and saw in the dullness of her complexion and the faint lines already beginning to form in her skin that life had not been kind to her. She also knew the likelihood was there wouldn't be a fairy tale ending for Jessica. No weekend stays at Chequers, no first-class travel, no luxury hotels. Jessica would likely live in poverty every day for the rest of her life unless more could be done to help her and women like her.

Kelvin doesn't care about Jessica, Anna thought. *But I do.* She glanced over at the refuge manager who was waiting to introduce her to another resident, before turning back to the young woman.

"I really wish you well, Jessica," she said. "It's been lovely to meet you – and thank you for talking to me."

Anna turned to find Libby sitting behind her in deep conversation with a middle-aged woman, and felt glad she had invited her along – even if her primary motivation had been for moral support. Meeting others who had been through similar situations was as therapeutic for Anna and her sister as it was for the women they were there to help. Libby beckoned Anna over and introduced her to Alice who had waited until her youngest son had left home before she decided to flee from a violent husband. As she listened intently to Alice's story of a life destroyed by a man who had lost all control, Anna's attention was momentarily distracted by the sight of Sandra sitting on the other side of the room, holding the hand of a young woman. Sandra's face was side-on so Anna couldn't be absolutely sure, but she could have sworn she was crying. To see this iron woman showing something that looked decidedly like emotion came as a total shock to Anna and she found it very difficult to turn her focus back to poor Alice. Could it be that Sandra wasn't quite as unreachable as she made out?

The forty-five minutes that had been allowed for meeting residents passed all too quickly and Anna promised both herself and the staff that she would come back again when the election was over, to spend more time there.

Anna and Libby walked along the corridor of the refuge together towards the front entrance where the press contingent was waiting for her to say a few words. Sandra walked in front alongside two protection officers who were increasingly becoming part of Anna's day-to-day life. It often crossed her mind that if she required an entourage of this size just as a wife of the opposition leader, what on earth the situation would be if and when they lived in Downing Street?

Once outside, Anna saw a large press pack had gathered and there were a few familiar faces among them of the reporters and photographers who were now regularly assigned to follow her around. She remembered Sandra's pep talk in which she was told not to answer any questions but just to say the few words Henry had sanctioned the previous evening. Standing in front of so many cameras and microphones, Anna began to feel a wave of anxiety-induced nausea. She searched around for Libby who instinctively read her cue and came to stand by her left-hand side. Sandra, sensing her discomfort too, came to stand nearer her right.

Anna tried to replicate Richard's calm, authoritative tone as she began to make her statement working from the prompt notes Henry had given her.

"My sister Libby and I have just spent the last hour meeting some of the residents at this refuge. Their stories were hard to listen to, and the suffering they have endured is as shocking as it is completely demoralising. To think that in this day and age women and their children still live under the daily threat of violence and abuse should be something that casts shame on all of us. We haven't done enough. Governments have not done enough – and it's time to change all that. The inclusion in the Social Democrats' manifesto of another fifty centres of this kind throughout the UK is a major step in the right direction." She looked up momentarily, blinking against the harsh flashlights, before returning to her notes. "Women and their children must be given shelter from harm – and the chance to rebuild their lives. We owe them this much and I will be fighting every step of the way on their behalf." Anna paused. She was now supposed to say *"thank you"* then immediately turn from the reporters to walk back to the car. But, there was something else she still had to say. Something she owed the women she had just met. This time there were no notes.

"Most of you will by now be aware of the abuse my sister and I suffered at the hands of our stepfather. It was violent, it was humiliating, and it destroyed any sense of self-belief we could have ever hoped to enjoy. The only thing that saved us from total destruction was each other. We were not alone..." Anna bowed her head as she fought the pricks of tears in her eyes and the tightness of the emotion threatening to claim her voice.

"I want every woman and child in this country who is suffering harm to know that they are *not* alone either, and I will do everything alongside my husband to help you." Anna swallowed hard again. "Thank you."

She felt Sandra's hand tuck under her arm as she began to lead her to the car. She could hear the cries of the reporters behind her: "Anna... Anna... Why did you not speak out earlier about your abuse? Will you separate from Richard Williams after the election?"

Anna tried to drown out their questions. She knew she was no fraud – and, as far as she knew, neither was her marriage. But she still had some way to go to convince the press of that. For now, at least, the public seemed to be on her side.

As Sandra marched the two sisters back to the car, protection officers in front and behind, Anna suspected she would be in trouble for straying "off message" as Henry would put it. Almost as soon as she'd had that thought, Sandra's mobile rang. As the caller didn't even give her the opportunity to say hello, Anna immediately guessed it was Henry.

"No, it wasn't planned, Henry," she heard Sandra reply.

Libby, who'd obviously picked up on the call too, smiled encouragingly at Anna.

A protection officer opened the car door and let Anna in first, followed by Libby and then Sandra who was still talking animatedly on her mobile.

"To be honest, I don't think it matters that she was emotional," Sandra told Henry, much to Anna's surprise. "You don't go through what she's been through and not feel something when you see others in a similar position. She spoke from her heart and I think people will appreciate that."

Anna turned to Libby, giving her a wide-eyed glance and raised eyebrow that asked, *"Did she just say something in my defence?"*

Sandra ended the call then gazed out of the window for a few moments, joining Anna and Libby in watching the chaotic scenes outside as photographers and reporters pushed and shoved one another in an effort to get near the car as they pulled away.

From behind the security of the blacked-out windows she finally turned to look at her travelling companions. Her face was devoid of the haughtiness with which she usually liked to greet them. Instead, it was a total blank, stripped of its hardness.

"I'm not so different from you two," she said quietly. Anna and Libby stared back at her, unsure of what to say. "My dad enjoyed a drink you see; but we certainly didn't enjoy the repercussions. At first he'd get all happy and silly, then he'd get a little sentimental and morose and then he would just get angry."

"Are you saying he was violent?" Libby asked.

"To my mother, mainly, yes."

"I'm sorry," Libby replied, quickly echoed by Anna. "That must have been awful."

"Not compared to what you went through. There were times I wanted to kill him to stop him hurting my mother, but I couldn't. That's the worst part of it. Watching and being able to do nothing. The guilt stays with you forever, even though I realise I was only a child."

They at once understood what was eating at Sandra.

"Well, now that explains why you've come to be such a sour-face," joked Libby.

Anna drew breath in anticipation of Sandra's reply. But rather than take offence, she threw her head back and laughed.

"You've got me," she said.

"Well," Libby continued, "now that we've shared our mutually miserable past lives, maybe we can conclude that, actually, we've all done all right considering."

"We're survivors," said Sandra, still smiling.

"No," corrected Anna. "We're fighters." She closed her eyes and sank a little further down in her chair, letting out a long yawn which she was unable to stifle despite the intensity of the moment. Her fatigue in pregnancy knew no boundaries.

"Sounds like you're a tired fighter," Libby said, putting a protective hand on her sister's arm. "Are you okay?"

"Yes," she replied wearily. "I could just use a couple of days off to catch up on some sleep but I guess that's not going to happen."

"Make sure you take it easy then," said Libby, her voice full of concern. "You're going to have to pace yourself if you want to see this campaign through."

16

WILLIAMS AND DAVIS GO HEAD-TO-HEAD IN LIVE TV DEBATE

Thursday, April 30th, 2009, UK Newswire

Prime Minister Kelvin Davis is set to take on Social Democrat leader Richard Williams in a live presidential-style televised debate this evening.

The head-to-head between the political rivals is the first of its kind in British politics and follows criticism from both sides of the House this week over negative campaigning.

Social Democrat MP Graham Hollsworth, told UK Newswire that he was "ashamed and embarrassed" over the mud-slinging that has been a feature of the election contest.

"We should be busy setting out our policies to the British people, but instead we're enduring week after week of tit-for-tat tabloid tales which do our cause absolutely no good at all."

Alliance backbencher Nigel Smillie said campaigning was now "descending to the depths of smear and counter-smear".

He added: "These lurid tales hitting the headlines each

week take away from the real issues that are so important to voters: health, crime and the economy. This TV debate is an opportunity to set out our stall on these matters and get back to a positive campaign".

R ichard glanced at the clock and realised the endgame was in sight with only ten more minutes of debating time left. Despite the make-up artist's furious attempts to mop and powder his brow between ad breaks, he could feel the sweat breaking through again and just hoped it wouldn't form into droplets. More than Kelvin's biting put-downs over the SDP's taxation policies, Richard feared the sensation of a trickle running from his forehead with the inevitable, and humiliating, drop onto his shirt collar. For those beads of sweat would undo any good he had managed to achieve in the last forty-five minutes of verbal duelling with Kelvin. They would tell the world that he felt out of his depth; that he didn't know if he was ready to be Prime Minister or not. That he was just hoping, and praying he could measure up to the expectations of a nation that needed to feel good about itself again.

The presenter, Simon Flaxon, was trying to get Kelvin to wind up his rather lame explanation of public spending cuts under the Alliance Party before they moved on to what would be the closing section of the debate; leadership qualities.

Richard smirked along with the rest of the studio audience as he watched Kelvin continue unabashed while Simon repeatedly tried to head him off.

"If I could just stop you there," Simon had begun. "Now we really must move on..."

"Thank you, Mr Davis, but there are other issues we must

cover..." Nothing worked, until Simon finally boomed, "That's it, Mr Davis. We're moving on."

Whether Kelvin had actually had to cut himself short or whether, conveniently, Simon's final interjection had coincided with him actually finishing talking was unclear. All Richard knew was they were into the last and potentially most hazardous section of the debate.

Simon turned back to the cameras and began his introduction: "It's been one of the dirtiest campaigns in political history with claims and counter-claims appearing in the tabloids on an almost daily basis. And the finger of blame for that has been pointed firmly towards the two men who stand either side of me now."

Simon switched then to stand side-on to the cameras and addressed the two candidates directly.

"How are voters to see you as leaders when you're covered head to toe in mud? The question goes to Kelvin Davis first."

"Well, this suit came back from the dry-cleaners only yesterday," Kelvin joked, pretending to check himself over, "so I don't believe I am covered in mud." He was forced to move on quickly when only a couple of his own staff among the audience laughed. "Tabloids will dig up their scandalous tales," he continued. "That's the nature of the beast and there's very little we can do about it. But if there's any mud thrown at me then I just brush it off because I have more important things to worry about – like running a country."

"So are you inferring that you weren't aware of some of the stories that your own press team have been accused of planting in the media?"

"If you're asking me did I plant a story in the press that Richard Williams had left his wife then I can tell you no, I didn't. Richard did that all by himself." Kelvin chuckled, this time more heartily backed by a small gathering of hardcore Alliance supporters towards the front of the studio.

Richard raised his eyebrows to show his displeasure at the remark before steeling himself for his turn to come.

"Richard Williams," Simon said, turning to face him. "What's your opinion of the dirty tricks used in this campaign. Are you proud to be associated with them?"

"No, I'm not proud to be involved in a campaign which has been, at times, overshadowed by personal issues. In fact, there have been many points over the last few weeks where I've had cause to question myself and my actions. What I can tell you, though, is that at no stage have I directed anyone in my team to dig up muck on Kelvin Davis, or anyone else in the Alliance Party for that matter."

The audience was totally hushed and Richard glanced back at Simon to indicate he was finished, but the presenter was simply nodding and obviously waiting for him to go on. Richard and Henry had spent hours planning for the debate the evening before, but Henry had been emphatic that answers about personal issues should be short and rehearsed. Sticking to that point, his final words to Richard before he stepped on stage were: "Don't go off script." But that was exactly what he was about to have to do, because a room full of people, along with the millions watching at home were waiting for him to explain himself. Richard rarely prayed, but in that moment he couldn't help but offer up a few silent words. *Please God. Let me say the right thing.*

He swallowed hard and began. "Much has been said in the press about my wife and I recently. Some of it was true, some outright lies. The full truth is, of course, that we did separate for a short period. This was a decision on my part which I will regret for the rest of my life."

End it there, Richard was urging himself, but the voice inside wasn't finished yet.

"My father was a very good man. Not a successful man, but an honest one. He worked hard every day of his life and he had no desire to be wealthy or grand in any way. Yet he told me several times as a boy that one day I would do an important job – and one that would change people's lives. Over the last few months and weeks I have had to ask many questions of myself about the kind of man I would like to be. Firstly, I recognised that to be a good leader, I needed to be a good husband and son. Because only in realising your own potential as a human being, can you help others realise theirs. But, I promise you this; I'm ready now. I have put my house in order, and I am ready to lead. I have the determination to bring us out of debt and into recovery and I have the single-mindedness to never waver from the task in hand. Let me worry about my personal responsibilities, and let us all focus on the fight we now have to make this nation great again."

Richard glanced back at Simon again who opened his mouth to thank the candidates but was drowned out by the loud clapping and cheering which was now resonating from every corner of the studio. Many of the audience were on their feet, save the hardcore Alliance supporters who remained firmly rooted to their chairs with arms folded. Simon began shouting over the cheers so he could wrap up the programme and, as the studio lights faded to darkness and the credits began to roll, Richard could feel a small bead of sweat make its way from the side of his forehead to the collar of his shirt.

In all the years she had worked in journalism, Marie had never been summoned to a venue quite as preposterous as this one.

She had actually laughed when Joy first suggested meeting on a bench by the duck pond at St James's Park. Wrongly, she had assumed she must be joking. But, in fact, Joy was that paranoid. Whereas before they had met in darkened corners of coffee bars, Joy had felt even that would be too risky in case she was recognised. Instead, she had chosen a bench tucked away from the main thoroughfare where, surely, no member of the Social Democratic Party or press could spot them.

Even worse, they were meeting over lunch so Marie found herself sitting on a park bench, wearing a raincoat, eating a sandwich and waiting for a contact. The only thing missing from this spy thriller was the code word.

Marie checked her watch. They had agreed to meet at one o'clock and it was already five past, prompting her to wonder whether Joy had changed her mind. She peeled back the seal of her sandwich pack and told herself she might as well stay for another ten minutes to eat her lunch and figure out what she was going to tell Damian if she had to go back to the office empty-handed. He made it painfully clear to her earlier that morning that he expected her to deliver. Why the political team weren't coming in for the same kind of pressure she didn't know, but it only went to show that there was very little about this campaign that had actually been about politics. So Marie had been faced with the choice of going out and getting something, or just sitting back and taking the consequences. She had been tempted to do the latter, with the half-hearted hope that Damian might even fire her. But, when it came down to it, she couldn't bear to fail.

It was Joy's red hair that caught her attention first, followed by the bottle-green coat. If she had wanted to go unnoticed, Marie thought, that wasn't the way to go about it. But Joy had chosen the venue well. In the fifteen minutes she'd already been sitting there, Marie hadn't seen a single passer-by, which made her wonder if this was the sort of thing the woman she was meeting did regularly. She certainly had form for shock tip-offs, that was for sure.

Joy strutted purposefully towards the bench, glancing around her before she sat down and examined Marie's sandwich enviously. "Damn, I was in such a rush I forgot to pick up a sandwich on the way over."

"Here." Marie tossed the second half of her lunch into Joy's hand. "I had a bacon roll earlier so I'm not that hungry," she lied.

Joy looked like a child on Christmas morning – a mixture of surprise and wonder at this kind gesture.

"Well, aren't you a sweetie," she said, before hungrily biting into her donated lunch.

"You mentioned on the phone you had something for me relating to Richard Williams," Marie said, hurrying her to the point. Joy had a bit of a reputation in the newsrooms as being someone who enjoyed talking about herself for long periods before giving the information the journalist was actually looking for, so Marie wanted to head her off before she started.

Joy frowned. She didn't like being hurried so she continued to chew slowly on her sandwich while she looked out over the duck pond.

"I do love it here," she said, oblivious to Marie rolling her eyes next to her. "When I first moved to London I missed Central Park so much until I found this place. There's so much space, you can just forget the city around you for a while and be somewhere else."

Joy continued to stare dreamily ahead, but Marie was in no mood for polite conversation – she was under way too much pressure to forget her reality.

"I need to have a front-page splash on Richard Williams by the end of today, Joy. That means I'm a bit pushed for time."

Joy finished the final corner of her sandwich before turning to look at Marie.

"You may have noticed there's an Alliance MP called Lizzie Ancroft who's always having a dig at Anna – which bugged the hell out of me when I worked for her. But you just had to mention her name to Anna and she'd get all fired up; because, apparently, she and Richard once had a thing going on."

"While he was seeing Anna?" Marie asked breathlessly.

"No, before," Joy replied. "But the thing is, Lizzie is sadly harbouring a dark secret in that she used to have a bit of a cocaine habit."

"I see," Marie said tersely, wishing Joy would get to the point. "Did she take it with Richard Williams?"

"You could say that," Joy said, casually brushing some crumbs from her lap.

"Well, did she or didn't she, Joy? I'm going to need something concrete here."

"Lizzie is about to be made aware that I am in possession of a picture in which she can clearly be seen at a function in a London hotel snorting cocaine. Richard Williams was also at the same party that night and can just be made out in the corner of the image."

"Did Richard know of her taking cocaine? And has anyone ever seen him taking it?"

Joy snorted. "I doubt Richard would be colourful enough to try that kind of thing. But he was there when she was doing it – and that's all you need to make a sensational headline, right?"

"Do you have the picture?"

"I do," said Joy, "and you can look at it, but it's going to cost you if you want to use it."

"How much?"

"Make me an offer." Joy smiled.

"Let me see the picture then and I'll talk to Damian."

With that, Joy triumphantly plucked an envelope from her handbag before prising the picture from inside and handing it to Marie. It was just what Joy had described. Lizzie Ancroft could be seen leaning over a table in the corner of a darkened room – where she surely thought she was sheltered by the group of people around her – clutching a rolled note which she was using to sniff a white powder. Richard could be seen standing talking to a man Marie didn't recognise, some way from Lizzie. It could not be construed that he had seen her from the picture, but she knew that wouldn't deter Damian from milking it for all it was worth.

Marie wrestled with her conscience as she faced the growing realisation that this could be an election winner for Kelvin. Her stomach churned at the thought. But she had neither the energy nor the heart to let Damian down.

"If we're going to run with this, then we'll need Lizzie Ancroft to spill the story on their relationship and her cocaine abuse. The picture's not enough."

Joy looked at Marie for some time, clearly trying to weigh the reporter up. "Leave that with me," she eventually replied. "But don't you know how explosive this story is? How much it calls Richard Williams' judgement into question for not only dating an MP in an opposing party, but one who had a cocaine habit? This could finish him."

"Yes." Marie sighed. "I'm aware of that."

"I don't want us to get overconfident, Henry. We haven't won this election yet." Richard served another reminder to his colleagues as he led Friday's planning meeting in his office. The mood around the SDP HQ was already turning to one of celebration which made their leader distinctly uneasy. "We just can't afford to drop our guard now," he added.

Following the press briefing earlier that morning, he, Ray and Henry had spent much of the day campaigning around Central London. Anna, Sandra and Libby, who had now formed an unlikely alliance, had separated from them after lunch to go and visit a home for the elderly in Finsbury Park. That left the three men plus Bob Guthrie to hold what was to be their last official planning meeting before the election. In the days ahead, they would be too busy out on the road fighting for every vote to sit down together in any number.

The first ten minutes of the meeting had been taken up with Henry crowing about the glowing press coverage of Richard's "victory" over Kelvin in the TV debate. Most political analysts had agreed that the opposition leader had appeared the more credible and trustworthy opponent throughout, but his win had been sealed with the impromptu closing speech he made which, they believed, had seen Richard put his past to rights.

"We can afford to have confidence now, Richard," Henry reasoned. "The Alliance can't catch us anymore – we're too far in front."

"I don't want any of us to take our eye off the ball. We need to finish this as though we're behind and battling like our careers depended on it," Richard insisted.

"He's right," said Ray. "We can be confident but not complacent."

"And we've still got Sunday to look forward to," Bob chipped in sarcastically.

"Well, we know the *Echo* will come up with something," said Henry. "They're not going to finish this campaign on a whimper, but whatever it is we'll get on top of it. And we'll have a much broader range of positive stories spread throughout the other Sundays."

"Would it be worth talking to Damian Blunt?" Ray asked. "See if he wants to wipe that egg off his face and back a winner?"

"No," Richard answered robustly. "As long as Viktor Nemov is pulling the strings, we're never going to get support from the *Echo* so we might as well just write them off and leave them to wallow in defeat. I'm prepared for whatever's coming on Sunday and I'll warn Anna too. There can't be any skeletons left in our closets, but that won't be an issue for them. If there's nothing there, they'll make it up."

"Then I'll warn the lawyers too." Henry smirked.

Lizzie Ancroft was just packing the final file into her briefcase before setting off for her constituency. She was due to address the local party members later that evening to give them their final pep talk before polling day. So far, campaigning had been going well and she was expected to win with a comfortable margin again.

She stopped briefly by the coat stand to collect her jacket and took a moment to check her appearance. She frowned at the dark circles under her eyes, but decided she looked all right otherwise. Not bad for forty-three anyway, she thought. Ever since the tabloids had started describing her as the "babe of the Alliance Party" she had become very preoccupied with her looks and was quite defensive of the position they had given her as "Westminster's hottest MP". This meant regular trips to the hairdresser to avoid any greys showing through her dark, sleek bob which she was pleased to note was still perfectly in place. She smiled fleetingly at her reflection and was turning to leave when her office phone rang; the call display showing the number she dreaded seeing.

She swallowed hard to clear the lump already forming in her

throat, before picking up. What had she done now was all she could think.

"Hello, Lizzie Ancroft," she answered.

"I have Reggie Caldwell for you, Miss Ancroft."

"Thank you," Lizzie replied as she awaited the onslaught. She knew whatever Reggie had to say to her would have come directly from the Prime Minister. Perhaps, she thought hopefully, he was calling with an apology from Kelvin for his blatantly sexist remarks about her. But the PM never was one for saying sorry or admitting mistakes so she guessed instead that he probably wanted something from her. Something he didn't have the guts to ask her to do himself.

"Lizzie, how are you?" Reggie asked in an unusually breezy tone, normally reserved for his party pets. Seeing as Lizzie had established a reputation for backbench rebellion and outspokenness, that wasn't a category she fitted.

"I'm fine, Reggie," she replied cautiously. "Just about to head off to Brighton, actually."

"Of course, of course. Well, I'll try not to hold you back but I do have a rather delicate matter that I need to discuss with you."

Lizzie's heart sank. She had been waiting for this phone call for the last eight years.

"Go on," she said.

"A Sunday newspaper is in possession of a photograph in which you can clearly be seen snorting a substance which looks suspiciously like cocaine. Were you aware of the existence of such a picture?"

"Yes, I was aware of both the picture and the person who took it. It was someone within this party who promised me they would destroy it."

"Well, they haven't and the *Sunday Echo* is publishing it this weekend. If you have any chance of your career surviving this then you'll need to talk to them to set the record straight."

Lizzie closed her eyes and let out a long sigh. Her parents would be devastated.

"Oh, and Lizzie?"

"Yes," she said, unable to disguise her dismay.

"Richard Williams is also pictured and the *Echo* are aware of your relationship so you'll be expected to talk about that – and in terms which don't present him well."

"I wouldn't exactly call it a relationship. We were both new MPs and he was trying to help me."

"It was a relationship. You need to work with us on this one, Lizzie. The Prime Minister's support for you depends on it. If he chooses to throw you out of the party for drug-taking, your career would never recover from it. So let's not waste time debating semantics. You know what you have to do."

Reggie abruptly ended the call leaving Lizzie holding the receiver in one hand and her head in the other.

17

COCAINE-SHAME MP TELLS OF RELATIONSHIP WITH SDP LEADER

MONDAY, MAY 4TH, 2009, UK NEWSWIRE

Social Democrat leader Richard Williams was again forced to defend himself against accusations over his private life following claims in a Sunday newspaper that he had a relationship with Alliance MP Lizzie Ancroft, who has admitted to being addicted to cocaine at the time.

Ancroft, 43, told the *Sunday Echo* newspaper that she dated Williams for "a couple of months" when he first became an MP in 2001. She spoke out as the newspaper published a picture of the Alliance MP apparently snorting cocaine whilst attending a party in the same year. Williams can also be seen in the background of the picture attending the same event, although he is not looking directly at Ancroft at the time.

The SDP leader fervently denies claims that he was aware of Ancroft's drug-taking, saying it was "complete news" to him. In a statement to reporters outside his London home yesterday he admitted to once having a "close friendship" with the Alliance MP but reiterated that this was well before he began a relationship with his wife, the actress Anna Lloyd.

"I was sorry to hear of Lizzie Ancroft's struggle with cocaine addiction, but I must make it absolutely clear that I had no knowledge of her drug-taking whatsoever", he said. "We were both new to the house and she had a number of personal problems at that time and I guess I became a confidante to her. That she has chosen to turn this into a tabloid story for the sake of political gain saddens me enormously.

"For my part, I have never tried cocaine, I have never seen anyone take cocaine and I do not condone its use in any way. I am pleased Lizzie appears to have been able to put her problems behind her and I wish her well for the future."

But Liberal leader Giles Henderson said the revelations of Williams' past relationship with an Alliance MP revealed "another gross lapse of judgement.

"Voters are fed up with being confronted with new stories every week about Richard Williams' chaotic personal life. In embarking on a relationship with an MP from another party, however long ago, he clearly showed either extreme naivety or complete ignorance of acceptable conduct".

A nna heard their six o'clock alarm go, but she didn't bother to open her eyes. Instead, she buried her head deeper into her pillow and half-listened to the news headlines, which were unsurprisingly dominated by the weekend's revelations, before drifting back to sleep.

Soon she was back in her old house, in the darkened, shabby bedroom she had shared with Libby. Just being there immediately brought on the sense of foreboding she had lived with for most of her teenage years. She turned to look for the door, aware that this was a dream from which she should be able to exit. But as she spun around sharply she found there was no way out. She threw herself back against the wall, panic rising in her chest. It was then she saw him looming in the corner like a large shadow. The scar across his left cheek, the cold, pale-blue eyes so filled with hate. Dennis reeked of evil. He was laughing at her again, as he had loved to do. "What you so frightened of?" he slurred as he moved towards her. "Anyone would think I was a monster. Do you not love me, is that it?" She tried to scream but no sound would come out. She thrashed from side to side, desperately trying to escape. He caught her arm, and she flailed at him with the other helplessly.

Suddenly, it was another face looking down at her. She stretched out her hand to push the man away.

"Anna," he was saying, "Anna, what's happening?"

"Richard," she replied blearily, pushing herself up onto her elbows.

"What's wrong with you?" he asked. "Are you sick?"

"Yes," she replied. Sick and bloody tired, she thought.

"Will you make Swindon this morning?"

"No, Richard. I need to rest." She turned away from him.

"Anna." His eyes searched hers pleadingly. "I hate to put pressure on you but you know how things look at the moment, particularly after that Ancroft story. If you're not out campaigning with me today, people will assume there's a problem between us – again."

"People? People will think? You mean the party will think, you mean the press will think, because most people don't actually give a shit about the state of our marriage, they just want someone who's man enough to run the bloody country without worrying about how the polls are going to react to every cough and spit."

"Oh Anna." Richard shook his head. "You're impossible. I can't believe you're back to this again."

"I'm tired," she yelled, surprising even herself with the anger in her voice. And then the tears came, and once they started she couldn't stop them.

Richard put his hand on her shoulder. "I'm worried about you. What can I do?"

"Just give me some time to rest, Richard," she said, leaning back into the pillow. "I'll be all right if I can just take today to get my strength back."

"Okay," Richard replied. He stroked her hair gently then kissed her on the cheek.

"I'll see you tonight."

"Bye," she said, without turning to look at him. Then she listened, trying not to feel guilty as he walked from the bedroom, down the stairs and finally out to the car that was waiting for him outside.

All things considered, she knew she should have got back on the campaign trail. But she felt drained of energy and motivation. Pregnancy was taking its toll, as was the intensity of a wretched and bloody political campaign that had deprived them of any dignity they once possessed. She believed Richard when he said his so-called relationship with Lizzie Ancroft had been little more than "a couple of drunken snogs" as he'd put it, but she also felt angry that he'd got himself into that situation in the first place. No matter how tame the truth was, the media had gone into overdrive and the resulting coverage was very damaging. To Anna it felt like the final straw.

The explosive mix of hormones and insecurity over her marriage had sent her spiralling into an almost constant state of fear and paranoia, transporting her straight back to the terrible past she hoped had been locked away forever. Memories of neglect and abuse now met her at every turning.

It had started just a couple of weeks after he moved in with their mother. Anna had been happily skipping down the hallway, about to run upstairs for her bath when Dennis had cornered her. "Bathtime is it then? That's nice. I like baths too. They can be so fun when you share with other people, don't you think?" Then he'd winked and Anna, speechless and confused, made a half-smile then ran swiftly past him up the stairs and bolted the bathroom door. But there had been no bolt on their bedroom door, and with a mother who was too drunk to try – or even care – to protect them, she and Libby had been easy prey. His threats increased in their frequency and intensity. He would kill their mother if they told; he would slit her throat and make them watch. He'd tie concrete to their feet and throw them into a river. So it went on. Week after week, month after month, until Libby put a stop to it.

Now here he was, back in her thoughts again. Those old feelings of fear and hate so palpable. Richard was the one man she had ever really trusted; now even that was in doubt. The insecurity that followed their separation caused her to ask herself daily whether he really loved her? Would he reject her again as soon as the election was over as so many commentators had speculated – or perhaps wait a few months to make it seem more respectable? Anna felt terrifyingly alone and vulnerable once again. She looked at the clock. It was too early to call Libby so she switched on the television for company and hoped she wouldn't fall back to sleep again where Dennis would surely be waiting for her.

Marie felt distinctly uncomfortable as she stepped through the doors of the plush Mayfair restaurant where Damian had suggested they meet. She wasn't supposed to work on Mondays, but he had caught her off guard just as she was finishing in the office on Saturday evening. She'd been putting her coat on and had turned to walk out the door when she found him standing right in front of her.

"Very good work this week, Marie. You pulled it out of the bag again." He smiled.

"Well, that's what I'm paid for," she'd replied. In actual fact she'd felt horrible about the Ancroft story from start to finish, not least because it was a serious misrepresentation of the truth. Richard Williams had indeed been right when he'd described it as "journalism at its worst". Not that Viktor Nemov would care about that. Provided the story added the extra sales he was predicting, he'd figured they could afford the legal damages. And he'd also betted on the fact that, if elected, Williams wouldn't want to get involved in an ugly legal battle anyway.

"Let me treat you to lunch on Monday," Damian had suggested brightly. "You deserve it for all the hard work you've put in over the campaign."

Reluctant as she was, Marie couldn't come up with an excuse fast enough. "Okay," she'd replied unenthusiastically before deciding she had better try to sound vaguely grateful. "That would be great, Damian."

"Excellent. I'll ask Helen to book us somewhere and drop you a text to let you know."

Marie had then spent most of the weekend dreading this very moment. She followed the maître d' across the restaurant, finally arriving at the back corner where she found Damian waiting at a table for her, ready to celebrate their work.

The first thing she noticed was the overpowering smell of aftershave. He's made a special effort, she thought, adding weight to her theory that he had more than a purely professional interest in her.

He smiled broadly as she approached and she swallowed

hard as she caught what looked like a glint of ardour in his eyes. She supposed she might have actually found him attractive if it hadn't been for the constant pressure he had put her under – which had finally led her to breaking any kind of moral code she had.

"You made it," he said, standing to attention at the end of the table. He leaned forward, took her by the arms and kissed her on each cheek

Marie smiled nervously before slinging herself into her seat. She wondered if her discomfort would be obvious to him, but then she remembered guys like Damian have a very thick skin. He beamed across the table as if they were lifelong friends.

"I've ordered some champagne," he said, pointing to the bottle sitting in an ice bucket at the end of the table. The maître d' filled her glass before wishing them a pleasant meal and, as Marie watched him walk away, she wished it was she who was making such an early exit.

She took a sip of champagne and smiled again at Damian. "This is lovely," was all she could think to say.

"Well." Damian leaned across the table. "Viktor is extremely impressed with your work over this election campaign. And, whatever the outcome, at least you and I know we pulled out all the stops and, at the very least, put a major dent in Richard Williams' popularity. The early polls suggest he's taken a bit of a bruising, so very well done, Marie." He raised his glass and indicated for her to do the same.

"To many more blazing exclusives to come," he said before taking a huge swig of champagne. Not wishing to be rude, Marie took a sip, but she was in no mood for celebrating.

"Viktor also asked me to pass on his personal thanks for your tenacity and dedication."

Marie felt nauseous at the thought of Viktor and Kelvin delighting over her stories.

"That's great," she said. "Just great." Unable to maintain eye contact whilst lying, Marie buried her head in the menu. She saw they served fishcakes and thought *that'll do*. There was no point in dwelling over what she was going to order as she wasn't going to enjoy her food anyway.

"I'm going for the oysters," Damian said, staring at her intensely. Marie swallowed again. If he tried to feed her one that would be her cue to flee, she thought, before flashing Damian another fixed grin.

"So while we're drinking champagne, I'm hoping we can make this a double celebration."

"Oh," Marie replied, trying to disguise her alarm. Surely, he wasn't about to ask her out – or worse.

"I wondered if you would do me the honour of becoming my deputy," he asked earnestly.

"What about Malcolm?"

"Leaving," Damian replied, without clarifying whether this was by choice or by force. "So what do you say?"

He leaned across the table again, fixing her with that same intense stare; one that suggested they shared some kind of bond, that they were similar animals with an unspoken understanding. It was an expectant, arrogant stare that didn't even question her loyalty. And it was a stare that soon turned to a shocked frown when Marie delivered her reply.

"No. Thank you."

It was noon before Anna finally managed to get hold of Libby on her mobile phone. She had been trying to contact her sister since waking at eleven but the number was constantly ringing out. Despite her best efforts to stay awake, she had fallen back to sleep only to have another nightmare – this time about Richard winning the General Election in a landslide victory before announcing to the world that he was leaving Anna so he could focus entirely on his work as Prime Minister. In her dream, she had been watching from the side of the stage and had stupidly nodded along as if she had been aware of the announcement before Henry quickly escorted her away. Though she realised the events in her dream were completely improbable, it had left her feeling even more agitated and uncertain than before and she really needed to talk to her sister about it. She dialled the number again and felt a burst of relief and anger in equal measure when Libby picked up.

"Where the hell have you been all morning?" Anna snapped.

"Sorry. I've been doing the weekly shop at Sainsbury's and I forgot my mobile."

"Libby, you committed to working for me and, although I don't expect you to be on call every minute of the day, considering we're two days off the election, I do need you to answer your bloody phone."

"Is something wrong?" Libby asked.

"I'm all over the place." Anna's voice quavered. "My hormones are raging anyway with the pregnancy and I'm just racked with anxiety. I hardly slept last night."

"What are you worried about, Anna? You're not taking that stupid *Sunday Echo* thing seriously are you? It was so obviously a complete crock of shit."

Anna let out a long sigh. "No. I know nothing much went on between Richard and Lizzie Ancroft, though I guess it has pissed me off. But it's more than that. I had a horrible dream about Dennis and it's because I'm feeling vulnerable again. I feel so exposed at the moment and I'm just not sure I can trust Richard anymore. Who's to say he isn't just stringing me along until the election is over? He could just be using me to get to Number 10."

"He could, Anna," said Libby cautiously, "but I don't think he is. I know he made a big mistake leaving you before and it's bound to make you feel anxious, but you've got to try and trust him again. The papers are going to be full of stories about your marriage for the foreseeable future so you've got to learn to draw a line between your public and private life and not let it get to you. You've got a baby to think about now too, Anna. These are exciting times so please put the past behind you. All of it."

"You seem to find that so much easier than me."

"Look... it still creeps in sometimes. I have my moments too. But we can't let it defeat us. We didn't do anything wrong. We were two terrified girls living a nightmare. But it's over, Anna. Finished."

Anna curled her knees up to meet her stomach and leaned into the side of the sofa. Her head was still spinning with fear and paranoia, but Libby's voice of reason was beginning to force its way through. She let the tears fall freely again as she realised that for the last twenty years she had been too afraid to accept happiness in her life. She had felt that if she'd dropped her guard and relaxed then something bad was bound to happen so, instead, she clutched onto the fear that had become her security blanket. Now she had to try and let it go in order to cope with the new life that lay ahead for her and her family.

"You still there?" Libby asked.

"Yes." Anna sniffled. "And I know what you're saying is right. I've got to try and get back on my feet again and help Richard. I just feel so tired."

"I know. That's only natural, but you've only got a couple of days of campaigning left and then you can relax a little bit – well, as much as is possible when you're a prime minister's wife."

"*If* I'm a prime minister's wife, Libby. The polls are looking shaky again after that whole Ancroft thing."

"Well, it's all the more important that you get back out there then. Where were you supposed to be today?"

"I should have been with him in Swindon this morning and then we were flying from Heathrow to Newcastle at two-thirty."

"Right, well you can still make it to Newcastle. I'll tell John to come and get you in fifteen minutes, okay?"

"Okay," Anna replied. She said goodbye to Libby then walked to the downstairs toilet to look in the mirror. Her face was heavily blotched and there were dark circles under her eyes. She would need a lot of make-up to disguise this, she thought. But then she was no stranger to disguise, it was reality she had to learn to face.

The air hostesses smiled broadly as Richard made his way into the cabin, closely followed by Henry, two special branch officers, Richard's PA and a small assortment of aides who all formed part of what was now a familiar entourage. They had been running seriously late and Richard thanked the crew profusely for holding the aircraft for an extra few minutes.

"That's all right," one of the hostesses replied brightly. "Pleasure to have you on board, sir. Your wife is already seated."

Richard smiled and tried to hide his surprise that Anna was on the flight. He rounded the corner into the cabin and spotted her sitting in the second row. He wanted to rush straight over and give her a hug, but already a couple of passengers in the rows behind had stood up to greet him.

"Good luck," a very rotund and red-faced businessman said, whilst firmly shaking his hand. Behind him, a ten-year-old boy was being pushed forward by his mother. He shook the boy's hand and asked him his name. "Lucas," he replied, smiling shyly, adding, "I hope you win." Richard thanked him then smiled and waved at the other passengers, many of whom, he noticed, were smiling back at him. He could sense their hopes and expectations – and he didn't want to let them down.

He turned back to find Henry chatting animatedly with Anna, obviously briefing her on the hell that had been that morning. The press had been all over them while they were out canvassing in Swindon, all desperate to know why Anna hadn't joined them on the trip. "It was never intended that she would be here," Henry had barked back. "So, when will we see her then?" a persistent reporter had kept asking. But they couldn't answer that one.

Richard moved into the row to sit between them.

"Glad you came," was all he said. He noticed Anna looked tired and drawn and his heart felt heavy with the guilt of all the pressure she was under when she should be sitting at home with her feet up. He had confided to Henry about Anna's pregnancy earlier that morning as it was the only explanation he could give as to why he couldn't force his wife to be permanently on the trail now.

"I spoke to Libby," Anna said. "She made me realise I can't keep getting upset over every story because there are going to be many more out there before our days at Number 10 are through. The important thing right now is to make sure you win; then we'll maybe get some time to work through the craziness of these last few weeks."

"You're a trouper," Richard said, touching her arm.

The safety announcement came on over the tannoy, and Richard, Anna and Henry dutifully paid attention while the flight crew gave their demonstration. Anna was an uncomfortable flyer – particularly during take-off – so she distracted herself by listening to Henry's anecdotes about how the local Alliance candidate in Swindon had been forced to cancel a planned speech he was going to make in contest to Richard's, because only a small handful of supporters had turned out for him.

Once in the air, the TV screens in front of them flashed into life to show a brief, five-minute *AllNews 24* bulletin. Both Henry and Richard reached for their headphones, but Anna preferred the silence. She glanced at the screen to catch Don Monteith's face appear above the headline *Director's attack on Anna Lloyd*. Anna felt her stomach disappear through the clouds below. She studied Richard's frowning face as he listened to the bulletin, knowing she would have to wait patiently until it was over before she could ask what had been said. The cabin had fallen almost completely silent and all eyes seemed to be on them.

Finally, Richard removed his headphones and turned to look at her with a raised eyebrow.

"What was he saying about me?" Anna whispered urgently.

"He called you an ambitious man-eater," Richard said, before bursting into laughter.

"What's so funny?" Anna asked, shocked by the flippancy of his response.

"I don't know," he said, shaking his head. "This is all getting so ludicrous now that I'm just starting to find it funny. Besides, he's only sore because you knocked him back."

"Is there no end to this, Richard?" Anna cast her eyes down forlornly as she fought back the tears.

"No end to what?"

"The constant criticism, the constant speculation, the constant pressure. It's awful."

"You're not worrying about Don are you?" Henry suddenly piped up, leaning around Richard so he could see Anna. "He was so coked-up he came across as a complete nutter. No one will take him seriously."

"It's not just Don," Anna mumbled.

"If it makes you feel better," Richard said, stroking her hand,

"I fully intend to sue over every false allegation that's been printed once we get the election out of the way."

"We'll have more important things to think about after the election," Henry sagely reminded them. "I promise you this means nothing. This is just the sort of shit we've got to start getting used to. Once again, Anna, the press are going to be scrutinising your every move for signs of marital disharmony after the Ancroft thing. We need to crush that dead, so let's just stay focused and keep our heads down and forget about idiots like Monteith." He paused as if he'd finished speaking, then added, "Politics is full of traitors."

Henry shook his head, sat back in his chair and crossed his arms in front of him, reminding Anna with those few words that she was not the only one who had made personal sacrifices in this campaign.

She supposed this was just another nasty story that she would have to try and brush off, though that was much easier said than done.

Newcastle came and went in a flurry of flashbulbs, handshakes, smiles and waves. They began with a tour of a new biomass power plant, the details of which passed Anna by, but she deduced it was essentially an "eco-friendly" power station. Richard appeared very interested during the tour, nodding his head fervently and asking lots of questions. Addressing the press outside, he told them he would work hard to support the creation of other similar plants around the country. All the while, Anna made sure she smiled, leaned in towards Richard as he spoke (lest the body language experts call them "distant") and simply laughed off the suggestion that the Lizzie Ancroft story had caused tension between them. The reality was that Anna didn't know whether it had or not. How can you analyse the state of your marriage when your husband is two days away from potentially being elected Prime Minister? For now, all she could do was stick dutifully to his side and hope they could somehow find their way through the craziness that had become their lives.

After a walkabout in Newcastle city centre, Anna, Richard and Henry sped back to London via Leeds, where Richard stopped to address an audience of SDP Youth members. Anna had slept most of the way home in the car while Richard and Henry took a succession of mobile phone calls and chatted animatedly between themselves. As they neared North London, though now awake, Anna continued to keep her eyes shut so she could be left alone with her thoughts. She had such little time to think these days and, increasingly, her life was ceasing to be her own as she gave in to the demands of her new role as Prime Minister's wife-in-waiting. She still loved Richard, but they were becoming strangers amid the daily onslaught. And as much as she now cared about Henry, having him living with them did increase the pressure. Add to that the fact they were now chaperoned by special branch officers wherever they went, there was barely a moment's privacy between them. How then could she know whether her reconciliation with Richard was for the right reasons? And what kind of life lay ahead for the child growing inside of her, destined to be born into a very unreal world?

18

DEMOCRATS' LEAD NARROWS IN WAKE OF "LIZZIEGATE"

WEDNESDAY, MAY 6TH, 2009, UK NEWSWIRE

The Social Democrats' lead over the Alliance Party took a knock in the polls today, falling from ten to six points on the eve of the General Election.

The sudden drop in support for the SDP raises for the first time in the campaign the spectre of a hung parliament should the Alliance Party be able to further capitalise on their gains.

Alliance spokesman, Reggie Caldwell, welcomed the poll results, saying: "We all know polls can vary widely from day to day and from pollster to pollster. But the latest results suggest the public are turning their backs on Richard Williams in their droves.

"Only an Alliance government can offer the experience and safe hands it will take to continue to steer this country out of the recession which has affected every major economy around the world."

But SDP campaign organiser Ray Mosley, widely tipped to become Deputy Prime Minister if his party wins tomorrow, dismissed today's fall in support as "a flash in the pan".

"Britain is still very much on course for the change of government it so desperately needs", he said. "Recent malicious and untrue headlines have no doubt had some impact on voters but, when faced with the choice of voting for change or the same old ineffective Alliance Party, common sense will prevail".

The dramatic turn in public opinion followed claims last weekend that Williams had once had a relationship with Alliance MP Lizzie Ancroft who, at the time, was battling a cocaine addiction which she claims he was aware of. Williams admitted to a "close friendship" but firmly denied any knowledge of her drug taking.

In the last day of campaigning, the leaders of the main political parties will each be embarking on whistle-stop tours of the marginal constituencies, before returning in the evening to their own constituencies where they will vote tomorrow morning.

Now a formidable trio, Anna was really looking forward to spending another morning with Libby and Sandra. They were due to meet at the Willows residential school in Croydon which helped children with emotional and behavioural problems. Anna had travelled alone, or as close to alone as it got these days, with John driving her while a couple of police officers followed in the car behind. It had only just dawned on Anna the previous evening that to top off her problems, she and Richard had now become significant targets for terrorists and lunatics.

As she looked out of the car window onto the rainy morning outside, she tried to suppress the butterflies rising in her stomach as she thought of how her every move would once again be picked over. She was becoming tired, very tired of this whole process. The thought that by winning the election the pressure might become even greater, was terrifying. And in all of this, the glaring irony that she had yearned for this level of fame for twenty years yet, when it finally came, she hated it.

The car swept into the driveway of the school and Anna turned to see what could only be described as a very characterless but enormous seventies block directly ahead. She could see Libby's Citroen sitting in the car park and she bet herself that Sandra would also have arrived before her, being the control freak that she most certainly was. Anna smiled as she imagined Sandra already inside, most likely bossing a junior press officer around as they planned the tour of the school. She would be on tenterhooks, knowing that the brief statement Anna made after the visit could seriously influence tomorrow's election vote if she was able to convince the public that her husband was a man to be trusted. A man who she trusted – or desperately wanted to.

Henry had tried to avoid putting too much pressure on her earlier that morning but he had left her in no doubt that she was their only hope of turning the situation around to win a strong majority. "The public love you, Anna," he had assured her. "They will believe you if you tell them Richard deserves their vote." He had then patted her on the shoulder as if to say *"go to it"*. Now here she was, ready to step out in front of the world's press with the party's hopes pinned firmly on her. She took a deep breath as she waited for John to open the car door. As soon as her feet hit the ground, the mayhem began.

The head of Willows school, Judith McCormack, was waiting – alongside Sandra, Libby and an SDP press officer – by the front door to greet Anna who walked purposefully towards them while the special branch officers held back the scrum. She made sure she smiled broadly as the cameras flashed all around her and photographers and reporters shouted her name over and over in an attempt to get her attention.

But just as she was about to hold her hand out to greet Judith, a young male reporter leapt forward and stuck a radio microphone barely a couple of inches from her face.

"Is yours a marriage of convenience?" the reporter shouted at Anna.

"How dare you?" she called back, infuriated by his lack of respect. "I'm a human being you know," she continued. "You wouldn't think it was appropriate to ask your neighbour that, so why are you asking me?" The reporter shrugged nonchalantly, only aggravating Anna further. "You think I don't love my husband, is that it? You think I'm just some money-grabbing actress out for all the power and fame I can get and hanging onto him for dear life?"

Sandra was at her side now, pulling on her arm as the special forces officers closed in behind, trying to move her on.

"No. No," Anna protested. "Let me speak, please."

The press pack had by now fallen into an absolute shambles of reporters, cameramen and photographers all clamouring to get in closer to witness this dramatic outburst. There were microphones being dangled from every angle in the hope of picking up her comments, while reporters viciously tried to elbow their way to the front.

"Is she cracking up?" she heard one reporter ask another.

"This needs to stop," she said firmly to the pack as a more dignified but stronger resolve came over her. "You need to know that I didn't marry Richard Williams for his career, and I didn't marry him so that I could one day live in Number 10 Downing Street. I married him because I love and admire him. Our marriage isn't a sham..." Anna felt her head start to spin and she stumbled back a little.

Sandra gripped her arm to steady her, but Anna was determined to continue.

With her voice restored, Anna continued. "I... we, are not fakes. We are two normal people who share the same ideals and desperately want to make a difference. And, yes, this campaign has been tough on our marriage. The never-ending stream of stories making ever more ludicrous allegations, has been hard to take. But if they are allowed to overshadow Richard's beliefs and determination to make this country a better place to live for us all then it will be the biggest loss in our political history. Please just let him get on and fight for the job he would be so, so good at."

The cameras moved in again, flashing over and over, while the assembled reporters were jostling to ask their questions, each trying to shout louder than the other to be heard above the din. Anna felt a rush of heat sweep through her before her hearing gave way to a single high-pitched tone. Her legs buckled beneath her and Sandra struggled to prop her up. A photographer rushed forward and picked up the other arm before a police officer was able to help carry her towards the car.

Libby burst into tears at the sight of her sister out cold. "Anna, Anna," she was shouting as she walked alongside, "Can you hear me?"

She dashed over to the car and yanked open the door of the front passenger seat to talk to the driver, completely oblivious to the press pack who were by now right behind.

"We've got to get her to hospital quickly," she screeched. "She's pregnant."

~

Marie fought back another wave of nausea as she again watched Anna collapse live on *AllNews 24* who were repeating the clip over and over.

She knew it must have been the strain of all the recent allegations that had finally taken its toll, and she felt worse still to think she had been central to it. But the final blow was the realisation that Anna was pregnant. What if she lost her baby? It would all be her fault. And though she had decided to quit her job at her lunch meeting with Damian, it was too little too late. She hadn't intended on resigning when she first arrived at the restaurant, but as he pushed her to take the promotion, Marie realised she could no longer contribute to a paper she didn't believe in. She hated its values – or lack of them – she hated her boss and she had come to hate herself. So now she was unemployed and watching a woman she admired, but had set out to destroy, buckling under the strain and in danger of losing her baby. A woman who she knew had faced the toughest of childhoods – the very, very worst of situations – when Marie had only ever known the safety and security of two loving parents.

She glanced at her watch. It was only four o'clock but she thought she could allow herself another glass of wine to try and relax. The black cloud of depression hung heavily over her again, not even slightly dispersed by her decision to leave the paper.

She headed for the kitchen and plucked the bottle from the fridge door before quickly returning to the living room to recharge her glass. She took a few gulps then filled the glass to the top again before taking a seat on the sofa and staring at the phone. She knew she should call her dad to tell him about her resignation but she had been dreading that conversation for fear he would disapprove of her rash decision. She picked up the receiver and dialled her parents' number.

"Hello Dad," she said cautiously when he answered.

"Hello dear, how are you?" he asked.

"Not bad, not bad…" She hesitated. "Just wanted to let you know that I've resigned from the *Echo*. I handed my notice in yesterday after being offered a promotion."

"I see," he said flatly. "Were you unhappy there?"

"Yes. I had been finding it more and more difficult to produce the kind of stories they wanted me to. Particularly the ones against Richard Williams and his wife."

"I can understand that. The one at the weekend seemed particularly unpleasant. The poor man couldn't help being in the photo after all. Didn't mean he was up to anything himself." The line went quiet for a few moments before her father spoke again. "What are you going to do now?"

"Well," Marie said, taking on a defensive tone. "I'll be sending my CV off to a few other papers this week. I'd be so much happier anywhere than the *Echo* – and I'm also thinking of applying to the Red Cross to be a press officer."

"I hope that something will come up for you soon then, dear."

Marie gulped back a few more swigs of wine and wondered why the alcohol wasn't relaxing her. In fact, she was feeling increasingly agitated. She couldn't understand why her father sounded so disengaged. Like he was just so disappointed with her work on the *Echo* that he'd almost given up on her.

"Is everything okay, Dad?" she asked anxiously.

"We're fine, dear. We're just about to head off to the supermarket to do the weekly shop."

"Okay." Marie wanted to ask if he was angry with her, but she couldn't bring herself to confront him. "Love to Mum then," she said. "Goodbye."

"Goodbye, dear. Thanks for calling."

Marie put the receiver back in the handset and started to cry. She felt so completely lost. She'd given up her job and her income on the spur of the moment and she'd soon be in financial trouble if she didn't come up with something else. In her heart of hearts she knew it would be tough getting work on another paper, broadsheet or tabloid, after the trash she had produced over the last few weeks and she couldn't imagine a charity would feel particularly compelled to take her on either. Her career was surely finished.

She would have to retrain and, to do that, she'd need to ask her parents for financial support. After the shame they'd had to endure over her work in recent weeks, she was going to top it off by asking them for money.

Her head spun. She felt nothing but self-hatred and despair. Then an idea came to mind that made her cry even harder.

She walked back through to the kitchen and opened one of the cabinet doors to reach for the little box she kept medication in. She looked inside and pulled out a packet of paracetamol before opening it up. She noticed there was only one missing from a box of twenty. That should be enough, she thought.

Richard eventually made it over to the hospital at six o'clock in the evening, having had to abandon the last day's campaigning and catch a flight to London from the Midlands. He was supposed to be travelling – along with Anna – to Bristol right now to spend the eve of the election in their constituency, but that would have to wait.

He rushed along the hospital corridor to Anna's room, easily marked by the police officer standing guard outside.

Once inside, he saw Anna propped up in her bed watching the evening news.

"You needn't have bothered phoning to say when you were

coming." Anna smiled. "I've been charting your every move from here," she said, nodding towards the television.

"A novel but effective way of keeping in touch." He laughed, then kissed her tenderly on the forehead. "How are you feeling?"

"I'm fine. Just tired. I've not had a chance to sleep for all the tests they've been running. Either I've been wired up to something or they've had a band round my stomach to listen to the baby. Neither of us have had any peace."

Richard felt a wave of complete devotion to Anna as he looked at her lying so serenely on her hospital bed, her face completely devoid of make-up, yet still so beautiful. He kissed her again lightly on the cheek.

"I love you," he said. "But you've got to take it easy from now on. I'm so sorry for pressurising you to come with me the other day."

"Don't worry. I'm fine. Just tired. If the doctors want to call that exhaustion then so be it. They want me to stay in another night but I should be out tomorrow to come with you to the count."

"Don't be silly, Anna. You go straight home tomorrow. I'll have plenty of company at the count and you can save your energy for Downing Street. Just pray that we get there."

His eyes widened with what Anna recognised as a mix of fear and excitement.

"You're going to do it," she said, suddenly sombre. "I can feel it."

"And will you be happy?" he asked, his eyes searching hers.

"I'll try," was the best she could muster.

Richard swallowed hard as he grasped her hand and hoped this wasn't going to turn out to be a no-win situation.

$\sim$

On the ground floor of the hospital two ambulance staff wheeled a new patient through the entrance to the Accident and Emergency Department. "Her name is Marie Simpson," one of them announced to the waiting medical team. "She appears to have taken a paracetamol overdose and she's been drinking heavily too. She had texted a friend who became concerned about her welfare and called the police."

Kelvin paced his Downing Street office while Joy and Reggie sat helplessly, just waiting to be verbally savaged. It was after nine in the evening and Kelvin should have been on his way to his Buckinghamshire constituency, but he had delayed his schedule by twenty minutes to talk with Joy and Reggie. Over the course of the day, it had become clear that one or both of them was to be blamed for the Democrats' unexpected publicity coup – and they were now being called to account. To prove his point, Kelvin was forcing them to watch a very animated Esther Yarleth on *AllNews 24* who was grilling two studio guests about the latest twist in the campaign.

"What is it about Anna Lloyd that is resonating so much with the British public?" she asked excitedly. "We have received literally thousands of messages of support for her from concerned well-wishers today, all saying how refreshing it was to see someone from the world of politics actually speaking their mind, and how awful it was that she had been under so much pressure. To what do you think she owes her popularity, Marcia?"

"Well," replied the Women's Alliance founder, Marcia Haynes, "Anna Lloyd has come to represent the struggle of many women; whether they are experiencing domestic abuse or marriage problems, or whether they simply admire her strength and resilience, there is something in her life that a lot of us can relate to. And, of course, she has become something of a voice for women both young and old."

"Patricia Drake," Esther said, turning to her second guest, the haughty chairwoman of Women for Families.

"I certainly think Anna Lloyd has come to represent a great many things over this campaign." Patricia smirked. "Not all of them positive. But I do admire the way she spoke out today and refused to be bullied by the press. I am also pleased to see how, over the course of this campaign, she has stepped back from her own work commitments to support her husband, and I certainly wish her a speedy recovery."

"Good God," Kelvin boomed. "When even Patricia Drake is eulogising about that woman, we know we've got problems. She is talking about a former call girl here for fuck's sake."

"Former escort," Joy instinctively corrected him, then immediately regretted it.

Kelvin glared at her in both anger and disgust.

"You've got the cheek to sit there and pick me up on something like that, when you've spent the last two weeks mooning around doing bugger all except ruining my chances of being re-elected. You've made a martyr out of Anna Lloyd thanks to your ridiculous tabloid stories."

Joy braced herself for the remainder of what was to come and tried not to notice the flush of red that was quickly making its way from Kelvin's neck to his forehead.

"I am seriously beginning to wonder, Joy, if you were actually deliberately planted within my party to screw up the Alliance campaign."

"I've wondered the very same thing," Reggie said smugly, clearly relieved that it was Joy who was taking the heat and not him.

"Just to remind you," Joy replied calmly. "It was you who

approached me to work for this party. I believe I have acted professionally at all times, and always in the best interests of the Alliance. I told you when I agreed to take the job that I have no particular political allegiances, but that I didn't want to see the Social Democrats win this election. However, having gotten to know you over the last two or three weeks, I can categorically say that is no longer the case."

"Get the fuck out of this building," Kelvin said, leaning menacingly into her face. "You're a disloyal bitch. You'd better get on the first flight back to New York in the morning because I'll make sure your name is mud in this country."

Joy collected her bag from under her feet and slowly stood up.

"Kelvin," she said, calmly fixing him in the eye. "After tomorrow, I'm quite sure no one will ever listen to a damn word you say again."

19

VOTERS TO DECIDE AS BRITAIN HEADS TO THE POLLS

THURSDAY, MAY 7TH, 2009, UK NEWSWIRE

Voters go to the polls today in the General Election that will decide whether Social Democrat leader Richard Williams can end eight years of Alliance government to become the youngest Prime Minister in over a century.

After a month trailing the length and breadth of the country in the quest for votes, the three main party leaders know their fate now lies in the hands of the electorate.

After a final day of campaigning, Prime Minister Kelvin Davis, Richard Williams and Liberal leader, Giles Henderson, will this morning cast their own votes in their constituencies.

Polling stations around the country open at 7am and close at 10pm – with the first results expected around 11.30pm.

The Democrats have led the opinion polls for the majority of the campaign, but dropped several points in recent days following claims that, in his early parliamentary career,

Williams was involved with the Alliance MP Lizzie Ancroft who was, at that time, addicted to cocaine.

Williams was yesterday forced to abandon campaigning for two hours to visit his wife, the actress Anna Lloyd, who was rushed to hospital after collapsing outside a residential school whilst making a public statement in support of her husband.

It was revealed by Lloyd's sister that the actress is in the early stages of pregnancy. Hospital officials said last night that she was suffering from exhaustion but both mother and unborn child were expected to make a full recovery after a period of rest.

Both the main parties are said to privately believe today's vote could be close, with the SDP facing a tough fight to win many of the key marginal seats where the election will be decided.

In the end, turnout could be crucial. The last General Election in 2005 saw a turnout of 59 per cent and there are concerns that there could be a similarly depressed vote this time around following what was considered to be a campaign marred by dirty tricks and smears.

There are private fears among Democrat strategists that some supporters may feel disaffected after a series of claims about the personal lives of Richard Williams and his wife, Anna Lloyd, and could simply stay at home.

The uncertainty over the result has been heightened by the large numbers of undecided voters, with the final opinion polls suggesting more than two in four may have yet to make up their minds.

F aced with the long wait at his Bristol constituency home, Richard had decided it would be best to walk to the polling station and he had risen early so he could be among the first to arrive. His mood was apprehensive as he braced himself for both the results and Anna's response. Her reluctance and unease at the prospect of becoming Prime Minister's wife deeply unsettled him.

He decided to distract himself by offering to make coffee for Henry and Sandra and the array of special branch officers camped around the house. Henry had leapt in to help him whilst Sandra sat watching the breakfast news.

"Any word on Anna?" Henry asked Richard quietly.

"I've not called her yet. She'll still be sleeping," Richard replied. "I thought I'd speak to her after voting."

"Good idea," Henry agreed, whilst loading a few coffee-filled mugs onto a tray. "I had noticed she'd been a bit quiet these last few days but I didn't realise she was so tired. I feel a bit guilty for urging her out on the campaign trail with us."

"Me too," Richard said flatly. "The last few weeks have been really tough on her, it would have been a struggle anyway but adding the pregnancy on top has really flattened her. I just hope she's going to be okay."

"Course she will." Henry smiled encouragingly. "Anna's a trouper. Here." He held the tray out to Richard. "You take these to the cops outside. It'll make for a good picture."

"Okay." Richard took the tray and headed through the hallway towards the front door. He balanced the tray against the wall and used his right hand to free the snib. As soon as the door was open the flashbulbs snapped into action and the photographers chortled loudly as they watched Richard struggle to rebalance the tray, the contents of the coffee cups beginning to slosh around.

"Sorry guys," he said sheepishly, as two male officers rushed forward to help him.

"Not a problem, sir," the older of the two said. "That's a lovely thought. We could all use a nice cup of coffee at this time in the morning."

"Precisely," said Richard.

"We'll take the others to the officers round the back for you," the policeman said as he scooped up the remaining cups and laid them out on the window ledge, ready to be distributed. "And I hope your wife makes a speedy recovery, sir," he added.

"Thanks. That's kind," said Richard before heading back inside the house, his thoughts turning to Anna again. Surely her fears for the future were simply down to exhaustion and a natural apprehension about what lay ahead, he reassured himself. But he wished they'd had more time to prepare themselves for this new life they could be about to embark on. They had, he knew, much to discuss when all this was over. He just hoped she would still be by his side, whatever the result.

Anna switched off the TV news and turned back on her side again in the hope of catching some more sleep before another nurse came in to take her pulse and disturb the very thing she needed most. She had watched Richard casting his vote and felt saddened that she couldn't be there to support him. But she was also relieved. Shut away in the hospital room, hidden from cameras and probing reporters, she felt more at ease than she had done in months, perhaps even years. With such security she wondered how she was ever going to face leaving and desperately hoped the doctors would encourage her to stay another night so she wouldn't have to face the pandemonium of the election result. She knew it was wrong. She knew that, in many ways, her exhaustion was a bit of a betrayal. Why couldn't she just take it all in her stride? And what had happened to her over the course of just a few weeks to prompt such a change of heart on fame – the very thing she had fought so hard, for so long to achieve? She should be desperate to have her moment in the global spotlight. In the end she guessed she had reached her saturation point. The revelations about her past had left her exposed and vulnerable. Then came the terrible and destructive rift with Richard, followed by the utter madness of the intense public scrutiny and becoming an overnight "People's Princess". And through this process she had come to realise that the only thing that mattered was the security of family life and the company of those you really love. Those ideals were pretty far removed from the insanity that would be life in Downing Street. How on earth would she be able to take her baby for a walk? A peaceful stroll down to a local café to meet with friends would surely be impossible. Life's simple pleasures were about to be wiped out in an instant leaving them as nothing but a pair of public figures going through the motions and never stopping to enjoy the most precious gift of family life. Was this the right situation to raise their child in? She clasped her hands to her head as her fears screamed and swirled in her mind. Would they ever stop, she wondered?

Back at the house in Bristol, Richard paced the living-room floor while Sandra and Henry huddled together at the dining table, their mobile phones constantly pressed to their ears as they barked orders down the phone. When they were not talking on their mobiles or to each other, they were glued to the television screens searching for clues as to the possible result or bickering between themselves over which marginals they thought the Social Democrats would win or lose.

Richard stopped for a moment to take in the scene. History in the making, he wondered? Either way, he was bound to write about this moment in an autobiography one of these days. He noticed how at ease Sandra and Henry were in each other's company and wondered if either of them had yet considered the possibility that they might become an item in future. He remembered how he and Anna had shared that same familiar ease with each other, before the pressures of public life had threatened to turn them into strangers.

At four o'clock, Dan arrived with the children who had been allowed to leave school early and take the following day off in light of the significant occasion for their family. They were supposed to have been joined by Libby but she had stayed in London so she could visit Anna. Richard's father and mother had also arrived from Cornwall.

Shortly after five, Dan volunteered to brave the press pack outside and went off to buy fish and chips for everyone. He arrived back twenty minutes later, loaded down with a large box containing their dinners and looking like he'd been pursued by wolves; his hair all tousled and his jacket hanging down over his shoulders because he'd been unable to stop and pull it back on.

"Blooming 'eck," he shouted as he slammed the front door behind him. "I wouldn't fancy being a Hollywood star if that's what life is like. They practically tripped me up on the path trying to get a shot of what I was carrying. They kept yelling 'What's in the box?' and 'Who are you?' Terrifying." Dan shook his head as he laid the box down on the table and allowed everyone to help themselves to their orders before taking their seats. The kids sat on the floor in front of the television in the adjoining lounge, trying to seem interested in *AllNews 24's* election coverage because they knew it was the reason they were off school.

At one point little Rupert made the mistake of asking Sandra if he could switch on to CITV, only to be shot down with an immediate "Not today, no." Though she did ruffle his hair afterwards in a peace-making gesture.

Richard stood silently yearning for Anna – for the feel of her hand in his, calming him, balancing him. He was achingly close to his dream now, yet felt so distant from the one person he most wanted to share it with. Tomorrow would be different, he reassured himself. Tomorrow she would be back and the celebration could really begin.

Marie opened her eyes and blinked rapidly as the light penetrated her skull like lasers. Her mouth was very dry and she felt extremely drowsy. She turned to her right to see the unfamiliar sight of a metal frame around her bed, with a small pine cabinet just in front of her. It was then she realised she was in hospital and she groaned with fatigue and confusion. Had she got drunk and fallen over somewhere? Had she been attacked? Marie turned to her left and found her father sitting quietly studying her.

"It's all right, dear." Her mother appeared by his side and patted her hand. "You're in hospital. You've been asleep for a long time."

Marie tried to open her mouth to ask why, but her lips were so dry they were sticking together. Instead, she put her hands down on the mattress and attempted to push herself into a sitting position. Her father stood to help pull her further up the pillows, while her mother held a glass of water for her to sip.

As she supped the liquid back slowly, a crushing memory

flashed in front of her. She saw the box of paracetamol, she remembered the drinking. *Oh shit*, she thought. *How could I be so stupid?*

She looked into the tired, concerned faces of her parents and started to cry.

"I'm so sorry," she sobbed. "I didn't mean to do it. I just got myself into a state."

"Please don't worry, Marie," her mother said, leaning forward to stroke her hand again. "We love you very much."

"I feel terrible, dear," her father added. "You called me wanting to talk and I was rushing out to the supermarket to get chicken stock for your mother. She needed it quickly. I only wish I had stopped to talk to you. I'm so, so, sorry."

Now it was her father's turn to cry, and he was quickly joined by her mother.

"What made you feel so low, Marie?" her mother begged.

"I'd been feeling down for a while, I guess." She sighed. "I felt so bad about my work, and all the rubbish I've been writing over the election campaign. All the people I'd lied about and hurt."

"Who did you lie about?" her father asked. "I thought you had to stand these stories up? Make sure they were accurate."

"I did, Dad, before I joined the *Echo*. But Damian got greedy and desperate to the point he just didn't care what we printed. He kept saying, 'It's not like they're going to sue, is it?' Because he thinks if Richard Williams is voted Prime Minister he won't want to get into a legal battle over his personal life. And he was probably right. It doesn't make me feel any better about it though. I feel really, really disgusted with myself."

Marie began sobbing again, her head now pounding with all the effort.

"I can't believe I swallowed a packet of paracetamol and I've still ended up with a headache," she joked between sobs.

"That's my girl." Her father smiled. "You can't be so hard on yourself. You were just doing your job. And if you're concerned that you've lied, then you still have a chance to put that right."

"How?" Marie asked.

"By saying sorry," he replied.

By ten o'clock the relaxed, jovial atmosphere in the house had turned to palpable tension as the reality of what was about to be decided sunk in. Henry was downstairs in the living room monitoring the BBC news for the exit poll, while Sandra was upstairs watching ITV. The bulletins started simultaneously.

"We're on," shouted Henry.

Richard rushed through from the kitchen where he had been talking to Ray on the phone. Ray had kept insisting all the signs suggested they were going to win big, but Richard was still refusing to agree, not wishing to tempt fate.

By the time he had squeezed past the three children, his parents and Dan, Henry was already on his feet.

"They're giving us nearly 400 seats. That'll do nicely." Henry beamed as though they had just won.

"It's good. It's good," Richard said quietly before being embraced by his proud mother.

"Oh Richard, darling. You're so close. So close."

He then turned to embrace his father who had tears in his eyes.

"I can't believe it," he said, shaking his head. "Richard's going to be Prime Minister. My son is going to be Prime Minister."

Dan stood slightly further back, absolutely speechless, but grinning ear to ear.

"Is Uncle Richard going to win, Daddy?" Jasmine asked.

"Looks like it, Jazzy." He laughed. Soon the three children

were bouncing up and down with excitement. It was impossible to suppress it. They were on their way, and everyone could feel it.

At 10.30pm, Les pulled up front to take Richard and his parents to the polling station while Sandra and Henry followed in the car behind.

"Don't worry, I voted for you," were Les's first words when Richard opened the car door, raising a half-smile from his anxious passenger.

By the time they reached the school hall where the votes were being counted the place was buzzing with press, party members, candidates and their families. Richard was swamped as soon as he entered the building with SDP supporters clamouring to shake his hand. The hour-long wait was agonising – and only made easier by the unending announcements of Social Democrat wins from around the country. Finally the moment came and Richard made his way up to the stage with the other candidates.

Sandra clutched Henry's arm as they listened to the results being read out. They were confident Richard would win, but he needed to increase his 12,000 majority in order for the critics not to say he had personally been hit by the series of allegations made about him over the course of the campaign.

"Michael Denton, Green Party, 2,127 votes. Gareth Hill, Alliance Party, 7,962 votes, Elizabeth Bramley, Liberal Party, 9,874 votes. Richard Williams, Social Democratic Party, 24,788 votes."

Richard had to wait several minutes before the raucous cheering settled enough to enable him to give a humble acceptance speech in which he carefully thanked all those from the local constituency party who had helped him. He was cautious, too, not to sound overly confident of victory, simply remarking: "The tide is turning for Britain and we are ready."

~

Joy watched their smiling faces as they left the polling station. A jubilant Richard, closely followed by Henry and Sandra who were deep in conversation, his hand touching her back protectively as he moved her past the waiting press. They had become quite a close-knit team, she could tell. She imagined the celebration they would soon be travelling on to, the totally overwhelming realisation that you had just fought and won a General Election campaign. That, in Henry's case, he would be working in the most powerful communications job in the land. Joy switched the TV off, threw her head back against the pillow and started to sob. The tears fell one after the other as she tried to make sense of the past few weeks. Losing her marriage, her job and one of her closest friendships in the space of a few days, then making the crazy mistake of agreeing to work for Kelvin.

She realised it had been a dumb move, made in the depths of her heartache. In the end, it had only worsened her pain as she worked day in, day out in a job she hated for a man she absolutely loathed. And of course, by choosing to work for the Alliance, Joy had ruled out any chance of a reconciliation with Henry. Something that now the dust had settled she deeply regretted.

She switched the bedside lamp off and tried to get to sleep, but it was no good. She had told herself over and over again that she wasn't going to sit up all night watching the election and obsessing about her husband. Now she realised there was no way she couldn't watch it. But in that moment she also made a promise she knew she had to stick to; in the morning she would book a flight to New York, pack her belongings and leave.

20

NEW DAWN FOR BRITAIN AS SDP SECURES ELECTION VICTORY

FRIDAY, MAY 8TH, 2009, UK NEWSWIRE

The Social Democratic Party today emerged victorious from a hard-fought and dramatic General Election campaign, ending eight years of Alliance rule.

The party now has 394 seats in the House of Commons while the Alliance Party was left with just 230.

Richard Williams, at 44, the youngest British prime minister in over 100 years, promised he would deliver "a brighter future, through courage and determination".

Kelvin Davis resigned as Alliance leader saying: "I want to give the party a fresh start, under a new leader. All we need is a little time to reflect and recharge, and we will emerge stronger than ever before".

Liberal leader Giles Henderson, hailed the election win of 12 seats for his party as "a turning point which marked the emergence of a new voice in British politics".

Meanwhile, many in the Alliance Party blamed their poor performance on Davis's failure to engage with the public whilst Richard Williams and his wife Anna Lloyd had been forced to open themselves up in the face of several allegations made about their personal lives. Lloyd's collapse on the eve of the election following an emotional public defence of her husband was also said to be a factor in winning public support – helping to secure the SDP's victory after a rollercoaster campaign which saw unprecedented fluctuation in the polls.

The actress, who is pregnant with the couple's first child, is expected to leave hospital this morning before accompanying her husband to Buckingham Palace where he will be asked by the Queen to form a new government.

An SDP party spokesman confirmed Lloyd had been suffering from exhaustion but had made a good recovery after "some much-needed rest".

A nna finished applying her lipstick and packed her make-up bag into her overnight case before perching herself on the bed again. She had been told the police officer guarding her room would let her know when Richard's car had arrived and would then escort her down to the front door to join him.

He had called her in the early hours from the car while on his way back to London to tell her the election result. She had fallen asleep in front of the television before midnight and was fast asleep when she heard the phone ring.

"We've made it, Anna. We won," Richard told her breathlessly.

"I'm so proud of you, Richard," she had replied woozily. "I knew you would make it."

"*We* made it, darling," he corrected her. "I can't wait to see you. Are you feeling better?"

"Yes, I'll be fine," she said, trying to reassure him, though she couldn't imagine how she was going to cope with what now lay ahead.

Now waiting to leave the hospital, her stomach was churning at the thought of facing the press again after a couple of blissful days away from the public glare. As soon as her outfit – a navy Joseph dress she had chosen with Camilla for this day several weeks ago – was delivered earlier that morning, Anna's nerves had started. She let out a long sigh and began her breathing exercises. She could just feel the tension starting to ease when there was a tap on the door. She immediately jumped off the bed and reached to pick up her case, ready to leave. The policeman stuck his head around the door, but instead of announcing Richard's arrival he said: "There's a Marie Simpson here to see you, madam. She said you know her?"

"Oh," Anna replied, dumbfounded. Richard had told her Marie had tried to commit suicide – a piece of news passed on from Henry that she hadn't had time to give much thought to, until now. "Umm... let her in."

A few moments later, Marie walked into the room looking suitably sheepish. Her face was devoid of make-up and Anna noticed she looked pale and drawn.

"It's true then?" Anna said, breaking the silence. "You were staying here too."

"Yes," said Marie. "I did something spectacularly stupid and ended up being admitted here on the same evening as you."

"That's pretty ironic." Anna laughed uncomfortably. "Are you okay?"

"I'm fine. Just very, very ashamed of myself." Marie's eyes were stuck to the floor as she struggled to compose herself. "What makes it worse is that I admire you so much for what you've come through and achieved and every story that I ever wrote against you felt totally and utterly wrong. I just came to hate myself."

"Oh Marie," Anne gasped. "You didn't do that on my part?"

"Not just you. It was a mix of things. I think I've probably struggled with depression for years and just hadn't done anything about it. The staff here have been great though, and I'll be getting the right help now. Anyway," she said, finally raising her eyes to meet Anna's, "I just wanted to say I'm sorry for what I did, and I really wish you well in Downing Street."

"Thank you." Anna smiled. "That means a lot. I know how it feels not to like yourself. I just hope you can get to a happy place again soon and know that you can move on from your past and build a good future."

"I hope so."

There was another knock on the door before the policeman opened it again to tell her Richard was waiting in the car outside.

"I suppose I'd better go and face the world again." Anna sighed.

"They love you out there." Marie smiled. "Enjoy it."

"I wish I could." Anna leaned forward and kissed Marie on the cheek. Looking at the journalist who felt she had sold herself out, she realised they had much in common. "We're not so different, you know," Anna said. "As a younger woman I also took jobs that only increased my self-loathing. I struggled for years to forgive myself but..." – she clasped Marie's shoulder – "you can make mistakes and still be a good person. It's the only way you learn."

Marie nodded, her head still bowed. "Thank you," she replied softly.

Anna gave her shoulder another squeeze. "Take care," she said before following the policeman down through the hospital corridor and back into public life.

Richard was waiting for Anna near the entrance of the hospital. As soon as he saw her emerge from the lift he rushed forward to embrace her while cameras flashed furiously outside. It was an awkward moment, they both knew, because it would appear to many to have been staged when, in reality, it was just a natural reaction.

"It's so good to have you back," he whispered. Anna smiled and followed him outside and to the car clutching his hand. "From hospital to Buckingham Palace. This is quite a journey," she joked nervously as she took her seat in the back of the vehicle.

"It's all just a great big show, Anna. Nothing you haven't done before." He squeezed her hand. "You need to think of this as another acting job. We smile and wave and everyone's happy."

Not everyone, Anna thought. But just as she'd learned from her acting coach, she took a deep breath and prepared for her next performance.

Marie clutched her coat tightly as she waited for her parents to collect her from the hospital. She glanced at the clock again and saw it was now five minutes to the agreed pick-up time, when her new life living with her mother and father and taking heavy-duty antidepressants would begin. She felt like a child again. And a naughty one at that. One who couldn't be trusted to be alone for any significant period and one whose future was now uncertain.

She heard a door swing open in the corridor and the sound of footsteps coming ever closer. Then she recognised the familiar throat-clearing that could only belong to one man. Before she could react, he was standing in the doorway.

"Hello Marie," he said, cautiously. "Do you mind if I talk to you for a minute?"

"Well, you're here now," she replied, avoiding eye contact like a sulky teenager.

Damian perched himself on the edge of the visitor's chair and looked up at Marie who was still sitting on her bed, swinging her legs under its rails. He thought she looked so tired and alone, it took him all his willpower not to get up and put his arms around her.

"I resigned today, Marie," he said, matter-of-factly. "The *Echo* Group put a statement out about it a few minutes ago, so it'll be all over the news soon. Course, they didn't mention the Ancroft story. They just said I wanted to move on to pastures new, but it won't take long before questions are asked about my editorial judgement."

"You just did what Viktor wanted you to," Marie muttered, only looking at Damian fleetingly as she spoke. She noted he was unshaven with dark circles under his eyes. She thought his posture was less assertive too, and she could see his ego had been deflated. Looking at him sitting timidly in the chair she couldn't help but feel a little sorry for him.

"I spoke to him this morning. I said he'd put both me and the staff – especially you – under a ridiculous amount of pressure to produce anti-Williams exclusives and that in the end we'd had to throw editorial standards out of the window to make a tenuous link between Williams and Ancroft's cocaine abuse. My decision to run with the *'My Cocaine Nights with Richard Williams'* headline is without doubt the biggest regret of my career. Whether he decides to sue or not we'll have to wait and see, but I didn't want to hang around for that. My resigning draws a line under what happened and allows the *Echo* to move on."

He leaned forward slightly and cleared his throat again. "I didn't just come to tell you that though, Marie," he continued. "I wanted you to know how sorry I am that I drove you to this. I can't tell you how ashamed of myself I am. I really, really admire you, Marie. More than anyone I ever worked with, but I just got things all wrong. I thought you felt the same. I…" Damian faltered as he searched for the words to continue so Marie decided to put him out of his misery.

"This wasn't just down to you," she said, gesturing around the room with her eyes. "I'd been struggling for a while and the whole election thing just tipped me over. The blunt end of tabloid journalism was not the right career choice for me. I never felt good about it and, considering I've never thought particularly highly of myself, it wasn't a good mix."

"Looks like we're both looking for new careers then." Damian laughed awkwardly.

"Yes." Marie smiled.

"I hope we can be friends," Damian said, searching her face for clues.

"We can try," she replied, glancing at him briefly again.

The door in the corridor swung open again and they listened to the footsteps which, seconds later, were revealed to come from Marie's parents. Her father entered the room first, his face flushed and his hair windswept.

"There are photographers and reporters all around the entrance. I asked them what they were doing there and one of them said it was about you and him," he said, pointing an accusing finger towards Damian.

"What do you mean me and him?" she asked, confused.

"They know he's resigned and you tried to…" He looked away, unsure how to complete the sentence. "I guess one of your former colleagues must have told them about your situation. Anyway, they're here now so we'll have to try and get out the back."

"Look," Damian began, "I'll go out the front and speak to them and that'll divert attention long enough for you to leave from another exit."

Marie studied Damian for a moment. A man who had been just as misguided as she was, but who was, ultimately, not a bad person. She thought about leaving with her mum and dad and going back to sit in their house, living by their rules. Would that really be the right environment for her to begin again? She had only moments to decide.

"Wait, Damian," she said. "I'm coming with you."

Though the journey from Buckingham Palace to Downing Street would usually take just a few minutes, the new Prime Minister's motorcade moved at only snail's pace through the crowded streets, every one lined with well-wishers and supporters. Richard continued to hold Anna's hand as they smiled and waved graciously to the people cheering and waving Union Jacks as they passed.

"There's so many of them," Anna remarked flatly. Ever since leaving the hospital she had felt on autopilot, going through the motions as a selection of officials guided her every move.

"It's fantastic." Richard beamed. "Isn't it?" He turned to her, seeking reassurance that she was as thrilled with this moment as he was, but she didn't have to speak. He could tell by her blank expression that her only feeling right now was one of bewilderment.

Sensing his eyes on her face, Anna smiled weakly at Richard. She wondered where on earth he found the energy considering he had only had one hour's sleep. She had done nothing but rest for the last two days yet still felt exhausted and completely removed from the situation. She berated herself for not being able to put on a show of happiness for Richard on what she knew was a momentous day. What kind of person was she? Why couldn't she do this for her husband?

The Queen had spoken warmly to him and he had emerged from their meeting at the Palace with a smile from ear to ear.

"I think she likes me," he'd whispered to Anna when they were out of the earshot of Palace officials. Yet all Anna had been able to do was offer a set of stock answers: "That's great" and "wow, amazing". Perhaps, she thought, this was all too much to take in at once and she would soon warm up to this celebration. She certainly felt proud of Richard and happy for him too, but it didn't ease the sense of disconnect.

As they continued their journey to Downing Street, they looked up through the tinted sunroof to watch the news helicopters circling above, slowly tracking the motorcade.

"Do you think you're ready for this new adventure, Anna?" Richard asked.

"Ready as I can be." She managed a half-smile.

"I couldn't do this without you," he said, squeezing her hand and continuing to wave to his supporters with the other.

Anna looked out of the window towards the cheering crowds and deliberately smiled widely so no one would guess her fear and insecurity. How was she going to fit into this new role? And if it turned out she couldn't, where would that leave her marriage?

Marie tensed as they neared the front doors of the hospital. She could see more than twenty reporters and photographers gathered outside, including a couple of TV crews. It seemed crazy that they would have been there for her and Damian, but then they were at the heart of a scandal connected to the two biggest names in the country right now: Richard Williams and Anna Lloyd. And, she had to admit, it doesn't get much juicier than the reporter who tried to sink them suddenly trying to attempt suicide while her editor mysteriously resigns. Given all that, Marie supposed they were lucky there wasn't more press here.

Damian put a hand around Marie's back and guided her straight into the path of the waiting pack. They stopped just a few feet in front of the hospital. Several reporters were shouting over each other.

"Why did you resign, Damian?"

"Why are you here, Damian?"

"Marie, Marie. What drove you to attempt suicide? Have you been telling lies about Richard Williams?"

"Guys." Damian held up the palm of his hand to try to silence them. "I'm prepared to say a few words. Marie will not comment today." He cleared his throat loudly, which made Marie want to burst out laughing. She put her head down, realising a fit of giggles would be most inappropriate based on what Damian was about to say.

"I resigned as editor of the *Sunday Echo* today because, in the last few weeks, I have not conducted myself according to the standards I believe an editor has to meet in order to produce the best journalism. The pressure under which I placed my staff, including Marie, was intolerable and unacceptable and I came here today to apologise to her. I ask now that you leave us in peace to reflect on what has happened and to move on."

Damian guided Marie to the left and they began to walk forward. Reporters pressed in on them from every angle.

"Damian, Marie. Where are you going now?" a radio

reporter was shouting as she pressed a microphone under Damian's chin.

"We're going to begin again," he said, smiling, before hailing a passing cab and quickly helping Marie inside. She wondered where they would go, then decided she didn't really care. She felt at home again; safe with the most unlikely of friends.

Anna eyed the living room of the Downing Street flat with disdain. She couldn't believe how dowdy the place was compared to what must be the grandeur of the White House or countless other official residences. Was she now expected to leave her home behind to raise a family in an unwelcoming apartment on top of a madhouse?

Richard, who had been busy making calls to appoint his first cabinet, came rushing back into the room, his face flushed with excitement.

"It's all falling into place now, Anna. Just a couple more calls to make and we'll head back to Highgate. The housekeeper says the rest of our stuff will be delivered tomorrow so we'll be official residents of 10 Downing Street within twenty-four hours."

"Great," Anna replied, unenthusiastically.

Richard looked behind him, checking they were alone before moving closer to his wife.

"What's wrong, Anna? You're just not yourself these days. Are you still feeling tired? Do you want to lie down?"

"I am still tired, Richard. But it's more than that." She turned to face him, realising that now she'd started there was no going back. "I've had the most gruelling few weeks, physically and emotionally, and I am struggling, really, really struggling to deal with this – Downing Street, you as Prime Minister, me. I'm a victim of abuse, a killer, a deeply damaged person, and now I'm supposed to be some kind of figurehead?"

"You're not damaged, Anna. You may feel bruised right now. You've been through so much, but you're a fighter. You have never allowed yourself to feel like a victim."

"Until now." She shook her head. "I desperately need stability. I need to know that our family comes first over all this," she said, gesturing around her.

"What are you telling me?" Richard asked, his eyes bulging with confusion and alarm.

"I mean, I have no idea where I stand with you anymore and the insecurity is killing me. Am I here as the wife you love, or am I here as the wife you need?" She stood tall now, defiant as she waited for her answer.

"Anna." Richard clasped her arm. "Of course I love you. You must believe that. It's been an absolutely crazy few weeks and I know it's taken its toll on you, but we've got to stand strong together. I love and need you, Anna. I can't do this without you."

"Well, you might just have to," she said, continuing to hold his gaze.

"What? What are you talking about? Anna, this is what we both dreamed of together. Don't you remember all the things we talked about achieving? All the people we can help?"

"You dumped me in front of an entire nation, Richard. Just a few weeks ago. Then, when the public jumped on my side you suddenly decided to ask me back. What part of that sounds like love to you? How do I know this isn't just some complete sham designed to suit your career? In a few months' time I will give birth to our first child and I will not allow him or her to live a lie. That's just not fair. I've spent my whole life chasing the spotlight, desperate to please, to be someone, to be loved, and I'm tired of the whole charade. I just want to be a normal mother. I want to give my child the stability I never had."

"Are you leaving me?" Richard asked, his voice unsteady, his eyes reflecting his desperation.

Anna leaned in close, her face just inches from his. "Would you give this up for me, Richard?"

"Give up being Prime Minister?"

"Yes."

"You seriously want me to walk into my first press conference tomorrow and tell them I'm giving up the job less than a day into it? Think what you're saying. Please."

"How will I ever be able to trust you otherwise? How can I live this life with you not knowing whether I'm only here as long as I help the poll ratings? I'm not strong enough for that." Tears welled up in her eyes and she turned away from him, reaching for her handbag.

"Anna." Richard reached for her arm again. "Please. I don't know what else I can say. I love you and I can't wait to be a father to our child."

"I'm sorry," she said softly. "I need to go home now."

Richard watched open-mouthed as Anna walked from the room, her head bowed as she tried to suppress her tears. His mind raced with the implications of what she had suggested. To leave Downing Street now would be to give up a lifelong ambition as well as being an absolute insult to the millions of people who had voted for the Social Democrats on the strength of his leadership. But then he thought of a life without Anna and their newborn child. The pain that separation would cause. The endless talk and speculation that would surround it and, all the while, he would be expected to lead a nation. Without her he knew he couldn't do it. Despite the turmoil of the last few weeks, or perhaps because of it, he realised he had never loved or needed her more. And when he looked at it like that, he realised there was no choice at all.

21

WILLIAMS GETS DOWN TO WORK WITH FIRST PRESS CONFERENCE AS PM

SATURDAY, MAY 9TH, 2009, UK NEWSWIRE

Social Democrat leader Richard Williams will today hold a press briefing in Downing Street as he celebrates becoming Britain's youngest-ever Prime Minister.

It is believed Williams will use the 10am press conference to outline the thinking behind his new cabinet, announced yesterday, which saw the appointment of his long-standing political ally, Bob Guthrie, as Chancellor of the Exchequer.

In another widely anticipated move, Williams appointed his election campaign organiser, Ray Molsley, as Deputy Prime Minister. Molsley said he was "thrilled and honoured to accept the post", adding: "To serve under the leadership of Richard Williams, a man so dedicated to helping turn this country around, is more than a privilege. I will support him every step of the way and I look forward to a bright new future under his direction".

Williams and his actress wife, Anna Lloyd, spent a night apart yesterday as she returned to their Highgate home alone while he stayed on at Downing Street. It is believed Lloyd will join the Prime Minister at their new residence later today once their belongings have been moved.

A nna awoke to a loud banging on her front door and instantly realised she'd overslept. The removal men were due to come at nine am but, glancing at the clock, she saw it was already quarter past and wondered how long they'd been knocking. She quickly threw on her dressing gown and rushed down the stairs to open the front door, taking care to keep out of view in case the ever-present paparazzi got a shot of her. Henry was always warning her of such things and the message had finally sunk in.

The removal men had been hired to pack, move and unpack and as they cheerfully piled in past Anna, she could see they were not in the least bit fazed by their task so she decided just to leave them to it while she went back upstairs to shower.

She checked her mobile but there were no messages from Richard. She knew he had the press conference at ten and she switched on *AllNews 24* so she could catch it as she got ready. Her heart was pounding as she thought through the implications of their discussion the night before. She felt terrible that she'd put him in such a position – choosing between his wife and child and the job he had always dreamed of, but how were they to make their marriage work otherwise? How could she ever really trust him when she was there to prop up his popularity?

Turning her attention to the TV, Anna watched Esther Yarleth flirtily flick back her hair before announcing her studio guests were "two of the most talked about people in the country next to Richard Williams and Anna Lloyd." Smiling into the camera she said: "Welcome, Damian Blunt and Marie Simpson."

Damian smiled confidently while Marie looked nervous. Anna found herself rooted to her seat as she watched.

Esther had, by now, finished her recap on the events of the last few days and was asking Marie, fairly insincerely in Anna's opinion, how she was now feeling.

"Better, thank you," Marie answered shyly. "I had backed myself into a very dark place from which I felt there was only one escape."

Damian immediately jumped in to rescue Marie from an uncomfortable situation. "She had been under a huge amount of pressure over the election campaign, for which I take full blame."

"And was that the reason for your resignation?" Esther asked with feigned confusion. "It's just I don't think you've made it clear why you decided to step down as editor."

"That was one of the reasons," Damian said, clearing his throat loudly. "But, ultimately, because of the pressure to come up with blinding exclusives, I made some very bad decisions which I feel were not about good journalism and were, instead, down to desperation."

Esther turned back to Marie. "And was it that sense of desperation that caused you to harm yourself?"

Marie sighed, carefully thinking through her answer. "Well... there were a number of reasons why I did what I did. Firstly, I think I was probably suffering from depression even before I took the job at the *Echo*. Secondly, I was writing pro-Alliance stories when I dearly wanted to see Kelvin Davis removed from office. I felt I was betraying my family and their values. All that meant I was in a bad place anyway, then I watched Anna Lloyd collapse on TV and faced the awful thought that I had caused a woman I admire hugely to suffer, and perhaps even lose her child." Marie looked down at the floor and took in a deep breath.

"Do you want to go on?" Esther asked, keen to show the more sensitive side her critics said she lacked when interviewing.

Marie nodded before continuing. "When I interviewed Anna Lloyd during the brief period she was separated from her husband, I was struck by her strength and courage. She had overcome hardships in her life that are the stuff of most people's nightmares. She told me that regardless of whether she remained married to him or not she desperately wanted Richard Williams to win the election as she knew he could make a difference to people who are suffering in just the same way she did. I think she's an extraordinary woman and I'm very glad that she'll be at the side of the Prime Minister as he runs the country because she will fight for those who most need a champion. I'm only sorry that this side of the story is one I didn't get to tell when I worked at the *Echo*."

Marie's words were ringing in Anna's ears as their truth hit home. Until her separation from Richard, she had always seen herself as a woman of courage who would fight to stop children suffering in the way she had, to stop women being abused over and over again with no means of escape. She had longed for them to reach Downing Street so finally they might be able to ease the chaos and turmoil that was the life of so many helpless people.

And just as though someone had turned a switch in her mind, she remembered why she had fallen in love with Richard in the first place. This was their shared dream. The very thing that had been forgotten in the run-up to the election. She had been focused on her career, and he on defeating Kelvin. They had lost sight of their very deep connection – something she now felt again for the first time in months.

She grabbed her mobile phone from the bedside table and noticed that she had a missed call and text message from Richard. She realised he must have called when she was letting the removal men in. She quickly clicked to open the message. It read:

Barely slept. You and baby must come first. I hope this will prove how much I love you. R.

"No," Anna shrieked as she frantically tried to dial Richard's Blackberry. It had been hard enough to contact him before the election, let alone now that he was ensconced at Number 10. And in her hurry to leave the day before, she hadn't taken any of the Downing Street numbers either. His phone rang out, then went to voicemail.

"Richard, it's Anna. Please don't resign. I had got myself into a really weird place. It was stupid... selfish. I want to help you achieve what you were born to do. I love you."

Anna started to tremble with the realisation that Richard could be about to end his career – and all because she had let herself become overwhelmed by fear and self-doubt.

Her mobile started to ring and her heart took a skip of joy with the hope it might be him, only to sink again when she saw Libby's name flashing on the screen.

"Oh Libby," she wailed. "I've messed up so badly."

"Why? What have you done now?"

"I think Richard might be about to resign. I asked him last night whether he would be willing to stand down for me. I just couldn't face being scrutinised and picked over anymore – my insecurities over our marriage being magnified every day for all the world to see."

"And now you've changed your mind?"

"Yes. I remembered what we had set out to do in the first place. I don't know how it all got so out of control, but it did. And now I have to get hold of Richard to tell him not to stand down."

"Have you tried calling him?"

"I can't get through," Anna wailed, the tears starting to pour down her face. "And he's giving a press conference in thirty minutes and I think he might stand down."

"Right." Libby swung into action mode. "I'm calling John to come and take you to Downing Street now. Meanwhile, I'll keep trying Richard and Henry and I'll call the switchboard too."

"Okay," Anna gasped, trying to get her breath back.

"Now go," Libby barked.

"Thank you, Libby. I'd be lost without you."

"Yes, you would." Libby chuckled. "I love you, you silly sod."

"You too." Anna ended the call and threw on a pair of black flared trousers and a crumpled blouse she found on an armchair near the bed. She swept her hair back into a low ponytail and quickly powdered her face, adding a little blusher and lipstick. She knew it would be all over the papers if she arrived looking dishevelled so she put a fitted jacket on and hoped she'd sufficiently covered up her chaotic state.

She glanced out of the window and saw John already sitting in the car outside. Grabbing her handbag first, she darted down the stairs, much to the alarm of the removal men in the hallway below.

"You all right, Mrs Williams?" one asked, concerned.

"Yes," Anna blurted in reply, before throwing the front door open. "Got to rush."

She slammed the front door and walked briskly to the car, trying not to arouse the suspicion of the waiting press. It was then she noticed the unmarked police car in front, waiting to escort them. Oh shit, she thought. Now there was no way John could break the speed limit, so the only option she had was silent prayer.

~

Marie stared intently at Damian as he finished the intriguing phone call he had been taking for the last ten minutes. She knew she was involved in some way because he had kept winking across the table at her in the café where they were having breakfast. "I'm pretty sure she'd be interested," he told the caller, "although it's really something I'd need to talk to her about before confirming."

Watching Damian relaxed and in full flight only warmed her to him further. A man she once saw as a bit of a bully, now seemed like a harmless puppy. Pressure does funny things to people, she reminded herself. And though things had not yet turned romantic between them, the fact that they seemed to find an excuse to spend their every moment together meant she knew they were heading only one way. Marie smiled and allowed herself to feel the first flushes of happiness in many weeks.

She tuned into Damian's voice again and, as the call seemed to be drawing to a close, realised he was setting up a time for the two of them to meet with the stranger on the other end of the line. "Monday at four-thirty is good, yes." He smiled back across at Marie again.

"We'll look forward to seeing you then."

When he finally ended the call, Marie could hardly contain herself.

"Well?" she demanded.

"That was Miles Hildon. He's setting up a new website called The Truth which will feature what he describes as journalism of the highest editorial integrity, and he wants to talk to you and I about working for him."

Marie laughed. "Let me get this right. He wants to talk to the two journalists in the country who have displayed the least editorial integrity in recent times, about employing us to tell the truth?"

"That's right, yes." Damian flashed another self-satisfied smile. "He said he greatly admired our courage in taking a stand against being pressurised into printing stories we didn't believe in."

Marie's mind boggled as to how opportunities like this were starting to present themselves when they were supposed to be in the journalistic doghouse. Miles Hildon was a former tabloid editor, turned TV star after a very public fall from grace.

In his press days he had been a young, brilliant and daring editor who was willing to take risks in the name of a good story – until he took a risk too far. Marie suspected that, although lucrative, his TV career wouldn't offer the heart-stopping thrill of chasing a great story, and that's why he wanted to start up this new online venture. And having just watched her and Damian speak of their shame in failing to work to proper editorial standards, he will have no doubt spotted a publicity opportunity. For they had each paid a heavy price for their mistakes and had publicly walked towards the light when it came to good journalism.

Marie looked across at Damian to find that he had been watching her being lost in thought for the last few minutes.

"You looked like you were thinking that one through." He smiled.

"I was just thinking that a few days ago a career in journalism seemed like the furthest place from where I wanted to be and now, suddenly, I feel excited about it again. Just like I did when I first started out."

"You and me both, Marie. We could do something really different here. Shake things up a bit. Worth a shot, don't you agree?" he asked, flashing an enthusiastic grin worthy of even the cheekiest schoolboy.

"Worth a shot," Marie agreed, returning his smile.

The police officer guarding the entrance to Number 10 could barely hide his shock as he watched Anna dash from the car, in full view of the world's press, and hotfoot it to the doorstep. And once inside the corridor, she left the house staff similarly stunned when she broke into another run, turning from left to right trying to remember her way to the State Dining Room where the press conference was scheduled to start within the next couple of minutes.

She spotted a member of staff further into the entrance hall and breathlessly asked for directions before rushing off again. As she rounded the corner she found Richard and Henry deep in conversation as they approached the dining room. She quickly caught up with them in time to hear Henry say: "I'll miss working with you hugely. Things are certainly going to be very different."

"No," she cried, grabbing Richard by the arm. Startled, he and Henry swung round to look at Anna.

"You can't resign. I've made a terrible mistake."

Henry and Richard looked at one another before both broke into raucous laughter.

"What's so funny?" Anna asked, bemused and a little annoyed by their reaction.

"Don't worry." Richard beamed. "I spoke to Libby. She told me you were on your way and that I didn't have to step down from the highest ranking job in the land after all." He reached out and touched her arm. "I'm so sorry you were feeling so scared and I didn't even stop to notice. Or maybe I just didn't want to notice, because I wouldn't have known how to fix it."

"No, I'm sorry," she replied meekly. "I wanted to talk to you about it. But things were so hectic I just never found the right time – until yesterday." Then, suddenly remembering the conversation she'd just overheard she turned to look at Henry. "But why were you saying you'd miss Richard?"

"Because one of us has just resigned, I'm afraid."

"Henry," Anna gasped, open-mouthed. "You're not leaving?"

"Just for a little while, yes. I'm going to take myself away to France for a few months to clear my head. I need to sort a few things out in my mind and this just isn't the place to do that."

"Sort things out?" Anna asked. "Are you okay?"

"Yes." Henry stuffed his hands awkwardly into his trouser pockets. "I need to take a bit of time to work through everything that's gone on in the last few weeks. My separation from Joy... and, also, some of the mistakes I made in the heat of the moment." He bowed his head momentarily, and Anna knew emotion was getting the better of him. "I'm sorry," he whispered.

"You know," Anna said, "I truly believe the things that happened during this campaign were meant to be, because we have learned and we've emerged stronger. So don't go all gloomy on me when you're getting out of this madhouse." Anna gave him a playful poke in the ribs.

"You two were born for this." Henry laughed. "You won't need me. And I'm not leaving the planet, I'll still be keeping in touch and sticking my oar in. And before you know it, I'll be back."

Anna could feel her eyes welling up with tears. She attempted to fight them back but realised her hormones were far more in control than her senses. Instead, she leaned forward to wrap a startled Henry into a bear hug.

"Thank you, Henry. We've all been through a lot together these last few weeks and we'll miss you terribly."

Henry's face flushed with a mixture of embarrassment and emotion.

"I'll miss you both too," he replied croakily. "I'm going to go now before this gets harder. But I won't be far away." He reached out and clasped them both by the arm. "You're going to be terrific."

With that, Henry turned and walked down the corridor of Number 10, heading for the front door.

Richard and Anna watched in silence until he was out of sight.

"And then there were two," Richard said quietly.

"I feel like we're missing an arm now," Anna replied, only half-jokingly.

A Downing Street press officer suddenly opened the door of the dining room to look for Richard, only to jolt back when he found him standing right there. "Ready when you are," he said, before closing the door quickly again.

"Will you sit in on the briefing with me?" Richard asked Anna anxiously.

"Course I will." She smiled reassuringly. "We can do this, Richard. We just have to stick together; no more letting other people talk us into decisions we're not comfortable with."

"No," Richard said, putting his arms around her. "This is strictly a double act from now on."

"Soon to be a triple act." She winked.

"Yes." He stroked her cheek fondly, his face turning serious. "Do you trust me now, Anna? Are you ready for all this?"

"I'm ready as I'll ever be." She smiled. "I guess I just needed to know you would put me and the baby before your career if it came down to it."

"I would – and you must trust me on that. I won't let you

down again. Now we need to go and tell the people who voted for us that we're ready to do what we promised to. Are you coming?"

"Yes," she replied, wrapping her arms around his waist. They held each other tightly and Anna allowed herself to relax into his embrace, feeling safe for the first time in months. After a few moments she stepped back and tucked her arm under his.

"After you, Prime Minister," she said before they stepped forward together into the packed dining room.

Turning to face the press, Anna smiled confidently, before leaving Richard's side and taking a seat next to a stunned reporter who clearly wasn't used to having a Prime Minister's wife as a seating companion.

"Don't mind me." Anna smiled at the now flushed young man.

"Will you be speaking today?" he asked sheepishly.

"No." Anna turned to look at him. "I'm just here to support my husband."

THE END

A NOTE FROM THE PUBLISHER

Thank you for reading this book. If you enjoyed it please do consider leaving a review on Amazon to help others find it too.

We hate typos. All of our books have been rigorously edited and proofread, but sometimes mistakes do slip through. If you have spotted a typo, please do let us know and we can get it amended within hours.

info@bloodhoundbooks.com

Printed in Great Britain
by Amazon

80992418R00161